Mansion On The Hill

by

Olmond M.Hall

Writers Club Press
San Jose · New York · Lincoln · Shanghai

Mansion On The Hill

ISBN: 1-893652-76-9

Published by Writers Club Press, an imprint of iUniverse.com, Inc.

For information address:
iUniverse
620 North 48th Street
Suite 201
Lincoln, NE 68504-3467
www.iuniverse.com

URL: http://www.writersclub.com

Mansion on the Hill

Olmond M. Hall

This story begins as a parody of a famous trial that took place in the 1990's. However, the travesty developes a life of its own. The spoof takes place in the 1930's in the deep south. It has similar names, and in a number of other ways parallels the 1990 trial. This satiric drama has hardships, fun times, romance, murder, suspense and mystery. It delves into the backgrounds of some of the key players. The title of the story is, Mansion on the Hill.

thanks FOR your Support
Best wishes
Olmond

Olmond M. Hall, Ocala, Florida

Wounds and Romance

While Donny had his second real stiff drink of White Ribbon Vitae, Lucy sipped hers and began to work. She mopped out the wound again and put some iodine on it. Donny let out a big whistle, as Lucy handed him another big drink. She put more iodine on the gash, then petroleum jelly. She put some gauze over the wound and taped it firmly in place. She added a damp cloth on his head, and being finished had another White Ribbon Vitae.

She took the rest of his clothes and his shoes off, and as he lay naked, she started removing her clothes. First she unhooked her stockings from her garter belt, sliding them down over her perfectly shaped legs. Then she unbuttoned her skirt, let it fall to the floor and stepped over it. She undid the buttons on her blouse and pulled it over her head.

Donny was transformed into a zombie. He was so taken back at the beauty of this girl. Lucy winked at Donny and pulled her white satin slip over her head. As she did, Donny saw the beautifully shaped, creamy skinned body, clad only in red panties and bra. When she reached behind her back to unfasten her bra and remove it, Donny's head was throbbing rapid fire, but not from the hit on the head. The Lil Thang slid her thumbs on top of each side of her panties, slowly lowering them to her feet and stepped out of them. There she stood in all of her glory. My God, Donny thought, I have died and gone to heaven. Then he saw her pubic hairs. The hairs were light brown, the color of her head, but trimmed in the shape of a heart. Now he knew the blow had killed him, for this was too good to be happening on earth.

Dedication

To my wife Mary Ann.
For putting up with my nonsense and laboring for hours proof reading, editing and spell checking.

To Fran Szutar
For her professional input and hours of proof reading.

To Paula Walker
Who laughed at everything I wrote, the good, the bad and wanting this book to happen.

Chapter One

Jim Paul Samson had been working with his Pa, Jim Curtis in Burntout. Burntout got its name from the moonshine stills in the area. When the revenuers couldn't find the stills, they set fire to the woods and burnt them out, but the stills kept popping back up. After six or eight times of burning them out, the revenuers gave up and the community was named Burntout.

Jim Curtis had lost all of his money and land when the banks closed at the beginning of the great depression. A few weeks after the bank foreclosed on the land, Jim Curtis started share cropping for Oscar Meadows, the owner of a sawmill and timber land, who had purchased the Samson land from the Federal Government after they received it from the defunct Three Notch Bank. Oscar wanted the land mainly for its timber. The land not harvested for its timber would be sharecropped out to interested farmers. Sharecropping was when the land owner would let a farmer move into a house on the land, supply the seeds, fertilizer, mules, plows and sometimes advance some money for food. At the end of the year, the money for the supplies would be deducted and the profits would be split 50-50. If any advance was made for food or loans, this would be deducted. A piece of land for a garden was used, so that the sharecropper could grow some of his own food.

In one respect Jim Curtis was lucky. Oscar Meadows let him have the back 40 acres of what use to be his land so he could live in the house where he was born. Meadows also made Jim Curtis a deal in writing, that he could buy back the forty acres and house after three years. During the depression, times were tough and the next year was just about a break even year.

The second year a dry spell came after the crop was put into the ground, and only 50 percent of the seeds came up. The plants were so small the corn was only three feet high with two or three ears per stalk. The cotton had only three or four boles on the stalks that came up. Oscar gave Jim Curtis some more seeds, and young Jim Paul stayed out of school to work with Pa from sunrise until sunset replanting the seeds, but very little rain came and there was no corn or cotton to harvest.

Jim Paul remembered the night his Pa died. He and Pa were sitting on the front porch, he in the swing and Pa in a rocking chair. Jim Paul looked at his Pa and thought, "Gosh he looks as old as Grandpa did when he died." Jim Curtis said to his son, "Jim Paul, I jest don't feel I can go on, I'm so tared and can't git nothing done. I'm 'fraid I won't be here much longer. When I go, will you promise me that you will look after yore Ma as long as she lives?"

"Don't talk that way Pa, we'll get the home place and land back, we jest have to," said Jim Paul. "I'll take care of you and Ma, jest don't talk that way anymore."

Jim Paul didn't sleep well that night, seeing his Pa looking older than his age and worrying himself to death about the land. He drifted in and out of sleep all night. Sometime during the night, he heard a shot down on Snit Creek. "Oh, I wish I weren't too tared," thought Jim Paul. "I'd like to be down on Snit Creek possum hunting with Bubba Moulton. I wonder if he got that possum." Jim Paul finally went sound to sleep in the early morning, and woke up just as the day was breaking. He could hear Ma in the kitchen cooking breakfast. "I wonder why Pa didn't wake me," he pondered as he went into the kitchen. Ma said that he had gotten up before her and left the house, to get some water from the spring.

Jim Paul went down to the spring and saw his Pa sitting against a big oak tree. As he got closer he saw the blood and the shotgun.

Jim Curtis Samson could not beat the great depression and had taken his life at the age of 38. The shot that Jim Paul heard was the shot that his Pa used to take his life.

All of the responsibility for the farm and the family fell on Jim Paul at the age of 17. He promised he would take care of his Ma, and that one day all the land that Grandpa and Pa had once owned would be back in the family. After the death of Jim Curtis, his Ma didn't seem to have any interest in living, and in less than a year she, too, was gone.

So at the young age of 18, Jim Paul took over sharecropping the farm. He worked in the fields, but at settlement time he was in the hole, a whole year's work plus $200 that he owed Oscar Meadows. Jim Paul vowed that he would pay Oscar Meadows and buy the land back. He set up a moonshine still as some of the other farmers did, hoping to earn extra money, however, he only made and sold enough of the illegal liquor to live on and saved little toward buying the land.

Delilah Kool grew up poor on a farm with her grandpa and mother. She buried herself in the Baptist Church where she met the handsome young, Jim Paul Samson. After a brief courtship, they were married in 1908.

When Delilah Samson was pregnant, she had a craving for orange juice. A couple of times a week, Jim Paul interrupted his moonshine making to travel five miles into town for orange juice. When the bouncing baby boy arrived in 1909, they named him Oscar James Samson and called him OJ for short.

OJ had a happy childhood around the moonshine still, playing string ball, marbles, knuckles, mumbly peg, seesaw and flying jenny.

When he was about ten years old, an incident shaped the future of his life. On a trip to town one Saturday with a bale of cotton for the gin, OJ saw a crowd and on a platform was a man, who wore a striking pair of fancy grey striped worsted pantaloon pants, a white doctor's coat and a J.B. Stetson Fedora style grey hat. He was selling medicine of all types. He had a deep voice, just right for singing. This day he was selling Somone Tonic and would chant, "Somone, for sweet refreshing sleep. We ask any of you fine folks who may be troubled with insomnia, who cannot sleep at night, to give this valuable remedy a try. No matter from what cause the sleeplessness, a sound sleep will be procured by its use and you will awake refreshed, strengthened, and cheerful, with no bad effects from its use. It is a vegetable preparation composed of herbs, soothing and healing to the entire system. Ladies troubled with sleeplessness and nervous spells should always have a bottle on hand, only $1 for the bottle. People started handing dollar bills to the man by the handful. OJ asked his Pa to get a bottle for Ma, and he never forgot the medicine man.

Jim Paul worked hard in the fields and the still, and although Delilah and OJ were a big help, he just couldn't save enough money to buy the farm. He thought maybe he should increase his moonshine production. OJ saw his Pa working and looking old and tired, and wanted to find a way to help out.

When OJ was 15, he still remembered the medicine man. In the Grit newspaper he saw an advertisement on how to make some extra money selling the Mexican Headache Cure. Buy the remedy for six cents each (by the dozen) and sell it for $.20 cents each. "Why, I declare," he thought, "This will more than double my money." He ordered two dozen boxes, and on Saturday after receiving the Mexican Headache Cure, he went into town and set up a table near the mule barn, where the farmers traded and bought mules on Saturday. His voice was strong from singing in the choir at the Shiloh Baptist Church. His sing song spiel went like this.

"A splitting headache cured immediately by our positive Headache and Neuralgia Cure. Almost everyone is more or less troubled with a headache. Some people are hardly ever free from them, and suffer martyrdom. Rarely is a second dose required except in very obstinate cases. Give it a try when you suffer and you will be sure to speak to your friends about me, and the Mexican Headache Cure."

OJ sold most of his stock that morning. Another way he found to help his Pa and Ma was selling the Grit newspaper. He would deliver the paper to the customers after church and, the ones that did not attend that Sunday, he would deliver to their house on old Matilda, a mule that was to old too plow, but could be ridden on errands. On Saturdays he would sell the Mexican Headache Cure at the mule barn, and before long they could start paying on the farm.

Jim Paul and Delilah were religious and attended the Shiloh Baptist Church at Burntout, where Jim Paul was a deacon. Delilah played the organ, and OJ sang in the choir. He had a deep baritone voice and sang very well, He wanted a guitar, but could not afford to buy one. If he could spare the price of the guitar in the Sears, Roebuck catalog, and learn to play, he might attract a larger crowd at the mule barn to buy his Mexican Headache Cure. They had some fine guitars in the Sears, Roebuck catalog, and would give his last pig knuckle for the "Seroco" model, but it was too much, $12 plus shipping. Maybe if next Saturday's sales were good he could get the "Troubadour" model for $3.50 plus $.30 cents shipping. The price included a valuable instruction book, a full set of strings, a fingerboard chart, with which anyone can learn to play the guitar without a teacher, and a song book with chords.

To increase his sales for the next Saturday, he got Ma to parch some peanuts that just dried on the peanut stack. He would give a bag of parched peanuts with every Mexican Headache Cure sold. OJ had studied people since he had been selling the Grit and the Mexican Headache Cure. They loved to think they were getting a bargain. For instance, all of the farmers grew some peanuts and could easily parch them, but to go to town on Saturday and buy a bag of parched peanuts was showing off. They would buy the nuts, then stand around, eating, gossiping, and bragging about, how much they were getting for their crops, livestock, and how much better their moonshine was than anyone else. The farmers felt it was a good deal, because they would get the peanuts free with the Mexican Headache Cure.

Saturday morning found him ready with his table displaying the Mexican Headache Cure, and a large supply of bagged parched peanuts. He started clapping his hands together to get the beat, and in his rich baritone voice started singing, "Amazing Grace, how sweet the sound to save a wretch like me. I once was lost, but now I'm found, I was blind, but now I see. Amazing Grace."

OJ opened a bag of the peanuts, looked over the crowd that had gathered and threw out some peanuts as he said, "Hi Jake, try these. Hi Jimmy Joe, have some peanuts."

He continued doing this until the bag of peanuts had been passed around. Again in his rich baritone voice, clapping his hand he started singing Peace In The Valley.

"I am so tired and so blue till you come to call me away. There will be peace in the valley for me, Oh Lord there will be no more sadness, no more sorrow, no more trouble for me, but there will be peace in the valley."

Then he started in his spiel, "Ladies and Gentlemen, do you want peace in your house? A splitting headache cured immediately by our positive headache and neuralgia cure, almost every one is more or less troubled with a headache. Some people are hardly ever free from them, and suffer martyrdom. We say to you that it is not necessary to suffer longer than the time it takes to get this package of our Mexican headache cure. I positively guarantee relief within ten minutes after the first dose has been taken. Rarely is a second dose required, except in the very obstinate cases. Give it a try when you suffer and you will be sure to speak to your friends about me and the Mexican Headache Cure. Have peace in the valley and your house, save a wretch from the neuralgia, you will find, no more sadness, no more trouble, just peace in the valley. A special offer for today, the regular price of $.20 cents a package, but free at no extra charge a bag of parched peanuts, parched fresh this morning by the best cook in Three Notch County, Delilah Samson. They are parched just right, cauz they are parched in sight. Step right up and hand me $.20 cents for each Mexican Headache Cure and a bag of the famous parched peanuts."

OJ made two more spiels that Saturday and sold 37 bags for a total of $7.40, making a net profit $5.45. He ordered the Troubadour Guitar, with the strings and instruction book, plus a song book with words and cords. He selected a book that had some sacred, popular and western songs. After purchasing the guitar, he put $1 in Ma's cookie jar to go toward the farm, and left $.65 for himself to be spent on having a good time, like going to the Saturday night square dance with Suzie Sweetwater.

Chapter Two

When OJ was 17 an incident happened that gave him more experience for marketing his product. Later in life these experiences came in handy for making a living. At the mule barn one Saturday, he saw his uncle, High Pockets Davis, the brother-in-law of Jim Paul Samson, who worked part-time for Jim Paul in the moonshine business. High Pockets got his nickname from being six feet six inches tall and weighing 172 pounds, making his pockets high off the ground. During cotton season High Pockets would put quart fruit jars of moonshine under the cotton and after the cotton was ginned, he would go to the mule barn and sell the moonshine.

In early March, High Pockets wanted some extra money to buy his wife Caroline a birthday present. They had been married five years, had five kids, and he never had the money to buy her a present. This year he was determined to get her a nice gift, for he thought she was still "a real cute lil gal."

High Pockets borrowed Jim Paul's car and hid 50 quart fruit jars of moonshine under the baskets of butter beans.

He figured that after all expenses were deducted, he should clear $22 for two days work, which is was more than he usually made in a month.

On a Wednesday he left for Montgomery, arriving about 3 PM. His destination was the Deep South Barbecue and Cocktail Lounge, on Highway 31 South. He went to see the owner, Curtis

Turnipseed, who told him to check into the cabin and he would be over in a few minutes and pay him. After Mr. Turnipseed payed High Pockets he decided he would see what the barbecue was like. He entered the lounge and thought, "Golly this is outer sight." They had a fifty-cent cover charge at the door. High Pockets said, "What the hell is this fer?"

"Well," said the man at the door, "Princess is going to dance tonight."

High Pockets thought, "Well I worked hard fer my money and I don't like to throw my money away, but now and then a man has to let go."

He gave the man at the door $.50 who said, " You just made your self a helluva deal," and seated High Pockets down in front.

Well, Princess came out, she was lean and tall and scantily clad. He thought to himself, "Ha, that's $.50 well spent."

Princess began to bump and grind and he almost went out of his mind. As she did a little song,

"One-two-three, wont you look at me, four-five-six, watch me do my tricks, seven-eight-nine, I have a perfect mind, a ten-ten, here I go again."

Later that night in the cabin bed, Princess kept dancing through his head. He just couldn't get her off his mind. He thought, "For nigh on to thirty years that I've been around, I never seen anything to beat that gal. I gotta go back and see her one more time. I'll say the car won't run, and I'll stay over fer another night." The next night he showed up again, and to his surprise when Princess walked in, she came over and sat at his table. She said, "How about later on we get together."

He was so excited he thought that he was going to die. He told her, "I'm in cabin 13, You are welcome anytime and I'll do my best to make you feel at home."

Sure enough about quarter to four she came knocking, and when he let her in, she was singing this little diddy.

"One-two-three, just look at me, four-five-six, watch me do my tricks, seven-eight-nine, we're gonna have a good time."

Princess went into the bath room to freshen her make up. High Pockets thought "Why is she taking so long?"

He opened the door, and there she was shaving her whiskers. HER WHISKERS!

He knew right away something was wrong, and he said, "What the hell is going on?"

She said, "Let me explain the situation. It's true, I use to be a man till I had my operation."

High Pockets said, "One-two-three, you better get away from me, four-five six, of all the low down dirty tricks, seven-eight-nine, you gotta be out of yore mind, I'm going home to Caroline."

While Princess was lighting her cigar, High Pockets bolted out the door and got an early start for home, swearing never to go back to the big city.

OJ was putting some white lightnin' in fruit jars when Uncle High Pockets, (it just struck him, that he didn't know what Uncle High Pockets real name was) told his Pa the experience he had with Princess. Putting the white lightnin' under the beans was a right smart thing to do. He would have to remember this and also when, if ever, he got to Montgomery, to go see Princess.

Chapter Three

During this period in his teenage years, OJ and his buddy, Frog Wiggins, were together most of the time. They were in same classes at school and went on dates with the Raye Twins. It didn't take much money. On late Saturday afternoons after he finished at the mule barn, they would hitch up the buggy and the four of them would go into Three Notch to the picture show. It cost $.10 each and a bag of popcorn cost a nickel. Twenty-five cents was more than he wanted to spend, but Fay Raye was worth it. The picture show had a continuing story for about six weeks and he hated to miss an episode. He and Frog would take the girls, Faye, his girl, and Maye, Frog's girl, down to piddle in Purdy's Pond after church for an afternoon of swimming and picnicking.

During the late summer and early fall, the four of them and another buddy, Booger Throckmorton, who dated Orra Belle Beesley, went to parties. One of the better ones was at Orra Belle's house. It was a candy pulling, cake walk and square dancing party. Bubba Jr. and Ted Bear had a little band with guitars, fiddles and a drum. Their slogan was, "Sweat and Swear with Teddy Bear."

On this night, OJ, Frog, Booger, and Bubba, Jr. sneaked around the house and put white lightnin' in the bucket of grape Koolaid. To get everyone in the party mood they even put white lightin' in the water buckets. Being a hot summer night, the band was playing and everyone was, "Sweating and Swearing with Teddy Bear."

The water buckets and Koolaid buckets were the most popular thing after the Teddy Bear Band.

Of course a good time was had by all, except Bubba, Sr. who at one in the morning had enough of the music and noise and tried to quiet everyone down, but no one could hear him. Well, enough is enough, so Bubba, Sr. got out the old twelve gauge shotgun, (painted white from the wedding of his daughter Sara Jane to Vern Hollis) and shot the double barrel twelve gauge twice in the air.

Everyone thought he was shooting at them and started running every which way. Booger thought it was him being shot at, because he and Orra Belle were in the barn nude. Booger jumped up, and ran out of the barn, naked as a jay bird. He was winning the mile a minute race when he came to a barbed wire fence. He hurdled the fence, but fell to his knees. He was going so fast, he couldn't get to his feet, he ran on hands and knees through the blackberry patch down to the creek where he sat in the water to heal his scratches and catch his breath. Later he sneaked home and went in through the window so his folks wouldn't hear or see him coming home naked. Ted Bear ran through the barn, scooped up Orra Belle's clothes and ran down to the corn field and lay there until it was safe to go home.

As Orra Belle came out of the barn with out anything on but straw in her hair, Bubba, Sr. ran up to her and demanded to know who the feller wuz that was in the hay loft with her, so he could use the white twelve gauge shot gun for another daughters wedding. Bubba said, "I'll see that young feller tomorrow, now put some clothes on."

OJ, Faye, and Maye ran down the road after Frog grabbing a pint of white lightnin'. They weren't too far from Purdy's Pond so they went skinny dipping.

About 3 AM. Booger heard a light knock on his window. When he looked out, there was Orra Belle. She told him what her Pa had in mind. As soon as Orra Belle was out of sight, he woke his Ma and Pa and told them the story. Ma said, "Thadeus (his given name) pack your clothes and Pa will take you to Three Notch to catch the 7 AM bus to Montgomery. From there you can catch a bus to New York and go to your Aunt Dorothy Sue Phyle and her husband. I'll go along and call her from the bus station and tell her you are on the way. You stay with them until everything cools down before coming home."

Booger packed his belongings in a cardboard box, tied it with heavy string and crawled in the wagon for the four mile trip to Three Notch. It was 4 AM and it would take about 30 or 40 minutes to get to the bus station. He lay down on some straw, hoping he could catch a nap and wouldn't have to hear Pa tell him how he went wrong and, "wus going to the Devil." He only wanted to get away and not have to marry into that Beesley family.

Chapter Four

After graduating from high school, OJ went to work with Jim Paul in the moonshine business. Relying on his experience as a medicine man and remembering the story of Uncle High Pockets trip to Montgomery, he took the old Ford touring car and cut it off behind the front seat, put a platform on it, and made it into a pickup car. Then taking hampers of various sizes, he put a jar of moonshine on the bottom and covered it with snap or butter beans. The small came with a pint, the half bushel size contained a quart, and the bushel size contained a gallon.

His set up was a takeoff of the Mexican Headache Cure. He had some labels printed with the name of his moonshine, White Ribbon Vitae-Likker Of Life. OJ's strong baritone voice rose as he started his sing song spiel that went like this.

"Step right up ladies and gentlemen and get a half bushel of fresh butter beans, picked early this morning by my mama with her delicate little fingers and in each basket under the tender butter beans you will find a gift, a bonus no less of one quart of White Ribbon Vitae-Likker of Life. You will feel the good effects immediately and you will get strong, feel bright, fresh and active. It fills every nerve cell with vibration and energy, and will stimulate your sexual desire. It is the ideal tonic to take before going square and round dancing. If you don't do any of the dances, get two half bushels of beans with two bottles of White Ribbon Vitae and you will learn to dance. Great for the shy, male and female, one bottle between the two of you and you can even have sex in the buggy while ole Roam takes you home."

His sales were extremely good and he decided to branch out.

To get the economy growing, President Roosevelt started the WPA, PWA, CCC, and the allotment to farmers to increase the selling price of cotton so they could earn more. The allotment worked like this. If a farmer planted 20 acres of cotton and got 20 bales, he would get about $17.50 per bale or approximately $350 for 20 acres.

The government told the farmers to plant only ten acres of cotton and the government would pay them an allotment of $175. Therefore, they would make the same for growing less and could plant other crops on the 10 acres. Jim Paul had twenty acres of cotton and 20 acres of corn for his moonshine still. OJ told Pa, "Why don't we take the cotton allotment and plant ten more acres of cawn, rent Elmore Meadow's 40 acres, where he went broke planting all cotton. We have to plant 20 acres of cotton to get paid for not planting 20 acres, and then plant 20 acres of cawn."

Pa said, "Why, OJ we can't sell that much likker."

"Look Pa. Leave the marketing to me."

OJ and Pa applied for the allotment on 20 acres of land and received approximately $350 per year for not planting 20 acres of cotton, and planted 20 acres of corn. OJ rented an old filling station with a gas pump in front, and cut a window in the back with a pass through shelf. This was the first drive-in of any type in the Three Notch area. OJ sold snap beans, butter beans, okra and other vegetables, with different sized fruit jars of White Ribbon Vitae-Likker of Life, in the bottom of the containers. The new business, was named Sad and Happy Drive-In. His slogan was "Drive in Sad and Drive Out Happy."

Chapter Five

OJ became very wealthy and soon started dating a beautiful young girl named Nike Brown from Turnip Hill. They met at the Three Notch Infirmary, when she went with her friend Mattie Lou, to visit Mattie Lou's husband Frog Wiggins. OJ was also visiting Frog and they were reliving some of their boyhood escapades.

The night before Frog was gigging frogs down at Purty's Pond. His wife Mattie Lou had tested her new nail polish on Frog's toenails, and while gigging frogs he saw his toes shining in the water and thought it was a mess of frogs.

Frog and OJ were looking out of the window and saw the picture show sign that read, Hoot Gibson in, WHO FLUNG MUD ON MY SADDLE. They reminisced about the first time they had gone to the picture show.

One February, when Frog and OJ were about 10 years old, Frog's Pa gave a peanut shelling party. He invited all of the farm families around the community. The boys had to help Frog's Ma shell peanuts. The object was to shell the seed peanuts for spring planting. Seed peanuts were selected from the peanuts harvested in the fall and graded. The party was held in the log kitchen, which had been the original house. When Frog's Grandpa built the house in 1875, it had one room, 30 by 40 feet, with a huge fireplace for heating and cooking at one end. The rest of the room served as the bedroom and living room. After adding to the house in 1900, the log house was made into a kitchen, A wood stove and a large dining room table and chairs were added. While the men and children shelled the peanuts, the women parched them, made peanut taffy and peanut candy.

On Saturday after the peanut party, Frog and OJ put some of the parched peanuts, in bags and took them to Three Notch, selling them for five cents a bag. Sales were slow, but eventually they sold four bags. This was enough to get two tickets to the picture show.

They couldn't believe what they saw, a picture moving and talking. The cowboy became Frog's and OJ's hero. His name was Tom Mix, and the serial was "Rin Tin Tin The Wonder Dog". They just had to sell more peanuts to see next week's show, Tom Mix in "Cement", and find out how would Rin Tin Tin save the pretty girl from being sawed in half at the sawmill.

After they got out of the pitcher show they noticed that they had been eating out of the bags of peanuts they had with them. They had four bags about half full. Frog thought, (as his Pa always told him), "SECOND THOUGHTS DO NOT COME FIRST, why not sell two bags for a nickel."

They sold the four bags in just a few minutes, so the second thought came second, that they had their picture show money for next week, and they would put peanuts in bags only half full and sell them two for a nickel. They just had to know if Rin Tin Tin saved that pretty girl.

As the two walked the three miles home at dusk dark, they day dreamed about Tom Mix and Rin Tin Tin, of Pa's mule Jack and the old dog Biscuit, that old dog loved biscuits, hence the name. The mule Jack, Pa said was one word from Jack Ass. Frog could see himself, OJ. Biscuit and Jack keeping Burntout free of revenuers and keeping Sue Ann Kitchen and Mattie Lou Spicer from that nasty old Dougie Musselwhite. Frog's heart thumped like a tired mule's as the stars came out on the dusty road home.

OJ knew from the first moment that Nike would be his girl for life. When they started dating, they made a handsome couple. OJ was six feet one inch tall, weighed about 190 pounds, with a ruddy complexion, black hair, blue eyes and a great body from lifting White Ribbon Vitae-Likker of Life, and vegetables.

Nike was beautiful, five feet two inches, 105 pounds, curved figure, long blond hair, blue eyes, full lips and an ample bust. OJ told her how beautiful she was and she was glad that she had ordered the Princess Bust Developer and Bust cream last year. She wore a 30A cup before using the Princess Bust Developer. The developer lived up to its advertising, promising that it "will build you up and fill out all shrunken and underdeveloped tissues, form a rounded plump, perfectly developed bust, and you will be happy over the results in one week." She now wore a 34C and was the envy of all the girls at church.

OJ asked her for a date to go to the Whitehurst's Social on Saturday afternoon and to the box supper that night. She said yes and she would make a fried chicken dinner for two and he could bid on it.

A box supper is when a girl or woman fixes a meal which is auctioned off to the highest bidder, with the proceeds going to the church. The man winning the bid, then eats the box supper with the lady who prepared it. Nike fried the chicken and put it in a basket with a white ribbon on it in honor of OJ's famous product.

She looked at her dresses and picked out the prettiest lawn dress. It was made of fine quality white India lawn. The waist was the Eton effect which was trimmed with embroidery and edged lace. The upper part had numerous rows of plaits extending from shoulder to waist, a collar and waist band embroidered to match, and a skirt with wide lawn ruffles around the bottom. After putting it on she looked in the mirror to see if it showed off her bust to her advantage. She liked what she saw and as she gazed at herself in the mirror she thought back to her childhood and how far she had come.

Her pa, Jebb Brown, was a dirt farmer and sharecropped twenty acres of land from old man Grover Haine. Her ma, Lulu Belle Brown, had four children, of which Nike was the youngest. All of the family worked in the fields to make ends meet. Nike was small, skinny and mousey, but she could pick more cotton than anyone. She chopped cotton, shook peanuts, pulled corn and all the field work that came along. Her ma and pa joined the Turnip Hill Pentecostal Church and she loved going to church and singing.

The kids at church and school teased her about being skinny, called her chicken legs and cackled like a chicken at her. They also called her Martha White, because being poor as the sharecroppers were, her ma bought Martha White Flour and used the flour sacks to make dresses, slips, underwear and night clothes for her and her two sisters and shirts for her brother.

One time she was picking okra and as she was bent over picking, that old Joe Ray Barley hollered at her, "Hi self rising."

She didn't know what he meant until that night when she took off her underpants and saw in big letters across the rear that said, "SELF RISING" and below "THE BEST IN THE WORLD." These things hurt her feelings and she stayed to herself. Nike vowed that one day they would be sorry that they teased her, she didn't know how, but she would find a way. She would not grow old, bent over, weather beaten and looking fifteen years older than she was like her Ma. As she looked at herself and thought back, the thought flashed through her head that her way out was through OJ, and she wondered if he would think her, "Self Rising is the Best in the World." She was ready for him. At three o'clock he drove up in the most beautiful new car she had ever seen, a 1934 Hubmobile. In fact, the newest car she had been in was a 1929 Ford Model T.

OJ was handsome in his white duck pants with bell bottoms, light blue shirt and a basket weave white vest covered with pin heads colored in dark blue and white, patent leather slippers.

They arrived at the Whitehurst home and were the envy of everyone. At the auction of the box suppers, several men bid on her box, and she held her breath, but OJ was rich enough that he outbid everyone.

They took the box supper down by the pond under some willow trees, and talked and talked and fell in love.

The two of them were seen at candy pulling parties, picnics, dances and other social events. Almost every Saturday night they went to the Cholly Hoss Honky Tonk and Country Club, where they danced and, on occasion, OJ would get up on stage and sing with the band. Nike fell in love with his rich deep baritone voice. Often on the way home from Cholly Hoss Honky Tonk and Country Club, they would stop under a big oak tree with lots of moss on the banks of Snit Creek. The moon would be full at times, the hoot owls would be calling their mates, while the whippoorwills would be singing their love songs. In the distance you would hear a hound dog that had treed a coon. Life could not be any sweeter than nights like this.

Some nights in the summer, they would go further up the creek to Purdy's Pond and piddle around in the moonlight. Nike loved these nights with OJ's strong arms around her and dreamed of the time when they would be together day and night. On one pleasant cool night while they were at Purdy's Pond and were laying on a quilt in the bright moonlight, OJ asked, "Nike would you cook for two and eat half of it?"

Her heart skipped a beat as she thought, "Is he really asking me to marry him or is he joking?"

"Yes, OJ," Nike said, "I'll cook for two and eat half of it and what we don't eat I'll slop the hogs with."

They had a big wedding with all the trimmings. OJ rented a social hall in Three Notch for the wedding. It was decided that this being a mixed marriage, Nike was Pentecostal, and OJ was Baptist, the social hall would keep the families happier.

The hall was decorated in white and pink flowers, white satin ribbons with lots of green plants.

Nike wore a white silk gown. Words cannot fully describe this beautiful gown with its long white train and close fitting bridal bonnet of fine white silk, laid in tiny folds on the edge and the veil draped in front and back with a wreath of velvet forget-me-nots with a little green foliage.

OJ wore a full dress tuxedo in all wool cashmere in a rich medium grey, full silk lapels on the coat, black full silk stripes one half inch wide on the outside of his pants legs, a white formal silk shirt, grey silk bow tie and a black silk top hat.

After the 10 AM wedding they left in the Hubmobile for Montgomery 85 miles north. It was a good gravel highway and OJ drove at top speed, averaging 35 miles an hour. They arrived at the Jefferson Davis Hotel in Montgomery about two o'clock, having stopped at the Coffee Pot Diner in Wing for lunch and a beer.

When they arrived they were hot, tired and dusty. Nike saw things she had never seen before. After all this was a city of 45,000 people and the capital of Alabama. The Jefferson Davis Hotel had the most beautifully designed rooms, and furniture which was all hand carved. The room even had carpet on the floor. There were colored photographs and water color pictures on the walls. They were waited on hand and foot. She thought, "I declare I believe I have died and gone to heaven." After a three day honeymoon they returned to Burntout.

OJ went over to Slap Out, (Slap Out got its name because it was slap out of sight) a few miles from Burntout, bought some land on the highest hill and built the largest most elegant home in the county. It even had three indoor privies and bathtubs bought from Sears, Roebuck and shipped from up North. The bath rooms looked liked the Jefferson Davis Hotel in Montgomery. Nike named the home "Mansion on the Hill," after a song in her church's song book, "When I Die I Will Go To That Mansion On The Hill."

Chapter Six

Life was in the fast lane for OJ and Nike. Every Friday and Saturday night they would go to the Cholly Hoss Honky Tonk and Country Club. It was the nicest honky tonk in the area and Cholly, (Charlie Spinks) the owner, was a good friend and customer of OJ's drive-in, where he bought his moonshine wholesale.

OJ was very jealous of Nike. In fact, if she looked at another man he cursed her out. The honky tonking, drinking, and his jealous outbursts became more frequent. Then he began beating her.

One night on the way home from the Cholly Hoss Honky Tonk as they came across Snit Creek Bridge, they were arguing about Nike flirting with the banjo picker. OJ stopped the car in the middle of the bridge, pulled Nike out, threw her in Snit Creek and drove off. Fortunately for Nike, snit. creek was only three feet deep, and when she hit the cold water it sobered her up. She walked home, arriving about daylight and found OJ passed out on the floor. She decided she had enough, so she hitched up Rhoda the mule to a wagon and went back to Turnip Hill.

OJ couldn't get over Nike. He would sit in the Sad and Happy Drive-In and cry when sad songs came over the radio from Nashville. He even wrote a song and went to Nike's mama's house and put it in the door. It went something like this.

"I'll love you til the day I die, whether you are wet or dry.
If you come on back to me I'll never throw you in the creek,

but I'll love you til the day I die. I am so lonesome I can't sleep at night, I keep seeing you in my dreams, up Snit Creek with out a paddle. Come back to me and get into the saddle. I'll love you til the day I die whether you are wet or dry."

He named this song, **"I'LL LOVE YOU TIL THE DAY I DIE".**

OJ would sing this and other sad songs while tending to the Sad and Happy Drive-In. One day an agent from Nashville, who came by for some White Ribbon Vitae-Likker of Life, heard him singing I'll Love You Til the day I Die. The agent offered OJ a contract, which he signed, and soon he was heard on the radio, doing concerts and even on the Grand Ole Opry. He became known all over the world, but he still loved Nike and would sing love songs to her over the radio.

True love won out and Nike went back to OJ and in the next few years two children were born, a girl named Nita and a boy named Oren. There were some happy years, but he was on the road a good deal of the time, singing at concerts and making records. He loved Nita and Oren and spent time with them when he was home, riding horses, swimming and having parties for them.

When Oren was about six years old, the fussing and fighting between OJ and Nike became more frequent. Finally, Nike divorced OJ and he moved out and only saw Nike when he was over to visit the kids.

One time Ludlow Potter was there with Nike, which made OJ very upset. Another night he went over to Slap Out to see Nike, but she was out with Ludlow. He went by the Cholly Hoss Honky Tonk and Country Club and saw Nike and Ludlow in a corner booth, snuggling up close and laughing. This made him furious and he had some words with Nike and Ludlow, then decked Ludlow and threw Nike on the floor. He was stopped by Cholly, but told Cholly as he left, "Hell I wouldn't pee on Nike's leg if she was on far."

Nike was dating Ludlow off and on and they seemed to get along fairly well. Ludlow was the preacher at Turnip Hill Pentecoastal

Church, until he backslid and the congregation threw him out for visiting the Sad and Happy Drive-In too often.

Nike had grown up in the Turnip Hill Pentecoastal Church and she did not like dating an ex-preacher from that church, but Ludlow was kind and did not hit or curse her, and they did have fun together. Ludlow had been going to see Preacher Oscar Wilcox at the church at night and Preacher Wilcox was praying for him to be saved again.

Ludlow was saved and began attending church, teaching Sunday school and even filled in as a guest preacher when Preacher Wilcox was preaching at a funeral in Red Level and couldn't get home in time for the service.

Chapter Seven

One night Nike, Nita and Oren went to a barbecue restaurant for dinner. After they got home Nike remembered that she had left her glasses at Shorty's Barbecue. Clem Hooper, who worked there, found them and left the restaurant to take the glasses to Nike.

On the morning of June 13, at daylight a neighbor, Nick Webb, who was on his way to get some corn ground into meal, passed the Samson farm where he heard some pigs grunting loudly. He thought that the boar got into the sows pen, but this sound was not like pigs making love, it was a sad type of grunting. Upon investigating the pig grunts, Nick found the children's pet pigs, named Root & Snoot, rooting at something.

Taking a closer look, Nick discovered Nike's and Clem's bodies slashed in the hog pen. Nike's throat was cut in a half moon from one ear to the other. Her throat laid open just like you were cutting the head off of a sow. The left breast was almost cut off and lay open with part of it on the ground. Her arms and stomach were slashed up pretty good. Clem's head was left hanging by a little piece of skin at the back. He also had cuts and slashes all over his body. The smell of blood and the stink of the pig pen was almost unbearable. Nick took a deep breath and heaved until he thought his stomach was coming out of his throat. He thought of the children, and as he went up to the house still heaving, his mind raced ahead to the house. "Oh Lord", he prayed, "let the two children be all right". Going into the house looking into a bedroom, he found the girl still sleeping in one room and the boy in another, both safe. He woke them, grabbed a couple of quilts, put them in the wagon and headed for Mathew's Grocery and Corn Mill, where he called the Sheriff's Office and told him what he found. Sheriff Jenkins told Nick to wait there at the store for him. Mrs. Mathew came out and got the children and gave them some breakfast while he waited for the sheriff.

The sheriff sent two officers out, one being Detective Van Otter, to investigate the crime. Another detective, Mack Burman came out later and they left to go over to the Sad and Happy Drive-In to notify OJ.

When they arrived at the Drive-In, they couldn't get anyone to answer the door, so they went around to the back and went in through the drive-in window. There they found the manager of the drive-in, Kaylow Kala, in a beer stupor. He said OJ left about nine PM on his tour bus for Shreveport, La. Detective Burman called the sheriff's office in Shreveport, asking them to notify OJ on his arrival.

While Detective Van Otter was questioning Kaylow, Detective Burman went outside to check a noise that Kaylow Kala said he heard about 8:30 the previous night. It went bump, like a cow had run into the wall.

OJ called the sheriff's office about eight AM and said he would cancel his concert and leave for Burntout right away. He got back in time for the funeral which was held in Turnip Hill.

It was the largest funeral the county has ever seen, Nike was laid out in a beautiful coffin in the Turnip Hill Pentecostal Church. She looked real pretty, as if she was just sleeping. She had on a stylish blue tailor made blouse suit, with a rolling collar, large lapels, bell sleeves, two rows of satin strap trimming above the flounce. On her head was a stylish dress turban, made on a silk wire frame to hold Nike in a prone position. The turban's front brim was covered with a narrow row of white chiffon, while the tam crown was made of a very fine white imported straw braid, trimmed stylishly and tastefully on the left with loops of white and blue silk to cover the slash marks on her throat.

Oscar Hawkins, the new preacher at the Turnip Hill Pentecostal Church, had the choir sing Nike's favorite songs. The first was "Mansion Over the Hill" and then "We Shall Gather At The River" and closed with "In The Sweet By And By." Preacher Hawkins gave a hell fire and brimstone funeral sermon. The Congregation cried, wailed and moaned. Some passed out in the aisles. When the sermon ended and mourners passed by the coffin, to view Nike for the last time, more mourners passed out. OJ was the last to come and as he stood there looking down at the beautiful Nike, remembering the good times, he could feel a song forming in his mind.

He just had to get back to the old Sad and Happy Drive-In to see if he could write it down. But before he could write the song, he was arrested and put in the county jail.

OJ had gone to school with a boy, who after high school took a correspondence course from UCLA at LA in law. (UCLA stands for Upper Corner of Lower Alabama and LA stands for Lower Alabama). He did so well in the law course, that he graduated the highest in his class.

OJ sent for him to come to the jail for an interview about representing him. Mr. Donny Kockran, Attorney at Law, arrived and told him that from what he had learned so far, he was in deep trouble.

"Mr. Kockran, Can you get me out of this mess?"

"Yes, I will put together the best legal minds in the South, if you can afford the cost."

OJ thought for a minute, "Well lets see, Pa is doing well at the still, I have a good manager, Kaylow Kala, at the Sad and Happy Drive-In, and my records are doing well, and I'll have some time to think. Maybe I can write more songs."

"Donny Kockran, get me the best justice money can buy, and get me out of this jail."

Donny went over to the courthouse and found that the Grand Jury had not handed down an indictment as yet and OJ could be bonded out for $10,000, but must remain within the city limits and report to the Sheriff's Office in two hours if indicted. OJ was in luck, the Sad and Happy Drive-In was located on the city limit line, just outside, so the city's policemen couldn't arrest him for selling White Ribbon Vitae-Likker Of Life. Only the county sheriff's officers could arrest him for selling moonshine, but the deputy that was in this territory was his close friend, and he passed along gifts of greenbacks. Also an addition had been added to the Sad and Happy Drive-In inside the city limits. This was his apartment when he wanted to get away from people. This is were he took up residence when he was bonded out of jail.

Two days later Donny came by the apartment to tell OJ that the Grand Jury had just handed down an indictment and he must report to the Sheriff's Office at 10 AM. It was now 8:30 AM and Donny told OJ he would pick him up at 9:40 AM for the trip to the Sheriff's Office.

When Donny arrived at the Sad and Happy Drive-In at 9:30 AM., OJ was no where to be found. Someone reported that he was spotted on Highway 29 North going toward Montgomery. Sheriff Jenkins and two other sheriff's cars loaded with deputies took off up Highway 29 to see if they could catch him, having called to Lucerne, 40 miles north of Three Notch, with the description of the black 1937 Hudson Terriplane touring car and the description of OJ and a man traveling with him, that fitted Cholly Spinks, of the Cholly Hoss Honky Tonk and Country Club.

They caught up to OJ about 25 miles up the road, behind a big log truck going about 20 miles an hour, kicking up so much dust they couldn't pass. The sheriff was behind the Hudson Terriplane and the dust on the gravel made it impossible to pass, so they followed the truck and Hudson Terriplane to Lucerne where the Chocktahathic County Sheriff pulled OJ and Cholly over. Cholly got out of the Hudson Terriplane with his hands up and palms toward the officers and was motioning them to step back. He approached the officers and said, "OJ is despondent over Nike's death and has a pistol up to his head."

Sheriff Clyde Jenkins told Cholly, "Go to the car and tell OJ that he is going back to Three Notch in a body bag by using his own pistol, by my 12 gauge shotgun or he can get his lanky ass out of that car and put these bracelets on."

Sheriff Jenkins handed Cholly a pair of handcuffs and told him to give them to him to put on or make a move. Cholly went back to the car and in about a minute OJ got out of the car with the handcuffs on.

The trip back to Three Notch from Lucerne was uneventful and OJ was lodged in the county jail with no special guards. Sheriff Jenkins said, "If he committed suicide the county would save lots of money."

Chapter Eight

The State Attorney's Office assigned the highly qualified, brilliant, and beautiful Martha Kluck as lead prosecuting attorney.

Martha graduated from Jones Law University in Montgomery, with the highest grade average of any student to ever attend the University. Martha joined the State Public Defender's Office where she proved herself in the highly publicized case of Cooter Ledbetter.

Cooter was a mean, ne'er-do-well, street type person that was always in trouble with the law and in and out of prison. Cooter had been paroled from a 15 year sentence for robbery and second degree murder.

He served three years and had been out of prison two weeks when he shot and killed a store clerk in an attempted robbery. There were two people in the store who saw the shooting. Martha, in a skilled cross examination of the witnesses, made it possible to get an acquittal.

One witness admitted under cross examination that she was facing the defendant.

Martha asked the lady, "How long have you been cross eyed?"

"Since I wus born," she answered.

"Well," Martha asked, "You saw the man on the opposite side of the store who was holding a big cigar and because you are cross eyed and have light gray eyes that make you see double and upside down, you are telling this jury that Mr. Ledbetter shot the victim with a cigar?"

"No Mam, I didn't say he shot the man with a cigar, I said, I think he stuck him with a cigar."

"Are you sure of that?" Martha asked as her voice rose, "That the victim didn't take the cigar and shoot himself? Can you look at the 12 jurors and say that Mr. Ledbetter shot the victim?"

"No mam," said the witness, "I can't tell them 24 jurors that Mr. Ledbetter shot him with a gun or a cigar."

The next witness swore he heard the shot and saw the flash of the gun as it was pointing at the victim.

"Which ear did you hear the gun with?" she asked.

"The one on my right side cause Mr. Ledbetter was on that side."

Martha asked the witness, "Why do you hear out of your right ear when you sleep on your left ear?"

"I don't rightly know," replied the witness.

"What type of work do you do?" asked Martha.

"Well I'm a cotton picker by trade and a darn good one," replied the witness.

Martha gave the witness a cotton Q-tip with alcohol on it and told the witness to clean his ears. Out of the right he pulled some cotton fuzz with a couple of cotton seeds. Out of his left ear he pulled lots of cotton fuzz and two boll weevils.

"Ah ha," said Martha, "Wasn't the noise you thought was a shot, the boll weevil rubbing his hind legs together in a mating call?"

"No, I didn't know the boll weevil was a fucking in my ear, maybe that's what I heard."

"You stated that you saw the flash of the gun, Are you sure?"

"Yes mam I know a flash when I see one."

"You sit there telling the jury, that with two nearly stopped up ears you know the flash was green and you heard the green flash, or did you see the mating boll weevils reflection in your eyes?"

"Well maybe the boll weevils was getting it on."

The jury acquitted Mr. Ledbetter in 10 minutes.

But as he walked down the courthouse steps he slipped on a big fat wet cigar, broke his neck and died instantly.

Chapter Nine

Chris Clock was also in the Public Defender's Office before he went to the Prosecuting Attorney's Office. His most famous case was "The Case Of The Too Short Rapist".

Shorty Moates who is five feet one inch tall, was arrested for raping Beulah Land who is six feet one inch tall. While Beulah was on the stand the prosecuting attorney asked her to describe the act.

She looked at the jury and began to sob. Between sobs she said she met Shorty at the Cholly Hoss Honky Tonk and Country Club where they had drinks and danced. About midnight she asked Shorty to walk her home. They stopped and hugged and kissed and Shorty raped her, and sobbing louder she said that Shorty raped her again.

"I'm tainted for life," she said, still sobbing.

On cross examination, Chris asked, "Miss Land, have you ever had sexual relations with anyone before?"

"Oh, yes suh, many times."

Have you ever had sexual relations with the defendant, Mr. Shorty Moates, in the past 10 years?"

"Yes suh," she answered.

"How long ago, Miss Land?"

"Oh about seven or eight inches, I guess," she answered.

"Miss Land, I asked you how long ago did you have sexual relations with Shorty, one year or less or was it more than one year? Answer me Miss Land."

"Oh I thought you wanted to know how long it wus. Well the time we done it wus five years, four months, two weeks, three days and six hours ago."

"Did you consent to the act five years ago, Miss Land?"

"It wus five years, four months, two weeks, three days and six hours I think I did as that wus what I wanted, yes, I consented."

"What position were you in, and where were you?"

"Well, suh, we wus in the cotton barn and I wus on my back."

"Where were you when the rape occurred and what position were you in?" asked Chris Clock.

"Well, suh, it was a little like this," she answered, "We got to the side of the barn when me and him got to hugging and kissing and he raped me right there by the barn."

"What position were you in Miss Land?"

"Uh, we wus standing."

"You both were standing, Miss Land?"

"Yes suh, we both wus standing".

"How tall are you Miss Land?"

"I'm six feet one inch tall."

"Tell this jury, Miss Land, how you being six feet one inch tall, and Mr. Moates is five foot one inch tall, how the defendant could rape you with the two of you standing. Tell them Beulah Land."

Looking at the jury, Beulah Land said, "Well I got Shorty a little feed bucket and I wus against the wall and Shorty got on the bucket."

"But Miss Land, the bucket is only ten inches tall and Shorty is five feet one inch tall, there is still a difference of two inches, How could he rape you?"

"Well, suh, can't a girl stoop just a little?"

"You stooped again when he raped you the second time?"

"No, suh, I got a bucket that wus a little higher, cause I wus too tard to stoop any more."

The Jury was out 12 minutes, including the time it took to get a drink of water and returned a not guilty verdict. Mr. Chris Clock was on his way.

Chapter Ten

The third attorney for the prosecuting team was Philip "Flip" Moore. Mr. Moore was also a graduate of Jones Law University, Montgomery. Flip could not decide whether to take up law or medicine, but law won out.

While in law school he got a job on weekends at the County Morgue. This gave him plenty of time to study as well as earn some extra income, which he sorely needed. Saturday nights at the morgue were quite busy, not only from the deaths of natural causes, but also from fights in the local honky tonks and from the county. Some were murdered by jealous lovers, married as well as single.

Flip began to study the bodies and made notes of how they died. As he had a flair for sketching, he would sketch the expressions on the faces on the deceased and study the sketches while reading the coroner's report. He began to get a pattern of what the expression meant, but was not quite able to put it together. As most of the people in the morgue died from causes other than natural, he decided he needed more experience on the causes of death. It would mean more work and an extra study load, but he got a job at night at a local funeral home assisting the mortician in preparing bodies for the funeral. After a few months he switched to a home study course to be a mortician.

After passing the state exams and getting his mortician license, he got a job at night as a mortician and still worked the morgue on weekends while continuing with the law school. He got back to studying the facial expressions from his sketches and found that he could almost predict how the deceased died. By doing the same to knife and gunshot wounds, he was getting good at determining what type of gun or knife was used to cause the deaths.

Going into his third year of law school, he had worked up a good method of detection about wounds and how the death occurred, and by the expression on the face, whether the victim knew the murderer. He wrote a book on practical scientific work on the human face embracing forms and character on all parts, including the forehead, hair, wrinkles, mouth, cheeks, eyelids, eyes, chin, ears and overall expressions at death. The name of the scientific work was named, "Faciology." Another scientific work that he wrote was the position of a body at the time the fatal blow was struck, be it gun, knife, poison, blow to the head, natural or any cause. He was able to estimate the time of death by temperature of the body when found. The name for this work was "Bodiology."

After getting his law degree he was hired by the law firm of Crook, Cheatem, Mays, Gill, Jones and Scannapieco, in Chicago as an expert in Faciology and Bodiology. He soon made a reputation for winning cases on more scientific facts than any other method.

Of the more famous cases he won, just before the Alabama State Attorney's Office hired him for the Oscar James Samson trial, was the case of, "The Lamb Baas at Midnight."

In early 1937, the chicago Police were called to 64 N. W. 10 Street where they found a grieving actor by the name of Billy Baxter, who said he just arrived home from the theater, where he was starring in the play, "Till the Doctor Comes". He arrived home and found his wife on the kitchen floor very cold, and surmised that she was dead. He said he left for the theater at 7:30 PM., the play started at 8:30 PM., and ended at 11 PM. It took him approximately a half hour to get the makeup and costume off and seven to 10 minutes to walk less than the quarter mile home, where he found his wife.

No weapon was found at the scene, and no wounds were visible on her body. The coroner found she had received a blow to the head that caused a trauma and this caused the death. The coroner fixed the time of death at 9 PM., the time that Billy Baxter was on stage.

Chicago police arrested Billy Baxter for murder, claiming that the coroner was off by approximately 40 minutes to an hour, and that the murder took place at 7:30 PM.

Because the apartment was warm, the body was slow in developing rigor mortis. The defense had witnesses to testify that the defendant could not have committed the murder, as it took him seven to 10 minutes to walk to the theater and 45 minutes to get into the costume and makeup and he had more than a hundred witnesses to prove he was on stage at that time.

The defense put on a forensic expert who testified that indeed the murder took place at 8 to 8:30 PM., the time Mr. Baxter was on stage and the room was extra warm and this slowed the rigor mortis.

Flip Moore, on cross examination, asked the forensic expert, Dr. Robin Hood, if a blanket was left in the ice box and got cold and put on the body at 9:15 PM., would this speed up the rigor mortis?

"Yes," Dr. Hood said.

"From the pleasant expression, on Mrs. Baxter's face, showing lack of fear or surprise, would you agree she was not confronted by a stranger Dr. Hood?"

"I would agree with that Mr. Moore," Dr. Hood answered, "but Mr. Baxter was at the theater and you do not have the weapon."

"Dr. Hood," Flip Moore asked, "do you know what the defendant had for dinner?"

"He stated that he had some roast lamb," answered Dr. Hood.

"Dr. Hood, could the following scenario be theoretically possible? Mr. Baxter, in his excellent physical condition, leaves the theater at the nine o'clock intermission, and jogs to his apartment.

Arriving home he takes a leg of lamb and hits his wife in the head killing her at 9:10 PM. He then puts the murder weapon, the leg of lamb, into the oven and roasts it at 350 degrees. After covering the corpse with a cold blanket, that had been chilled in the ice box, he jogs back to the theater in time to go on stage after the 20 minute intermission. Since he was not on stage five minutes before, and three minutes after the intermission, this would give him a total of 28 minutes to commit the murder. After the performance, he went home at 11:30 PM. removed the blanket, and sat down to a dinner of roast lamb, thereby destroying the evidence. Would that be possible, Dr. Hood?"

"Yes," replied Dr. Hood.

"Do you agree that a stranger would not have cradled her body in their arms as she was dying."

"I'll agree, but there is not proof that this happened."

"Dr. Hood, as a forensic expert have you examined bodies that were in a position, where it was as if someone tenderly held a person and gently laid them down and the rigor mortis set in on the body in that position as well as the facial expression as if they were looking at someone lovingly."

"Yes," replied Dr. Hood.

The jury after hearing more evidence and weak rebuttal from the defense, brought in a guilty verdict of murder in the first degree.

Chapter Eleven

Donny Kockran had been visiting OJ in the county jail, where they had been planning their strategy for the upcoming trial. They were putting together a witness list. By law, a defendant's witnesses have the right to visit the defendant in jail. One of the witnesses was Barbé Paulieri, a tall, leggy brunette, with a long full head of hair, full lips, uplifted breasts, size 34C. Barbé and OJ had been seen together at the Cholly Hoss Honky Tonk and Country Club. They had been together at various concerts in several cities and she also traveled on his tour bus. Barbé used the witness list as an opportunity to see him.

Donny told OJ that he was putting together the best legal minds in the South. A couple of names he mentioned to him were some outstanding southern attorneys that he thought might fit the team, and put on a good defense.

After graduating from UCLA, Donny went to Montgomery, but found it very difficult to get a job as a law clerk or intern. He had an uncle who worked for a law firm in New York and told Donny to come to up and he would help him get a job. Kelvin Kockran was an attorney in the firm of, Frankenbush, Gladfelter, Rabinowitz, Pawloski, Kamiercyk and Cook.

Kelvin handled cases that involved lawsuits that the firms clients filed in accidents and other disasters. The firm had tipsters who would report accidents and other suspected opportunities for lawsuits. Donny became an ambulance chaser and was soon promoted in the firm as their newest trial attorney.

Donny made his reputation with his charm and southern drawl, for winning every suit he tried while with the firm. Some of the tactics he used, were like those in the case of the, "Priests in the Trolley Car."

A milk wagon delivering milk hit a little old lady, Mrs. Magoo, on the curb in the Bowery. Mrs. Magoo who was blind in her left eye, was looking for cigarettes butts on the sidewalk with her right eye, and walked into the milk wagon just as the delivery man told the horse, "Giddy Up."

A tipster reported this accident to Donny, who talked to the milk company, Milk On The Way.

The attorney for Milk On The Way, refused to pay any damages due to the fact that the evidence showed it was the fault of Mrs. Magoo. Donny sued Milk On The Way for two thousand dollars.

On the first day of the trial, he called Mrs. Magoo to the stand.

He asked Mrs. Magoo, "Mam, as a Suthun Gentlemen to a charming nice grandmotherly lady who is blind in the left eye and can't see good out of the right eye, tell the jury what you were doing on the day in question."

"Well Sir, I am a penniless little old grandmotherly type person, and I have no money and my only son, may God have mercy on his soul, sits on death row for a crime he did not commit. I was looking for cigarette butts to save money for an appeal. So a penny found is good for four cigarettes. I can have two and send two to my son, may God have mercy on his soul."

"Mrs. Magoo, were there any witnesses to this terrible accident?"

"I'm not sure Mr. Kockran, I couldn't see farther than the trolley car."

Donny pointed to three men in the front row, who were dressed as priests. Donny then asked Mrs. Magoo, in his best southern drawl, "Are these the Fathers you saw?" (The men were married, with children, as Mr. Kockran did not want his witness to lie).

"Yes Sir, they were in the trolley car," said Mrs. Magoo.

The attorney for Milk on The Way, a Mr. Anthony Simonovitch, said to himself, "My God, a trolly car full of priests for witnesses."

He requested a side bar conference, and asked the Judge if he could have a recess to confer with his co-council and Mr. Kockran. He was given a 15 minute recess.

During the recess Mr. Simonovitch and Mr. Kockran agreed on a settlement for Mrs. Magoo, the little old lady who couldn't see so well.

A few more cases like this and Mr. Kockran felt he had enough experience to open his own law firm. He moved his practice to Three Notch and was doing very well,

Chapter Twelve

One of the best legal minds (beside his own) was a young attorney named Barry Kall. Barry had been a pilot in the airline industry. It was a fledging industry and Barry did not want to struggle with a low income, so he switched his career to sales, where he was a success.

He was interested in law, so he enrolled in the University of Alabama Law School at night and began the study of law. After graduating, he was hired by the firm of McCann, Hertz and Howe, which specialized in defending bootleggers, smugglers, robbers, murderers and other hard core criminals.

During prohibition, some moonshiners went to the Bahama Islands and Puerto Rico, set up stills and started smuggling moonshine to Miami and around Key West, and up the Gulf of Mexico to Mobile, where it filtered up to the southern states.

Some of the moonshiners added rum from Cuba and Jamaica to their moonshine load. Later the Colombians in South America sold some cocaine to the smugglers and that added to their inventory. With all of this activity, many smugglers were being arrested, and the law firm of McCann, Hertz and Howe had many cases to defend.

Barry soon made a name for himself in that 95 percent of his cases won acquittals. One of the most publicized cases was "The Barefoot Smuggler With Eleven Toes".

Pegleg Williams had been arrested for smuggling rum and cocaine. He had picked up rum in Havana, Cuba, and cocaine from Cartagena, Colombia. He brought a number of loads like this one in on a cargo ship he rented to bring in bananas, rum and cocaine. Pegleg came into the waters off the coast of the Florida and Alabama line. The ship would anchor out in deep water and the smugglers would bring the rum and cocaine in by small boats and run the boats ashore on a sandy beach near a community named Two Egg.

Two Egg got its name, because it was the only store for 10 miles, and the farmers would trade eggs for merchandise. The most popular product was a triple shot of rum for two eggs. This drink became so popular they named the community Two Egg. Pegleg would pay the locals with rum for their work of unloading the illegal cargo. The problem was that Pegleg Williams' leg would sink down in the sand at the landing, causing him difficulty in walking, especially if he had to run from the customs agents and revenuers.

On one of his trips to pick up rum and cocaine he had to lay over in Cartagena, Colombia. "Pepe" Hernandez told him of a man back in the mountains who could make him a wooden leg with a soft type foot on the bottom so he would be able to walk in the sand and mud without so much difficulty.

Pegleg found a guide to take him up the mountain to see Señor Juan Lopéz about the special peg leg. After two days of hiking through the jungle and up the mountain, they came upon a small clearing with two huts made of small tree trunks, about three inches in diameter and tied together with vines at the corner and spaced about seven or eight inches apart. The huts were about 10 by 20 feet, and had two windows and a door. Between the small tree trunks had been placed red clay mud, which had dried. The roof was made of banana and palm leaves, with burlap bags over the windows and the door.

He would stay in one of the huts with two Colombian men, who he thought were guards as the camp looked as if it was a cocaine processing operation. He had to be careful to try not to see too much as the men were ill clothed, hadn't shaved or bathed in weeks, and used the stuff they worked with. They arrived late in the afternoon and spent all night swatting mosquitoes. The mosquitoes didn't seem to bother the Colombians. "They were too smelly," he thought.

In the morning, a Colombian came and said he was Juan and would make him a new leg, but he would have to take the present leg with him. He thought that was what he said, as the Columbian spoke very poor English. This left him to get around with only one leg.

When he was twelve, Pegleg had lost his left leg at the knee, while he was in the woods hunting some wild boar. One of the boar found him and chewed so much of the leg that by the time they got him to the doctor, they had to amputate at the knee. However, he got a wooden leg and learned to walk, jump, and became an accomplished dancer, doing the waltz, square, round, and jitterbug dances. He also participated in walk-a-thons, winning many dance contests.

So Pegleg hopped around the hut and swatted mosquitoes for the two days. Finally Juan appeared with the leg. He tried it on and the fitting at the knee was perfect as Juan used the old one and added some llama skin leather to make it softer. The foot didn't look too much like a foot, except on the bottom, but he could walk better and he went outside to try it in the mud and it worked great.

It was tough going as they went down the mountain through the jungle, but with each step he seem to be doing better with the foot. By the time he arrived back in Cartagena he could walk better than before. He contacted Pepe, got his load of cocaine, and the freighter slipped out of the harbor at midnight. The freighter would anchor east of Mobile and west of Pensacola, always on Saturday night.

The reason was that the Coast Guard and Custom Agents (they were housed in the same building) would listen to the Grand Ole Opry from Nashville on Saturday nights, therefore they paid little attention to the few ships coming and going. It was on one of these trips that Pegleg had come ashore and he walked well in the sand.

The next morning the Coast Guard and Customs Agents came to Two Egg having heard that a shipload of goods had come in and some of the Two Egg boys were having a good time with their rum. Seeing the tracks in the sand and the odd shaped footprint they had plaster of Paris casts made of the prints. A tipster told the customs agents that a peglegged fellow in Montgomery had a foot like that.

Juan Lopéz had put six toes on the foot he made for Pegleg and the plaster of Paris cast had six toes.

After his arrest Pegleg contacted the law firm of McCann, Hertz, and Howe and the case was assigned to Barry Kall.

Pegleg told Barry that the customs agents had taken his leg and he had to hop around, until he could he get his leg back.

Barry was able to get Pegleg out of jail on bail, but customs would not release the leg as it was impounded as evidence. His bail required that he stay in the county and report in each Monday.

Pegleg and Barry had a conference and decided that Pegleg needed to get another leg made just like the one that the customs agents impounded.

Juan Lopéz had no telephone, and the only way to see him was to go into the mountainous jungle. Barry took a vacation, (as an excuse) and got a plane out of Atlanta for Miami. From Miami he hired a plane to Santiago, Cuba. Here he was able to hire a pilot that would take him to Cartagena, Columbia, by way of a stopover for fuel at Santo Domingo, then to Riohacha, Columbia, the last leg to Cartgena. It took five days to get there, and he still had to go into the jungle. He found Pepe who got him the guide and took him to see Juan Lopéz.

Juan said he had all of the measurements of the leg and foot, except for the stump of Pegleg's leg. Besides, he could have gained or lost weight. They agreed that the best thing to do was to bring the measurements and raw materials to Miami, and make the leg there. The fee would be high, so Juan Lopéz agreed to go with Barry to Cartagena so he could cable Pegleg for approval.

In Cartagena, Barry sent a cable to Pegleg that read, "If you want to learn how to dance the rhumba, it would be $1,000 to teach a two legged man to rhumba to the tune of "Five little Twinkle Toes."

Pegleg cabled back, "Let me know where the floor is, I'm ready to dance."

When Barry and Señor Lopéz got to the plane, the pilot was ready for take off. Barry reversed the trip as far as Santiago, Cuba. Because Juan Lopéz did not have a passport they flew into Nassau, Bahamas, where Barry chartered a fishing boat for two days of deep sea fishing, picked up Señor Lopéz at Paradise Key and headed for Miami, coming in at night into Haulover inlet and anchoring at the Sunny Isles Motel.

Barry took two rooms and gave instructions to the captain of the fishing boat to be back at the Sunny Isles Motel in one week.

When they had arrived at the Sunny Isles Motel on Sunday night, Barry called Pegleg and told him to go see Jasper White who would fly him to Miami. They were to leave within the hour after reporting to the customs agent on his weekly report. He reported at 10 AM on Monday and by 6 PM. was at North Perry airport outside of Hollywood, Florida. By 7 PM they were at the Sunny Isles Motel having dinner.

Barry told Pegleg that this is no vacation. "You have to go to room 313 and Señor Lopéz will measure the leg stump so he can start on the leg". Barry told him.

At the meeting Barry told Juan Lopéz to make it identical to the previous leg, except with only five toes. After looking at Pegleg's right foot Señor Lopéz got to work. By Thursday Juan Lopéz had a leg identical to the old leg, except there were only five toes, and he made the artificial leg adjustable at the stump so that it could be adjusted in the event Pegleg gained or lost a little weight.

Juan Lopéz left to get the charter fishing boat on Sunday and retrace his steps back to the jungles of Columbia. Barry and Pegleg flew back with the pilot, Jasper White, landing in a cow pasture near the Deep South Barbecue and cocktail Lounge on Highway 31 South.

Barry told Pegleg to eat lots of sweets and other fattening foods, so that he would gain weight. He wanted Pegleg to gain at least another 10 pounds by the trial date, and bring his weight up to 20 pounds over his normal weight. The trial would begin in about six weeks.

By the date of the trial, Pegleg had gained the extra weight. He arrived in court in a Schaffer & Co. medium gray and white check patterned suit, a white percale shirt, with a four-ply pure linen collar with cuffs to match, a pair of silk suspenders with medium light gray stripes, gilt buckles and fine leather ends, with a four-in-hand silk gray stripe tie to match his suspenders. On his head, cocked to the left side, was a medium gray fedora hat, that he removed at the defense table. On his feet he wore a beautiful pair of black patent leather oxfords.

As he walked down the aisle to the defendant's table a sigh went up from the lady spectators in the courtroom, for he was a handsome man, impeccably dressed, and his walk was nearly a waltz. No one would guess that his left leg was artificial. The jury consisted of four women, ranging from 25 to 50 years of age. The two men were in their late 20s.

The prosecutor called a customs agent who was on duty the night of the crime. Mr. Joe Bartow, the prosecutor, asked the witness, Ira Badger, the customs agent, "Mr. Badger tell us what happened on the night of the smuggling."

"Well Suh, about 11 to 11:30 we heard noise like a small boat off shore, and low talking, but we thought it wus some local fellows from Two Egg with their girl friends and we didn't want to disturb them, so we didn't go out. The next morning we heard that the boys in Two Egg was still partying, and we went over and found that they had gotten some fresh rum. A man called Peanut, cause he is so little, told us that a fellow from Montgomery had a foot like the print we saw in the sand."

"Describe the footprint you saw in the sand . Was there anything unusual about it Mr. Badger?"

"I saw this footprint that was long and slender and looked like it had six toes."

"Did you see the suspected smuggler, Mr. Badger?"

"No, Suh."

Mr. Barry Kall, faced the jury, smiled and said, "We will show that Mr. Nathan (Pegleg's real name) Williams is an innocent man. You can look at him and see that he is innocent. However, we will prove that the nice clean cut young fellow you see at that table, pointing at Pegleg, is not guilty of the crime he is charged with."

"Mr. Badger, I notice you have long slender fingers, I would guess you can play the guitar, is this true?"

"Yes Suh, Mr. Kall. I pick a pretty mean guitar, I love guitar music."

"Mr. Badger, do you listen to the Grand Ole Opry from Nashville on Saturday nights?"

"Yes Suh, I do every Sat'dy night."

"Tell me," asked Barry Kall, "who was picking and singing on the Grand Ole Opry from 11 to 12 o'clock on the Saturday night in question?"

"Well Suh, it was a number of stars, Roy Acuff played three songs, one wus my favorite, Orange Blossom Special, The Billy Bob Gospel Quartet wus on the last half hour, singing some of my favorite gospel songs, like, Rescue The Perishing, What A Friend We Have In Jesus, Bringing In The Sheaves and more."

"Isn't it true, Mr. Badger, that you was listening to the Grand Ole Opry with the volume of the radio so loud that it was heard one quarter mile away, and you could not hear anything outside, and you were singing with the gospel quartet and your mind was not on your duty. Remember, Mr. Badger, you are under oath and if you do not tell the truth you can be charged with perjury. Now did you hear any noise or voices outside between 11 and 12 PM on the night in question?"

"No Suh, I didn't and that's a fact."

Mr. Joe Davis, the prosecutor called another witness, Mr. Marvin "Peanuts" Koons to the witness stand.

"Mr. Koons, have you ever met Pegleg Williams?"

"Yes suh, I seen him once when we wuz unloading rum."

Mr. Bartow the prosecutor, asked Peanut if he ever saw Pegleg's left leg and foot.

"Yes Suh, when he pulled his shoes off to carry the rum up on the beach."

"What did you notice, if anything, about his foot?"

"Well Suh, he had six toes on his left foot. I saw this and took notice cause I never seen anybody with six toes before."

"Did you see the defendant on the night in question, and if you did, how did you recognize him?"

"Well Suh," said Peanuts, "he had this unshaven look and was a skinny fellow with a pegleg and a funny foot."

Barry Kall was ready to cross examine Peanuts Koon, and as he looked at Peanuts with his steel blue eyes, he asked, "Mr. Koons what was your pay for helping unload Mr. William's cargo ship?"

"Well you see Suh, I don't ask fer pay. Mr. Tommy, the boss man fer Mr. Williams, gives me all the rum I can drink while unloading, plus a quart when I finish."

"I understand, Mr. Koons, you can carry a big load, that is you can drink a good bit of rum, can't you?"

"Yes Suh, I can hold a right smart amount of rum."

"Are you sure you saw Mr. Williams after you had all of the rum you could drink?"

" Yes Suh."

"Mr. Koons, look over at the defense table and point out Mr. Williams from the three men sitting there."

Peanuts looked over at the defense table and picked the man on the left end.

"Why did you pick this gentlemen, Mr. Koons?" asked Mr. Kall.

"He is small and has a beard, and skinny legs."

Barry asked the gentlemen to stand and state his name.

The man stood up and said his name was Irv Stanley and he was a law clerk.

Then Barry Kall asked Mr. Nathan Williams to stand and walk across the room and stand in front of Mr. Koons and then the jury. Mr. Williams sort of walked/waltzed across the room and stood in front of Mr. Koons and the jury. "Can you, Mr. Koons, tell the jury that this is the man you saw on the night in question, with six toes?"

"No Suh, the man I saw wus not that big, and looked real mean."

Mr. Joe Bartow on recross asked Mr. Koons if he would recognize the foot if he saw it.

Mr. Bartow had the clerk to give him the peoples exhibit number 21, the leg with the six toes.

"Is this the leg with the six toes that belongs to Mr. Pegleg Williams, the defendant, who is sitting in the middle of the three men at the defense table?"

"Yes Suh, that is the leg with the six toes."

On recross, Mr. Kall asked that the defendant to take off his artificial leg and showed it to Mr. Koons.

"Is this the leg you saw on the night in Question?"

"I don't know as I can't see the toes, and I didn't see the top part of the leg." answered Peanuts.

Mr. Kall took the shoe off of the foot and asked Mr. Koons to count the toes.

"One-two-three-four-five-si, there is only five toes here," answered Mr. Koons.

"Mr. Koons will you count the toes on exhibit 21?" asked Mr. Kall.

"One-two-three-four-five-six." counted Mr. Koons. "That is the leg I saw at the beach."

Mr. Kall then asked Mr. Nathan Williams to put on the exhibit 21 leg, the one with the six toes.

Mr. Williams tried to put the leg on, but the stump of his leg would not fit the six- toed leg.

Mr. Kall said to Mr. Williams, "Walk over to Mr. Koons and the jury in the six toed leg?"

Mr. Williams walked a couple of steps and fell down, then he got up and walked over in front of the jury, as he walked he had very bad limp as the right leg was one and a half inches shorter than the artificial leg due to the fact Mr. Williams couldn't get the stump of his leg far enough into the leg to make both legs even.

Mr. Kall then asked Mr. Koons, "Is this the man with the six toed leg you saw that night?"

"No," said Mr. Koons, That ain't the man, but it is the six toed leg."

Barry Kall turned to the jury and said, "If the leg don't fit, then you have to acquit."

The jury was out 15 minutes and returned a verdict of not guilty.

Chapter Thirteen

Donny wanted to get some expert attorneys lined up. He had in mind an expert in wounds by knife, gun shot, blunt instruments, and fists, among other type weapons. The attorney was named Rufus Cobb. Donny would contact him.

Another attorney who was an expert in blood typing, finger-prints, and other indemnifications he would get, if available, was Israel Zolowitz.

In the meantime, Donny had to gather all information, meet with the attorneys, assign duties to them and lay out the plans for the best brains in the South.

While Donny was making plans, OJ was in a small cell, with only family and people they could get on the witness list for visitors. His girl friend Barbé Paulieri visited once a week, and OJ asked Donny to see if they would let Barbé visit more often. Sheriff Clyde Jenkins said, "Absolutely not, it may be cut down to once every two weeks."

Boredom set in on OJ. He was lonesome for Barbé, but most of all he missed Nike. He wished he could be at the Sad and Happy Drive In, where you "Drive In Sad and Drive out Happy", and even visit the Cholly Hoss Honky Tonk and Country Club, get up on stage and sing.

Gosh, I wanna be free, he thought. Maybe he could write a song. He asked the jailer for lots of paper and pencils and as he started writing his thoughts turned to freedom. After two days he had his song, but had to have a tune. He asked Donny to get him a guitar, which was delivered to his cell. As he practiced and practiced and practiced, the prisoners in his cell block began to holler for him to shut up.

Finally, he had his tune, and named his song, "ALABAMA STAR", he sent word down the cell block to listen to his new song all the way through to the end. In his rich baritone voice he began to sing.

I am an Alabama star and I wanna be free,
To hell with the O.C.P.
(Office of the County Prosecutor)
Let me drink and let me cuss,
Cause all I wanna do is ride my tour bus.
I am an Alabama Star, and I wanna be free,
To hell with the O.C.P.

He finished all four verses and chorus.

When he had finished the song, he knew he had another hit by the hooping and hollering from the other prisoners, and they wanted more. He sang some of the popular songs and threw in some gospel favorites. The prisoners began calling requests for such gospel songs as, In the Sweet By and By, When the Roll is Called Up Yonder, Amazing Grace, Precious Memories and others. It seems as if these songs reminded the prisoners of home and when they were young. The guard came by and asked that he stop the singing, as it was only ten minutes to lights out.

OJ asked the guard if he could use the phone, to call one of his attorneys. The guard escorted him to the jailer's office, where he called Carl Dash, and informed Carl that he was going to trial tomorrow and he would like him to bring some clothes that he could wear to court.

"We will have to wait until court is in session and ask the judge's permission. We will do that the first thing in the morning."

OJ didn't sleep too well thinking about the beginning of the trial.

Chapter Fourteen

Three Notch County 2-1/4 Circuit Court had assigned the highly experienced Judge Vance Ego as the Presiding Judge.

Judge Ego was appointed to the circuit court four years before and made his reputation in the notorious case "The Governors Wife is a Congenital Liar."

While Governor of the State, Hill Klinton and his wife Millary Bodam-Klinton, received 2,000 shares of stock in Ucheatum Holding Corporation for payment of fees payed to Millary for legal advice. The stock was priced at $.50 cents a share. In the thirties, anyone receiving the equivalent of $1,000 for a few minutes work was considered among the brightest of attorneys. However, the law firm that Millary was associated with was the legal firm for the newly formed Federal Farm Loan and Saving Association, created by FDR to help restart the economy, along side of the WPA and PWA. Ucheatum Holding Corporation purchased 5,000 acres of farm land under the name of one of their subsidiaries, Pofolks Community Farms.

The law firm of Lilly, Dilly and Bodam, of which Millary was a partner under her maiden name, recommended to their client the Federal Farm Loan and Saving Association to loan them $25 per acre on the Pofolks Community Farm, this coming to $125,000. The same day of the transaction, Ucheatum sold 500 acres of the Pofolks Community Farms to another subsidiary the Springwater

Resort and Country Club, for $10 an acre. The 500 acres that Ucheatum sold was the most prime piece of property of the 5,000 acres. It had ten natural springs and beautiful trees, creeks and landscaping. Ucheatum purchased the stock from Millary for $1 a share and five hundred shares of stock in the Springwater Resort and Country Club. This brought Millary $2,000 dollars, and the stock in the Springwater Resort and Country Club was worth $10 a share or $5,000. Not bad for a few minutes work and recommending a loan. In the next few years the Pofolks Community Farm was not heard from and three years later the Federal Farm Loan and Saving Association foreclosed on the Ucheatum loan.

The federal government paid to the Federal Farm Loan and Saving Association $120,000 for the unpaid loan. Ucheatum Holding Corp. had payed $5,000 on the loan. Some two years later the Ucheatum Holding Corporation and the Springwater resort and Country Club surfaced again. This was during the Governors election, but nothing could be found to connect the Klintons, as Millary did not own any stock in either corporation.

In the second year of the Governorship, an associate of Millary's in the law firm of Lilly, Dilly and Bodam had committed suicide and papers were found in his personal belongings, pertaining to stock in the Ucheatum Holding and Springwater Resort and Country Club and some of the records showed that Hill and Millary Bodam-Klinton had previously owned stock in both Corporations. Millary stated she did not or had not ever owned stock in either of the corporations. When she was shown the papers, she stated it was a minuscule amount that she didn't remember. Millary also denied to the grand jury any knowledge of anything to do with these corporations, except she invested an amount she couldn't remember in the Ucheatum Holding Corporation and lost that when the Corporation went under. She was indicted and went to trial where Judge Vance Ego was the presiding judge. Millary Bodam-Klinton was found guilty of perjury and contempt and Judge Vance Ego sentenced her to two years in prison, two years probation and a $10,000 fine. Judge Ego was pressured to reduce the sentence to one day and no probation or fine, but Judge Ego stuck to his ruling.

The case went to the Supreme Court and was upheld. The last day of December, one day before Millary was to report to start serving her sentence Governor Klinton, who had only three more weeks in his term gave, Millary Bodam-Klinton a pardon.

Chapter Fifteen

Judge Ego set the Samson trial to began on Monday, September 5, 1938. They would begin by meeting the attorneys and laying down the procedures and ground rules for selection of the jurors and other court room rules.

On Monday, September 5, the court was called to order, and as Judge Ego looked out from the bench, on his right was the defense team of Donny Kockran, Barry Kall, Rufus Cobb, Israel Zolowitz and an attorney who was not on the list. Judge Ego asked Donny Kockran who this attorney was.

"Your honor," answered Donny, "This is Mr. Carl Dash who renewed his license after not practicing for several years, because he is a friend of Oscar James Samson and is very capable of aiding in Mr. Samson's defense. I request the court to allow Mr. Dash to be one of the defense members in court."

Judge Ego approved the request.

Carl Dash is the friend who removed a suitcase from the tour bus on the morning that OJ returned to Burntout from Shreveport, La., after Nike's and Clem's bodies were found. The suitcase had never been located or seen since that fateful morning.

On the left side of the court room was the prosecution team of Martha Kluck, Chris Clock and Phillip "Flip" Moore.

Judge Ego informed the attorneys, court reporters, Merl Monroe and Dorthy LaTour, and Bailiff Dean Autry, that under no circumstances would he tolerate any nonsense such as, name calling, badgering of witnesses or demeaning the court.

The court began selecting the jurors and instructed the defense to have the defendant in court. Mr. Kall asked the judge to let the defendant wear his own clothing rather than the jail house uniform and said that the defense would pay for deputies to guard the defendant so that he could appear in court without handcuffs. The judge granted this motion, but said Mr. Samson had to be conservatively dressed and adjourned the court until 1:30 PM.

Carl Dash spent the lunch period going out to The Mansion On The Hill to gather some clothing that would make OJ look good in front of the jury.

When the court reconvened at 1:30 PM all participants were in court and ready to go. Judge Ego entered, took one look at OJ and said, "Mr. Kall, I said, I would not tolerate any nonsense and the defense had violated this rule."

Mr. Kall asked, "Your honor, what has been violated?"

Judge Ego answered, "Look at how Mr. Samson is dressed."

OJ was dressed in a white cowboy suit with tight legs, tassels hanging from the sleeves, sequins of several designs on the jacket and down the outside of the pants legs, white cowboy boots and a white cowboy hat on the defense table.

Judge Ego said, "This is not a county barn dance or honky tonk, and I stated, that Mr. Samson would be conservatively dressed, and that implies, dressed in a suit, coat, white shirt, tie and matching shoes, or Mr. Samson will appear in jail white and black stripes and be handcuffed and shackled. I recess the court for 45 minutes to let Mr. Samson change into the clothes I have described for this time only. Court is adjoined until 2:15 PM."

When the court reconvened at 2:15 PM., Mr. Samson had on a medium blue cashmere suit, white shirt dark blue tie, black shoes and medium blue socks.

Judge Ego took a look at the court room and OJ's clothing and with his gavel banging on the desk said, "Let the trial of the State versus Oscar James Samson begin. Bring in the first prospective juror."

The first juror was Arnold McKinley, a farmer of about 50, who was weatherbeaten, from tending the fields in the hot summer, and from caring for the farm animals in the winter. Mr. Mckinley answered the questions asked by Martha Kluck.

Mr. Kockran asked a couple of questions, "Mr. McKinley, could you listen to the facts and make an honest judgement in this case?"

"Yes, Suh, I shore can and my honest judgement would be he kilt dem." Mr. Kockran dismissed Mr. McKinley.

Judge Ego recessed the court until 10 AM on the next day.

On Tuesday, September 6, the court called Mr. Kit Carson, a rancher, farmer and an old style cowboy.

"Mr. Carson," asked, Mr. Kockran, "Do you know Mr. Samson?"

"No, but I have heard him on the Grand Ole Opry, and all I can say is he is a good singer."

After a few more questions, Mr. Kockran turned Mr. Carson over to Miss. Kluck.

"Mr. Carson, did you ever visit the Cholly Hoss Honky Tonk and Country Club when Mr. Samson was performing there?"

"No mam, when I wasn't ranching and tending to my cattle, I was in California working in cowboy pictures."

Mr. Carson was accepted by the prosecution and the defense and another juror, Kathy Tillman was called. Martha Kluck asked a few questions and then asked, "Did you know Mr. OJ Samson?"

"Yes um, I shore did, I usta go to the Cholly Hoss Honky Tonk and Country Club and dance when he played there. He shore wus a good singer and guitar picker."

Miss Kluck dismissed this juror.

Another was called, a Tom Watson, son of a business owner, who didn't do much but hang around the Three Notch Country Club with other well to do people of Three Notch, and play golf on the nine hole newly constructed executive course.

It was the defense's turn to start the questioning of the prospective juror.

Mr. Kockran asked, "Mr. Watson, what do you do for a living?"

"I am a golf professional and play golf for money."

"Have you ever won any tournaments?"

"Yes Sir, I won the county championship up there in Wahoon County."

"How much money did you win?"

"I won $50 but the promoter, Silas Crabgrass, bet $25 on someone else, so he only had $25 dollars to give me."

A few questions later Mr. Kockran concluded his examination of this prospect, as he would do for the defense.

"Mr. Watson, have you ever played golf with Mr. Samson?" asked Miss Kluck.

"No Mam," answered Mr. Watson.

"Have ever given instruction on how to play golf to Mr. Samson?"

"Yes Mam, I did," he answered.

"Tell us, Mr. Watson. Where did the instruction take place and if you were payed, how much were you payed?"

"Mr. Samson asked me to go out to his home, Mansion On The Hill, where he had a two hole putting green and chipping area, and I gave him instruction on chipping and putting. He payed me $5 and a bottle of White Ribbon Vitae-Likker of Life."

Ms. Kluck dismissed Mr. Watson as a juror for being to close to the defendant.

Judge Ego recessed the court for the noon hour and would reconvene at 1:30 PM.

When the court was called to order at 1:30 PM a Mr. Tom Mix was called, also a rancher and a part time cowboy for the picture shows.

Tom Mix was another clean cut cowboy type and did not know of Mr. Samson. He was accepted by the prosecution and defense.

A Mrs. Kitty Kat was the next person called. Mrs. Kat, a housewife, was the wife of businessman Freddy Kat. She had two children, a girl, named Scary Kat, and a son, named Tom Kat. She had one year of college and met all the requirements of the prosecution and defense. She was accepted.

Mr. Rhett Cutler was the next prospective juror called. Mr. Cutler worked for the Dixon Sawmill as a logger. Miss Kluck started the questioning, with, "Mr. Cutler, tell us what a logger is?"

"Well, Mam, I don't work for the Dixon Sawmill full time, I contract out to them on a job basis. Dixon, Dozier, Brantley and other saw mills use me."

"How do they use you and exactly what type of work do you perform?" asked Miss Kluck.

"Well, Miss Kluck, I have four oxen. Old Blue, he has one blue eye, Red, he wus redder than the others, Whitie, he wus red but has an all white face, and then there wus Marbelle, this ox wus no female, but I named it after my wife Marbelle, cuz it is just as stubborn as my wife. If Mr. Dixon hired me, I take the oxen, my seven foot bull whip and go out in the woods or swamps and hook up to the logs after the timber people cut 'em down and trimmed the trees. I hook my chains to the log and the harness of the oxen, then snake them out of the woods or swamp to a road where the trucks pick them up."

"Have you ever had a business dealing with Mr. Samson?"

"No Mam, I did snake some logs out of his swamp, but it wus fer Mr. Dozier who hired me to do the work, I never seen Mr. Samson."

No questions were asked by the prosecution and Mr. Cutler was accepted.

It was now 4:30 PM and Judge Ego recessed the court until the next morning.

The court convened on September 7, when Judge Ego called the court to order and the first prospective juror, Mr. Spencer Macy, a school teacher, was called.

The prosecution started the questioning by asking Mr. Macy what subjects he taught.

"I teach a number of subjects to the high school students at South Three Notch High, math, civics, arts and drama."

"Mr. Macy," asked Miss Kluck, "Do you know Mr. Samson?"

"No."

"Do you know me or any member of the prosecution or defense team?"

"Yes Mam, I knew Mr. Kockran when he went to South Three Notch High School one year."

"Mr. Macy, what subject did you have Mr. Kockran for?"

"Mr. Kockran was in my art and drama class and he was a good student of drama."

"Could you, Mr. Macy, hear the evidence, making a fair judgement on what you see and hear and not on whether Mr. Kockran was a good or bad student, but on the facts?"

"Yes Mam, I can do that Miss Kluck."

The prosecution and the defense accepted Mr. Macy as juror number five.

The next prospective juror was Mr. Al K. Haul.

Mr. Kockran started the questioning, "Mr. Haul, tell us the name of your company and the nature of the business."

"Well suh," answered Mr. Haul, "The name of my company is Y'all Haul, and I rent out wagons and mules to people here in town who don't have any way of moving their furniture when they move, or to go out in the country and get their fire and stove wood. Sometimes businesses and farmers rent my wagons or mules or both to help out in their busy seasons."

"Mr. Haul," Mr. Kockran asked, "Do you know Mr. OJ Samson?"

"I know Mr. Samson only by his records and songs," answered Mr. Haul.

"Tell us, have you ever done business with Mr. Samson?"

"No Suh, I ain't."

"Are you sure that you haven't visited the Sad and Happy Drive-In?"

"No Suh, I make my own."

"Have you ever rented your wagons or mules to Mr. Samson or the Sad and Happy Drive-In?"

"No Suh, I did rent a wagon and two mules to Mr. Kaylow Kala, but I don't know if he wuz working fer Mr. Samson or fer the Cholly Hoss Honky Tonk and Country Club," answered Mr. Haul.

Mr. Kockran concluded his questioning and Miss Kluck asked Mr. Haul, "Can you listen to the facts in this case and render a just and fair decision, whether it is in favor or against the defendant?"

"Yes Mam I can," answered Mr. Haul.

The prosecution and the defense accepted Mr. Haul.

The court went to the next prospective juror, Mr. Marion Butler, a bartender.

Miss Kluck asked Mr. Butler to state his occupation, to which Mr. Butler replied that he was the bartender at the American Legion Club on Pea River.

Miss Kluck then asked, "What other bars have you been a bartender for in the last 10 years, Mr. Butler?"

"Well let me think, I was at the Moose Club for a while, then I worked for J. T. Brassy at the Roadhouse off of County Road 13, and a number of others up state."

"Mr. Butler, did you ever work for Cholly Spinks at the Cholly Hoss Honky Tonk and Country Club before you went to work for the American Legion Club?"

"Yes Mam."

"Why did you leave the Cholly Hoss Honky Tonk and Country Club?"

"Well," answered Marion Butler, "Cholly said I was off too much from work."

"What was the reason you were off of work so much Mr. Butler?"

"OJ wanted me to go with him sometimes when he went on tour and make his drinks and sandwiches while on the tour bus."

"You are referring to the defendant, Mr. Orscar James Samson?" pointing at Mr. Samson.

"Yes Mam," answered Marion Butler.

Miss Martha Kluck looked up at Judge Ego and said, "I challenge Mr. Marion Butler's character to be seated as a juror."

"Ruled in the favor of the prosecution," answered Judge Ego, as he recessed the court for lunch and instructed everyone to be back in court at 1:30 PM.

As soon as court was in session, Mr. Kockran requested a side bar conference and asked if he could skip to the last person, a man in the jury pool.

"For what reason, Mr. Kockran?"

"I heard that he said to a couple of the prospective jurors, that if he got seated he was going to say to his wife on Christmas night, 'Momma don't turn no Christmas lights on tonight, cause Mr. Samson will be using the electric chair.' I think a remark like that is out of order and the prospective juror should be admonished and dismissed from the jury pool."

Judge Ego excused all of the jurors, except the last man, and after all the other jurors were out of the courtroom, Judge Ego called the man forward.

"Please state your name to the court," Judge Ego said.

"Sir, my name is Leroy Bunbar."

"Did you make the remark, 'Momma don't turn no Christmas lights on tonight, cause Mr. Samson will be using the electric chair?'

"Yes Sir, I rightly did."

"Mr. Bunbar," Judge Ego said, "Why did you make that remark?"

"Your Honor, I know this man, and if he is mean enough to throw Nike in Snit Creek, then he is mean enough to kill her and that is what I think."

"Mr. Leroy Bunbar, you were out of order to say anything about this case while in the jury pool. I should hold you in contempt of court, but I will only admonish you and tell you to give some serious thought to what you said, when you have not heard any of the facts in this case. You are hereby dismissed from the jury pool. Good day sir."

"Bailiff, call the jurors back into the courtroom."

After the jurors had been seated, Judge Ego looked at the pool of jurors and said, "Ladies and gentlemen, forget the remark you overheard by one the members of the jury pool, because you cannot make judgements on your personal feelings. You must listen to all the facts to arrive at a verdict. Be seated and let us continue the selection of the jurors. Call the next prospective juror."

The next juror was a lady by the name of Mae East, who was a seamstress at the local shirt factory, in her thirties, married with two children. She lived in the Burntout community.

Miss Kluck questioned the prospective juror, "Mrs. East, do you know the defendant or any of his relatives?"

"No, Mam, I don't know any of his relatives, but I have heard of them, as their farm is on the other side of the Mt. Zion Baptist Church, about four miles."

"You have heard Mr. Samson on the radio and his records haven't you?" Miss. Kluck asked.

"Yes Mam, but he ain't my favorite singer, I like Jimmy Rodgers better."

Miss. Kluck accepted Mrs. East as a juror.

Mr. Kockran asked only one question, "Mrs. East, being you don't like Mr. Samson's singing, would this have any effect on you listening to the facts and making a decision based on those facts, and if they found Mr. Samson to be innocent of the charges against him, could you vote not guilty?"

"Yes Sir, I said I liked Jimmy Rodgers better, not that I didn't like Mr. Samson's singing." Mr. Kockran accepted Mrs. East, making this the seventh juror seated.

The next witness was a Miss Thelma Jitter, 21 years of age. This was the first time she had been called to serve on a jury, and she was quite nervous. Miss Jitter had a very strong resemblance to Nike Brown Samson, light blond hair, blue eyes, full lips, full busted, and a nice figure. OJ couldn't keep his eyes off of Thelma, and his thoughts were, if he was acquitted, would he be able to get in touch with this lovely creature. He had to get her off his mind as he was fighting for his life, he would think about this later.

Mr. Kockran asked Miss Jitter if she knew Mr. Samson or the late Mrs. Samson.

"No Sir, I have heard his music, and I didn't know there was a Mrs. Samson."

"Miss Jitter, you live in Three Notch don't you?"

Yes Sir, but I was away at college in Birmingham for the past four years, and when I came home I went with my family on vacation. The rest of the time I was with my friends and we would go to the Three Notch Country Club to play tennis and swim."

Both Mr. Kockran and Miss Kluck accepted Miss Thelma Jitter as juror number eight. It was 4:10 PM and Judge Ego recessed the court until 10:00 AM September 8.

OJ was escorted back to the jail by two of the sheriff's deputies, Wyatt Herp and Matt Millon. He asked them to get in touch with Barbé Paulieri, his girl friend at the time he was jailed.

Wyatt Herp said, "You know we can't do that, you must contact your lawyer."

"I can't do that, my lawyer don't want me to see her so often. I just wanted to get this letter to her. If you will do this for me I'll give you a note to the new manager, Fred Flint, at the Sad and Happy Drive-In and you will drive out happy."

Just before they parked the paddy wagon at the jail, Wyatt and Matt had a discussion, and told OJ they would do this for him. He gave Wyatt an envelope sealed for Barbé and one to give to Fred Flint at the Sad and Happy Drive-In with instructions to give the envelope marked Barbé to her and $5 each to Wyatt and Matt, also Wyatt and Matt could go through the Sad and Happy Drive-In each week, "Drive in Sad and Drive out Happy" with a basket of beans and a pint of White Ribbon Vitae-Likker Of Life under the beans. This would continue as long as Orange was in jail and Wyatt and Matt would do little favors for him.

Barbé Paulieri had met OJ at a party in Nashville after an appearance at the Grand Ole Opry. She was a young aspiring country singer. Her voice was yet untrained, but she had a very good natural voice and was very talented. She was a beautiful girl, with light brown hair, and unusual light blue eyes, perfect neck and arms, smooth skin, weighed about 110 pounds with a very curvy five foot five inch frame. Her bust was filled out to nature's full proportions, giving that swelled, rounded, firm bosom, that queenly bearing, so attractive to the opposite sex. OJ being the opposite sex was attracted to Barbé and Barbé thought he was an attractive man, but did not have the manners of a gentlemen she preferred. However, he was famous, rich and had connections in the music business. With the latest development that had happened, her plans must be changed. In place of being with him for his ego, to show her off, being his lover, she would now say she loved him, and did not have to have sex with him. With OJ in jail she did not have to put up with his drunkenness, or his crude and clumsy love making. The note Barbé received from him told how lonely he was, how much he wanted her, and asked her to marry him, so that she could have more visitation privileges. Barbé decided she would marry him and have access to his money. Maybe he would write a song for her and she could become a famous singer in her own right, after all he may never get out of jail. Barbé went to Donny Kockran's office early the next morning and showed him the note from OJ and said she would accept the proposal.

Donny sat there thinking. If she tells OJ that she will marry him, this would change the tactic he had in mind for a defense, plus she would drain off too much of his money. He had to talk Barbé out of accepting the proposal. An idea entered his mind. If he was able to sell it to Barbé, all would not be lost, he could read Barbé like a book. In fact, like the first reader such as " Ned has a dog. His name is Spot. See Spot run. See Ned run, etc."

"Barbé," Donny said, "how would you like to be a big country music star, make plenty of money and not always be tied to OJ?"

That sounded good to her, but how long would she have to wait for the money; after all, if she married OJ now, she would have access to a bank account immediately.

"Mr. Kockran, I want to marry OJ as soon as possible, unless it would be more profitable immediately for me to postpone the marriage," she answered.

"Hmm." Donny thought." She is shrewder than I thought. As long as she has him thinking the marriage is postponed until after the trial, it may work."

"Barbé, I'll talk to OJ and try to persuade him to postpone the marriage until the trial is over. You will get visitation privileges four times a week, and we will set up a partnership with OJ for promotion of your career. A bank account of $5,000 will be deposited in the partnership, which will be named, "Barbé Doll." You will have 60 percent ownership, OJ 25 percent and I will have 15 percent. You will be President and run the organization at a salary of $200 a month and expenses. After all, $200 a month is a lot of money in these times, when bread is five cents a loaf, milk six cents a quart and an extra nice dress is $3. You can live like a queen. And after five years you can buy Oscar James and me out for $5000, but I must have your decision now, as I have to be in court at 10 AM to finish the jury selection."

Barbé thought for a minute, "Mr. Kockran you have a deal, lets shuffle the cards and deal."

Donny arrived at the jail at 9:20 AM on the morning of September 8.

"OJ Barbé wants to marry you, but I asked her not to at this time as it will greatly jeopardize your case. Not only will it give ammunition to the prosecution, but tarnish the good name and reputation of the woman you love. You and Barbé can sign a declaration of love and a promise to marry when you are released from jail."

He then explained the partnership, which would benefit the three of them, and he fully expected Barbé to be a big star and keep the money coming in. OJ agreed and Donny left for the courthouse for the 10 AM jury selection.

Another prospective juror was called and seated in the witness chair and was asked by the prosecutor, Martha Kluck, to state his name and occupation.

The prospective juror said, "My name is Fruit Jar Black and I am a filler."

Martha Kluck asked, "Mr. Black, is Fruit Jar your given name or is it a nickname?"

"It wus given to me when I wus a young'n cauz I wus too scared to go to the outhouse at night, and my mama gave me a fruit jar to pee in."

"What were you called before your mother gave you the Fruit Jar, Mr. Black?" asked Martha.

"Well, the best I can remember it wuz Clem, but when I wuz 13 or 14 yars old I went with Mr. Andrews putting white lightnin' in fruit jars and I have been thar for going on 'leven yars, so I have been called Fruit Jar Black ever since."

"Do you know the defendant, Mr. Black?"

"Not that I recall, unless I see him." said Fruit Jar.

Mr. Black, I'm speaking of Mr. Oscar James Samson sitting there at the defense table, do you know the defendant?"

"No Mam, but his Pa and Mr. Andrews done some trading'. When Mr. Jim Paul ran short of white lightnin' for the Sad and Happy Drive-In, Mr. Andrews would let Mr. Jim Paul have some white lightnin' for half price."

Martha Kluck dismissed Mr. Black as a juror for being too close to the family of the defendant.

Mr. U. R. Short was called as the next prospective juror.

Mr. Short was born in the community of Rosehill, some five miles out in the country, and after finishing high school his father, a moderately successful farmer, was able to send Mr. Short to Montgomery for a course in bookkeeping, at the Madison Business College. After two years of studying bookkeeping with the last six months on the job as a trainee, Mr. Short was able to get a job back in Three Notch at the Family Classic Clothes Co.

Family Classic Clothes Co. sold more than just clothes. Mr. Ham, the only Jew in Three Notch, had a wife and two children, and sold hardware, cookware, groceries, linen supplies, a real mercantile store and had a large business that needed a trained bookkeeper.

Mr. Short was christened Richard Udell Short and being short in stature at five feet tall had been teased with short jokes all his life. He had often thought of a unique name to play the jokes down. After being with Mr. Ham for about a year, they were taking a break one night while counting inventory.

"Mr. Ham," Richard said, "I have been thinking of changing my first two names around and using my initials as my real name. Then when people make fun of my name I can say I was born under the sign of Caprashort and most people born under this sign are short. Short people are actually tall midgets and if God had meant for the world to have short people he wouldn't have invented basketball."

Mr. Ham said, "Go ahead and change your name, I did. My name was originally Hamberger and people were asking me if I had any beef burgers or how can a Jew have ham in a burger or can you have kosher hamburgers."

Richard thought that Moshe Ham had an odd ring to it, so Mr. Richard Udell Short became U. R. Short.

Martha Kluck asked, "Mr. Short could you listen to the facts and make an honest judgement in this case?"

"Yes Mam, I can, but I would need a high stool to sit on, or I can bring my own, as I have a stool I stand on to say the Pledge of Allegiance at the Three Notch Business Luncheon."

Mr. Kockran accepted the juror and agreed with the defense team that Mr. U. R. Short could bring his stool. Mr. U. R. Short became juror number nine.

Judge Ego recessed the court for the noon hour and would reconvene at 1:30 PM.

The first prospective juror of the afternoon was called, Mrs. Lucy Walker.

Donny Kockran of the defense team had the first questioning period for this prospective juror.

Mrs. Walker, about the same age as OJ, was a perky little brunette, 4'11" tall, with brown twinkling eyes, and a pleasing smile that makes you think it is just for you. Her body was curved in the right places and full busted, with a Betty Boop hairdo. She wore a light blue skirt that showed her figure off to the best advantage, just short enough to show her well proportioned legs when she was seated. A white short-sleeved blouse, with light blue trim, that fitted her so well you could see the nipples of her breasts.

Everyone in the court room sat up straight when Mrs. Walker half waltzed and half danced down the aisle of the court room. Old Len Tiller in the aisle seat of the fourth row looked up as she waltzed down the aisle and, thought, my God I bet she could kill a good man, and he would be buried with a big grin on his face. She shore is a tiny li'l thing. I bet when she was a kid, instead of jumping rope, she had to jump a shoe string.

OJ thought, "She looks familiar, I think I have seen her before. Gee I hope she will be seated, it would be nice to look at this creature all day. God, I've got to keep my mind on the trial."

Donny asked, "Mrs. Walker what is your occupation?"

"Sir, I work for the WPA as a Director of Activities for the State of Alabama Indigent Homes, also known as the poor folks homes or farms. I see that they have some type of activity to keep their mind off their problems and are taken care of."

"Do you know the defendant seated at the defense table?" asked Donny.

"I believe that I saw him when I was in high school, but I haven't seen him since then."

While Donny was asking Mrs. Walker some of the standard questions, OJ sat upright and thought, "Oh Lord, is this who I think it is? Whatever made me let her go?"

Donny had finished his questioning and accepted Mrs. Walker as a juror. It was the prosecution's turn for questioning.

Flip Moore, of the prosecution, started the questioning.

"Mrs. Walker, what was your maiden name?"

"My maiden name was Lucy Locket, Sir."

"Mrs. Walker, are you the same Lucy Locket that was suspended from high school for two weeks at the same time the defendant Mr. Oscar James Samson was suspended?"

"Yes Sir."

"Tell us, Miss Locket, oh, I mean Mrs. Walker, what was the suspension about?"

"I object," shouted Mr. Kockran.

"You can not object, Mr. Kockran. Answer the question, Mrs. Walker," Judge Ego said sternly.

"Well," Mrs. Walker answered, "OJ and I were an item during our last year of high school, and one Saturday afternoon after he finished selling his Mexican Headache Cure at the mule barn, he asked me if I wanted to go to Slap Out to a round and square dance. "Sure, I said."

"He picked me up at five clock in a horse and buggy, and we started for Slap Out, which was about five miles from our place and 10 miles out of Three Notch. That is why it is called Slap Out, because it's slap out of sight."

"Why were you and the defendant suspended, Mrs. Walker? Please answer the question," Mr. Moore said raising his voice.

"It was after nine when we got to the dance and OJ had brought along some of his Pa's white lightnin' and we was having a few drinks along the way, letting the horse take his time. We left the dance at one o'clock and we decided to go to a fish camp down on Yallar River where some cabins were. We was there until Tuesday night when the sheriff and his deputies found us. When we didn't come home Sunday, my Pa went to the Sheriff's Office for help. They looked and couldn't find anything. On Monday and Tuesday the sheriff got the students to help search for us. My family was afraid we were dead or something, and that is why we were suspended, because the high school was out two days looking for us."

"Were you in bed when the sheriff and his deputies came in the cabin?," asked Mr. Moore.

Mrs. Walker dropped her eyes and at this time she looked like the little girl that was small enough to be jumping a shoe string in place of a jump rope.

"Yes Sir."

Mr. Moore asked for a dismissal of this juror, and it was granted by Judge Ego.

Judge Ego made an announcement. "Ladies and Gentlemen, it is taking entirely too long to seat the 12 jurors and three alternates. It is now 3:30, I am going to recess the court until 10 AM tomorrow, and I want the defense and prosecution teams to have a plan for asking pertinent questions and wrapping up this phase of the pretrial so we can start the trial. Good day Ladies and Gentlemen."

At five PM Barbé visited OJ for the first time since the new arrangement. With her she had a letter of love and declaration to each other, stating they would marry as soon as he was released from jail, and in the eyes of each other and God, they were truly man and wife. After reading the declaration, OJ called the guard to witness their signatures on the document. After the guard went back to his post, Barbé said, "OJ, I need a hit song and I want you to write one for me."

"I don't know, Barbé, if I can get in the mood to write a love song in this place, but get Donny to bring me some new guitar strings and I'll give it whirl.

On the way home from the jail, Barbé thought that if he did not write a song soon she would go out to Cholly Hoss Honky Tonk and Country Club and sing. She would flirt with the band members and some of the regular customers that hang around the Club. Word would surely get back to OJ about her and then he would write some breaking my heart type crap. She could always tell him it was a lie, that she cared only for him, and he would be fool enough to believe her.

On Friday, September 9, Judge Ego convened the court for the jury selection. The prosecution was first to question the prospective juror, a Miss Iola Bridges.

"Miss Bridges," said Martha Kluck, "To save time I would like for you answer these questions. One, what is your occupation? Two, do you know the defendant, or have you had any personal contact with him? Three, in reading the newspaper and listening to the radio have you formed any opinion about this case one way or the other?"

Miss Bridges thought for a moment and said, "I am a third grade school teacher and have been employed by the Three Notch County School Board since I completed college five years ago. I do not know, nor have I had any contact with the defendant. I have read the Three Notch Banner, and have heard the news broadcast on WTNC radio. One day I think he may have done the deed, the next I think he couldn't have done the deed."

"Miss Bridges, if you listen to the facts in this case and find, that the State proves the defendant guilty, could you, Miss Bridges, bring in a guilty verdict?"

"Yes Mam, I could," answered Miss Bridges.

"The prosecution accepts Miss Bridges as a juror, Your Honor," said Miss Martha Kluck.

Mr. Rufus Cobb for the defense team, "Miss Bridges, if the defense proves the defendant is innocent, would you vote a not guilty?

"Yes, Sir, I would," answered Miss Bridges.

Mr. Cobb said, "The defense accepts Miss Bridges as a juror, Your Honor."

When the next prospective juror was called, Mr. Zolowit for the defense asked, "Sir, what is your name and occupation?"

"My name is Leroy Rogers and I own a cotton farm in the southern part of the county, in the Foxhollow community."

"Do you know the defendant, sitting at the table?" pointing at Oscar James Samson.

"No Sir, I do not know the defendant. I have only heard him on the radio singing."

"Mr. Rodgers, if a doctor testified that scientific testing proved that the blood found at the scene of the crime was not that of the defendant, could you honestly believe this testimony is correct and vote accordingly?"

"Sir, if it was put into the language, that a simple cotton farmer could understand, then I would believe it," answered Mr. Rogers.

"If the defendant is proven innocent, could you vote a not guilty vote?" asked Mr. Zolowit.

"Yes, sir, I could." answered Mr. Rogers.

"The defense accepts Mr. Rodgers a juror Your Honor," said Mr. Zolowit.

The next prospective juror was called, Mr. Terry "Bubba" White.

"Mr. White," Mr. Chris Clock, of the prosecution team, asked, "What is your occupation?"

"In the season, I travel with a carnival," answered Mr. White.

"What is the season you travel with the carnival, Mr. White?" asked Mr. Clock, "and what is your job with the carnival?"

"I travel with the carnival from the first of May until the first of September, and my job is picking up the bull," answered Bubba White.

A little laughter broke out in the court, as Judge Ego banged his gavel on the bench, and said, "There will be no display of emotions in this court room."

Bubba White's job or act was picking up a bull. When Bubba was about 10 years old and was a little underweight kid, his Pa gave him a new born bull calf. After about a month, Bubba was lifting the little bull calf off of the ground. One day the little bull, who he named Blackie, because he was black all over except his left hind ankle which was white, was on the loading chute, (this is a chute where the trucks or wagons back up to and the cattle go up the ramp chute into the truck or wagon).

Bubba backed up to the chute and got Blackie on his shoulders and fell down. Each day Bubba would run Blackie up the ramp chute, back up and put Blackie on his shoulders. It wasn't long before Bubba could walk around with Blackie on his shoulders. By doing this every day, as Blackie gained weight, Bubba gained strength. This went on every day for several years, and now Blackie weighed 1150 pounds and Bubba who was six feet one inches tall, with extra large shoulders and chest, narrow hips and big strong legs, weighed 280 pounds and was still picking up Blackie each day.

Robert Rippley heard of this feat and put Bubba and Blackie in the "Believe It Or Not" column. Before long the United-Ace Carnival hired Bubba for his bull act. Bubba was very impressive sitting there in the juror chair, a big mass of a man, with coal black hair and beard.

"Where do you reside in Three Notch County, when you are not with the carnival Mr. White?" asked Mr. Clock.

"I live with my Pa and Ma when I ain't with the carnival and they live in the Harmony community," answered Mr. White.

"Isn't that close to Burntout, the community where Mr. Samson lived?" asked Mr. Clock.

"Yes Sir," answered Mr. White.

Then Mr. Clock asked, "Mr. White, do you know the defendant Mr. Oscar James Samson sitting in this courtroom?"

"Yes Sir, a little as he is older than I am. I only saw him when I was about eight or 10 years old, but after I got older and was doing my act with the carnival, he played a concert at the Iowa County Fair and we got together for a few drinks one night and would do the same from time to time as we met on the circuit."

After this answer Mr. Clock asked for this juror to be excused.

Judge Ego excused Mr. White and recessed the court until 1:30 PM.

The Three Notch 2-1/4 Circuit Court reconvened at 1:40 PM a little late, but called the next prospective juror, a Mrs. Minnie Curl, who stated that she was a widow, and worked at Cora Bell's Beauty Shop and sometimes worked at local functions as a comedian.

Mr. Cobb started the questioning off by asking, "Mrs. Curl did you ever perform at any place the same time as Mr. Samson, the defendant?"

"No Sir," answered Mrs. Curl.

"Do you know Mr. Samson or anyone close to him?"

"No Sir," she answered.

"Can and will you listen to all the evidence before you make a decision, and then reach a fair verdict?"

"Yes Sir," she answered

"The defense will accept Mrs. Curl as a juror, Your Honor," stated Mr. Cobb.

Mr. Moore of the prosecution team asked only two questions.

"Mrs. Curl, did Nike Brown Samson ever come into Cora Bell's Beauty Shop?"

"No Sir, not while I was at work," she answered.

"Mrs. Curl, if the evidence shows that Mr. Samson was innocent of the charges placed against him, could and would you render a verdict of not guilty?" asked Mr. Cobb.

"Yes Sir, I could and would if he is not proven guilty to me," answered Mrs. Curl.

"The defense accepts the juror Your Honor," said Mr. Cobb.

This completed the selection for the twelve jurors, however, it was time to select the alternate jurors. The first prospective alternate juror was a Mr. John Paul Pope. After Mr. Pope was seated, Miss Kluck started the questioning by asking, "Mr. Pope what is your occupation?"

"I am pastor of the Church of Luke in the Victory community, and an Evangelist. I go where the Lord calls me and hold services in churches, tents, or arbor meetings under the branches," he answered.

"Are you a Reverend or should I call you Mister?" asked Miss Kluck.

"You can call me whichever you like, but I am a pastor, and ordained by the Lord. People do refer to me as Reverend," answered the Reverend John Paul Pope.

"Reverend Pope, I remember when I was a young girl in school a Preacher Pope who preached and sang songs on the street corner, while a young boy played the harmonica and took up offerings, are you the same man Reverend?

"Yes Mam, that was about 15 years ago and I'll admit I was preaching under another church's name and I took to drinking to excess. The devil had my soul and I wrestled the devil day and night, until one day my boy, bless his God loving soul, came home and told me he was leaving because he couldn't take the drinking and deceiving the Lord any more. I asked my son Clifton Paul Pope to pray with me and help me. We prayed for 10 hours and the Lord chased that devil from my soul and I haven't even been tempted to drink in over 10 years, the Lord is my witness," stated the Reverend John Paul Pope.

Miss Kluck asked, "Reverend Pope, would your religion prevent you from arriving at a guilty verdict if the State proved beyond a reasonable doubt that the defendant is guilty of the crime charged?"

"No Mam, if the defendant is proven guilty I can vote guilty, if innocent, I can vote not guilty," answered Reverend John Paul Pope.

"Reverend Pope," asked Mr. Donny Kockran, "Tell us here in this courtroom, is the "Church of Luke" in the main stream of churches in America?"

"Yes Sir, it is but it does have a major difference and that is that the Protestant Churches, such as the Baptist, Methodist, Pentecostal, etc., believe that Jesus Christ is the Messiah. We in the Church Of Luke believe that Luke is the Messiah, because when the Messiah was born he was born at night in a stable, the same night that Mary had her child. There were no lights and they did not have I D bracelets so the babies were mixed up that night, and the true Messiah is Luke," answered Reverend John Paul Pope.

"Reverend Pope, because the defendant believes that Jesus Christ is the Messiah, would this keep you from voting not guilty if the State can not prove beyond a reasonable doubt that Mr. Oscar James Samson is guilty?"

"My job on this earth is to tell the story of who the Messiah is and those that do not believe the way we teach the gospel, that is their loss and they will have to answer to a mightier force in the hereafter. I can come to a decision of guilty or not guilty based on the evidence I see and hear so help me God," answered the Reverend Pope.

"We will accept The Reverend John Paul Pope as a alternate juror Your Honor," said Mr. Kockran

The second prospective alternate juror was Miss Shirley Pimple.

Mr. Flip Moore asked, "Miss Pimple, what is your occupation?"

"I am retired and live alone," she answered.

"What did you do before your retirement?"

"I was a child actress on stage and in the movies," Miss Pimple answered.

"Did or do you know Oscar James Samson from the entertainment profession?"

"No Sir, I have only been in the South for the first time in 51 years, I left when I was five years old."

"Would Mr. Samson being in the entertainment field have any bearing on your judgement as to his guilt or innocence?" asked Mr. Moore.

"It would have no bearing one way or the other on his innocence or guilt," answered Miss Pimple.

"The Prosecution will accept Miss Pimple, Your Honor."

A couple of questions by the defense team and Mr. Dash accepted Miss Pimple.

It was now 4:05 PM and the judge recessed the court until Monday .

Chapter Sixteen

Upon returning to his cell, OJ called Mr. Kockran and asked that he get his Ma and Pa to come visit on Saturday afternoon, as he wanted to talk to Pa about the business.

On Saturday Barbé visited OJ in the morning. They talked about their love for each other, and he wanted to know how she spent her time.

"Well," Barbé said, "I stay busy practicing my singing, writing to the different music companies trying to find some suitable songs, and I have been trying to write a song, but I am not as talented as you. I wish you would write one just for me."

"I'm just not in the mood now for writing songs. I hear that you are singing often at the Cholly Hoss Honky Tonk and Country Club. Which band is playing there now?"

"Yes, I sing on Friday and Saturday nights. The band is, Sweat and Swear with Teddy Bear. They have just returned from Bakersfield, California, where they broke all records at a concert."

"Is this the same Ted Bear that you dated in high school?" he asked .

"Yes, but I haven't seen him since, though I have heard him sing on the radio and have a couple of his records. He is a good singer and has an excellent band. I may be able to get on a record with him."

"Someone told me you went to Pensacola last Saturday after leaving here to play at the Barefoot Roost with Ted Bear, did you?" quizzed OJ.

"Yes, OJ, I did, but it was a gig and nothing went on between me and Teddy. As soon as the gig was over I went to the cabin alone and went to bed. You know I love only you and I am dreaming of the day you are free of this mess. I'm doing all I can to see that you get free. Please believe me." Barbé kissed him and said, "Darling I must be going as I have to do some shopping. My heart is always with you."

"I know you have my best interest at heart, but I get so lonely without you and I couldn't stand it if I thought you were with someone else. Please don't see anyone else and keep loving me."

Barbé thought on her way shopping and to the Cholly Hoss Honky Tonk, that she had him just where she wanted him, working up a good jealousy complex, but she'd tighten the screws a little tighter, if she didn't get a song soon.

After Barbé left, OJ got to thinking about the trip to Pensacola, and wondered if Barbé really did go to bed alone. He dwelled on this subject for a couple of hours, until his Pa and Ma came in at two o'clock.

He was glad to see Ma and Pa. It seemed that they were the only people that really loved him. The next two hours were a very pleasant time for him, having his Ma fussing over him and telling him how good he looked and how much she loved him. She had brought some sausage and biscuits, cold baked sweet potato and cookies. It was like he was a little boy again, eating his Ma's cooking. However, Pa got serious, and said that the corn crop was yielding so much corn, and the white lightnin' sales were off. The prices were down on corn and it was hard to sell. He said that the Sad and Happy Drive-In was using a little more than the usual amount, but the barn was still running over with corn, and he didn't know what to do.

"Pa, are the Cooper boys still buying the same amount of likker?"

"No, son, they ain't. I haven't sold them any likker in over two months, I jest ain't seen them boys."

"Pa, I know from my marketing experience, that first you must find out what the problem is, and then correct it by salesmanship, quality, price, or sometimes maybe a little of all three. Go to the Sad and Happy Drive-In and ask, Fred Flint to visit the Cooper boys, and soft soap them, asking if we can do anything to get their business back. Tell Fred to do this at once and I'll call him tomorrow night and we will make plans on how to combat this situation."

The rest of Saturday and Sunday, his mind went from Barbé to the business, then back to Barbé. He was getting moody, and jealousy was gnawing at his heart. He had to do something to be sure of her. Yes, maybe a song would do it. As he lay on his cot this fall afternoon, his mind and feelings went back through the years.

On Monday as Wyatt Herp and Matt Millon were leading OJ back to his cell, he inquired how their credit balance was doing at the Sad and Happy Drive-In. They both admitted that the credit was about down to zero.

"Boys, if you will get me a quart bottle of White Ribbon Vitae-Likker of Life from Fred Flint at the Sad and Happy Drive-In, I'll give you a note to him for a credit of $5 each."

That night after supper Wyatt delivered a package to OJ, a quart of White Ribbon Vitae-Likker of Life.

As he was sitting in his cell and sipping Vitae through a straw, a song began forming in his mind. "While sitting at a bar and sipping bourbon from a jar." I am not setting in a bar, this song must be for Barbé. Barbé loves beer, and she loves to sit on the stool at the Cholly Hoss Honky Tonk and Country Club and sip a beer between sets. Oh well, he thought this is going to be a long night. Hmmm....

Sittin' on a bar stool, sippin' a cold beer through, a straw,
Feeling oh so lonely caus my love ain't here.
Hoping that the beer will finally drown the pain.
If it don't I'll order up another one and gulp it down again.

He thought that this song could be sung by Barbé and maybe he could write a song to be sung by him when he got out of jail. He thought that this may work. As he took a drink of White Ribbon Vitae he began to sing.

While sippin' bourbon from a jar,
I dream of my love from afar.
Every time I take a sip,
I can feel her hot, hot lips.
I got the bourbon jar blues.

He wrote on the songs until he had both of them complete. Just as he was about to get his guitar, hum until he got the right tune and then put it to music, the guard informed him that he had a visitor.

"Well," he thought, "this is a start, I'll see who is in the visitors room. Maybe it's Barbé but it is too late in the day for visitors except attorneys and family members."

When he arrived in the visitors room, Carl Dash was waiting for him.

"Hi I know it is late to be visiting, but I have an important matter to discuss with you. It is about the suitcase that I took off of the tour bus on the night you returned from Shreveport. I have not opened the suitcase, and I don't want you to tell me anything about it, what was inside or what condition the material inside is in. The sheriff is trying to get a search warrant for my property, but being that I am one of your attorneys, at this point has been unable to get one."

"What do they want it for, I have--"

"Hold it OJ, I said I did not want you to tell me anything about what is on the inside. I can not testify, as I am on the defense team, but I had the suitcase stored in my garage and someone broke into the garage and the suitcase is one of the items missing."

"Why are you telling me this Karl?"

"In the event the suitcase is found and the sheriff's officers question you, do not answer any questions until one of your attorneys is present. Maybe it will never be found, but, I wanted to warn you what to do if it is, just sit tight and do not mention it at all."

"Tomorrow is Monday and that means court. Do you think they will select the last alternate juror?"

"That is a good possibility. I'll see you in court tomorrow, OJ."

When he returned to his cell, it was getting late. He would finish the songs and music another time.

Chapter Seventeen

Judge Ego called the court to order at 10 AM on Monday, September 12.

The next prospective juror was Mr. Hoot Gibson, typesetter and pressman for the weekly newspaper, The Three Notch Banner.

Mr. Kockran started the questioning by asking, "Mr. Gibson, have you formed any opinion of this case by the type you set for the newspaper or the paper you print on the press?"

"No Sir, when I set type it is upside down and backward, I don't read it, I only look at each letter. When I put the type on the press the press is going too fast for me to read it."

"You are telling us, Mr. Gibson, you have not read about the Samson case?" asked Mr. Kockran.

"No Sir, I didn't say I have never read about the case. I said I did not read 'bout it when I was settin' type and runnin' the press."

"Have you formed an opinion about the case while reading about it in the paper?"

"No sir, I haven't seen or heard any facts about this case."

Mr. Kockran concluded his questioning.

Miss Kluck asked Mr. Gibson, "Can you listen to the facts in this case and render a just and fair decision whether it is for or against the defendant?'

"Yes Mam, I can," answered Mr. Gibson. The prosecution and the defense accepted Mr. Gibson.

Judge Ego announced to the courtroom, "Ladies and Gentlemen of the jury and alternates, you are excused until tomorrow, Tuesday, September 13, at 10 AM when the trial of the State vs Oscar James Samson for the first degree murder of Nike Brown Samson and Clem Hooper will begin. Good day Ladies and Gentlemen."

On Tuesday night about 7:30 PM Jim Paul came to visit OJ and report the findings of Fred Flint on why the Cooper boys weren't buying as much moonshine as they had been buying.

"Son, Fred said that the Cooper boys told him that our prices are higher by 10 percent over Joe Jack Thomas.

"Well, I thought something like this was up, and I have been doing some thinking about this. If we gave 15 percent off, it would be more than Joe Jack could give off, as he buys his stuff from Matt Davis out of Montgomery. Matt has to deliver this 80 miles, so he can't give any more off. Now, if we will give the Cooper boys a bonus of 20 percent of their purchases in white lightnin', that would be equal to 50 percent when they sold the free stuff."

"I don't understand it son, but you know what you are doing, I'll tell Fred."

"Well, its like this Pa. Say they got $20 in moonshine. Joe Jack would sell it to him for 40 percent off or for $12, and he would make $8 when he sold it. From us he would buy $20 worth of moonshine we would give him 40 percent off which would still cost him $12, but we would give a bonus of 20 percent of the $12, or $2.40 in extra moonshine, and when he sold the extra moonshine for $4, he would make the original $8 plus $4 on the bonus for a total of $12 profit, rather than the $8 he now makes. That is 100 percent profit. It will cost us only $.60 to produce the extra moonshine for total off $3.55, still a profit $8.45 on each $12 deal, $68 on every hundred dollars sold wholesale. As we have enough profit in retail, tell Fred to have a sale of about 10 or 12 percent off. I'll write the deal down, you give it to Fred to deliver to the Cooper boys, then go home and start using the cawn that you are over stocked with."

Jim Paul left the jail feeling good; he had a smart son.

At 10 AM on Tuesday, September 13, Judge Ego entered the courtroom.

"All rise," spoke the Bailiff, Dean Autry.

The attorneys, courtroom members, and spectators rose while Judge Ego took his seat in the chair behind the large courtroom desk, above them.

"Be seated, Three Notch 2-1/4 Circuit Court, is now in session. Judge Vance Ego presiding," spoke Bailiff Dean Autry.

Looking over the courtroom Judge Ego saw on his right at the defense table, Mr. Donny Kockran, lead attorney, with his co-council, Mr. Barry Kall, Mr. Rufus Cobb, Mr. Israel Zolowit, and Mr. Karl Dash. As he looked to his left at the prosecution team he saw, Miss Martha Kluck, lead prosecutor, with her co-council Mr. Chris Clock, and "Mr. Phillip "Flip" Moore. The court reporters, Mrs. Merl Monroe and Miss Dorthy LaTour were in place, and he noted that a newspaper reporter, Hedda Popper, was in the front row."

"Good morning Ladies and Gentlemen. Before we bring the jury and the defendant in, I would like to lay a few ground rules. Under no circumstances will I have disorder in this courtroom. All of you will obey the common courtesy and rules of this courtroom. There will be no personal remarks about each other, to each other. When a remark is overruled, do not argue with me or any attorney on the ruling. Bailiff, bring in the defendant Mr. Oscar James Samson."

OJ was let into court without handcuffs or leg irons, but had three sheriff's deputies escorting him, Wyatt Herp, Matt Millon and Billy Kidd. They led him to the defense table, and then Deputy Herp sat a few feet behind him, while Deputy Million was at one door of the courtroom, and Deputy Kidd at the other door. He was neatly dressed in a dark blue cashmere suit, a light blue silk shirt, dark blue tie with grey stripes, and black shoes, with dark blue socks.

"Good morning, Mr. Samson," Judge Ego said.

"Good morning, Your Honor," OJ replied.

"Bailiff, bring in the jurors in."

"All rise," spoke Mr. Autry.

The jurors filed in the order in which they would be seated each time they entered the courtroom.

First was Mr. Kit Carson, a rancher with about 500 acres, and a part-time cowboy movie actor. Mr. Carson was about 38 years old, with rugged good looks.

Next was Mr. Tom Mix, also a rancher with about 500 acres, who also did a little movie work when recommended by Mr. Kit Carson. He too was a rugged type person.

Mrs. Kitty Kat, a housewife married to a local business man, was number three.

Mr. Rhett Cutler, a logging contractor, was number four. Mr. Cutler was a medium size man, with big broad shoulders, which he developed from driving oxen, and snaking logs out of the swamps.

Mr. Spencer Macy, a local school teacher, was juror number five.

Mr. Al. K. Haul, owner of a rental mule and wagon company, "Y'all Haul", was juror six.

Mrs. Mae East was juror number seven. Mrs. East was married and worked at the local shirt factory.

Thelma Jitter, the youngest and prettiest, was juror number eight.

Mr. U.R. Short, who came in with his own stool with a back to it, was juror number nine.

Miss Iola Bridges, a third grade teacher, was juror number 10.

Mr. LeRoy Rogers, a cotton farmer, from the southern part of Three Notch County was juror number 11.

Mrs. Minnie Curl, a beautician and a part-time comedian, was juror number 12.

After the 12 jurors were seated, the Bailiff brought in the three alternates.

Mr. John Paul Pope, a pastor of the Church of Luke, was alternate number one.

Miss Shirley Pimple, an old maid and ex-child actress, was alternate number two.

Mr. Hoot Gibson, a typesetter for The Three Notch Banner, was alternate number three.

This completed the seating of the jurors and alternates.

"Ladies and Gentlemen of the jury, and when I speak of the jury, I am speaking to the regular jurors and the alternates, who will be referred to as the Jurors. Ladies and Gentlemen of the jury, we are beginning the trial of the State vs Oscar James Samson on two counts of first degree murder. One count is for the murder of Nike Brown Samson, the second count is for the murder of Clem Hooper. You will listen to all the evidence from the prosecution and the defense witnesses. You will see exhibits from the prosecution and the defense. Some may be offensive and sickening to you, however, you must endure with the court and judge for yourselves whether the evidence is valid. You are to render a verdict of guilty or not guilty, based on what you hear and see in this courtroom, not what is said or published outside. I will instruct you on the law and how it is applied. You will not talk to anyone outside of this courtroom or to any member of this jury about this case."

"Ladies and Gentlemen, while the court discusses the ground rules with the attorneys, I ask that you retire to the jury room and do not talk about the case, but get acquainted with each other. Talk to each other of your occupations, hobbies or other interests in life. In other words, introduce yourselves to one another.

The jurors retired to the jury room and began the process of getting to know each other. Iola Bridges said she enjoyed her work as a third grade teacher, and was engaged to be married in the fall to a sixth grade teacher.

Kit Carson, the rancher, said that he liked to ride horses, and when a movie company was in this area he was hired as an extra. They liked his work and he starred in a number of movies. He didn't like the big city ways and came back to the ranch life he loved when he was not making movies.

LeRoy Rodgers said he loves fishing. He likes to take the family down to Yallar River to camp out at night. He, his son, and son-in-law would set a trot line across the river. The next morning they would have enough fish to eat for breakfast and lunch and then would go home on Sunday afternoon. They would do this three or four times a year.

Spencer Macy, a school teacher and part-time basketball coach, said he always wanted to be a big time coach and loved working with young people.

Minnie Curl said her hobby was telling jokes, and she sometimes got jobs as a comedian. She wanted very much to do comedy. Her husband of 10 years was her biggest fan.

Tom Mix said he was also hired to do movie work when the movie company was here making movies. "But I don't get enough work to stay in Hollywood and live the big life I would like to. Some day I hope to be a star so I can live there."

Reverend John Paul Pope said he liked preaching and saving lives. He had some out-of-life experiences and healed a few people. This is his life, joy, and work.

Al K. Haul said he grew up on a farm, but had met a salesman for Swift and Company, who dressed real nice, worked in a suit, drove a new shiny red automobile, and wrote orders. "I was 15 years old at the time and I guess being in business was the next best thing to being a salesman."

Kitty Kat said she was a housewife and her husband owned a hardware store. She sometimes worked in the store and loved it, but didn't want to work there full-time. She liked cooking and keeping house and going to the church socials.

Rhett Cutler said he liked his business of snaking logs, that had been cut for the saw mill. He had been around oxen all his life and could handle them well. He loved to go possum hunting, also coon hunting. He had a coon dog, Zeb, that won the championship in Three Notch County for coon hunting.

U.R. Short, who worked for Mr. Ham at The Classic Clothes Co., said he would like to get a sales job traveling, or, like Minnie Curl, be a comedian.

Hoot Gibson, the typesetter said he was happy working where he was. He didn't have any hobbies, because of his health. Someone asked what was wrong with his health, that he looked healthy. He then told of being in the war and was gassed in Germany.

Thelma Jitter the 21 year old, said she liked college, swimming, dancing and going to parties.

Before everyone had told of themselves, the bailiff called them back into the courtroom.

Chapter Eighteen

"Ladies and Gentlemen of the jury, we are ready for the opening statements by the prosecutor and defense."

"Is the prosecution ready?"

"We are ready, Your Honor," answered Miss Martha Kluck. "Is the defense ready?"

"We are ready, Your Honor," answered Mr. Donny Kockran.

"Start the opening statement Miss Kluck."

"Good morning Ladies and Gentlemen of the jury, members of this courtroom, and Your Honor. We of the prosecution team will present you with facts, proving that Mr. Oscar James Samson, who is seated at the defense table, did murder Mrs. Nike Brown Samson, and Mr. Clem Hooper in cold blood. We will prove without a reasonable doubt, that this was a premeditated murder of Mrs. Nike Brown Samson and Mr. Clem Hooper. We will show that the defendant had motive and opportunity to murder Mrs. Samson. Mr. Hooper was an innocent victim. We have the evidence to prove, beyond a reasonable doubt, that the defendant did commit these horrible murders. You will hear the phrase reasonable doubt, from Judge Ego and the defense team. Reasonable doubt is the term referring to the amount of certainty that you, the jury, must have before deciding on the guilt of this murdering defendant."

"I object," shouted Mr. Kockran.

"Overruled, Mr. Kockran Continue with the opening statement Miss Kluck."

"May we have a side bar, Your Honor, as to the reference of my client being referred to as a murdering defendant?" asked Mr. Kockran.

"No, continue Miss Kluck."

"When you hear the witnesses, see the evidence, hear the coroner, hear the forensic experts, see the murder weapon, and hear from an expert witness on blood and knife wounds, you will not have any doubts whatsoever of the murderer.

"Yes Ladies and Gentlemen of the jury, we have the weapon, and during the proceedings of this trial we will show you the weapon, and you will see the connection between the weapon and Mr. Samson. You will hear the witnesses testimony of the beating the defendant gave to the late Mrs. Samson. You will hear testimony in this court of the cursing and kicking of the late Mrs. Samson, and the abuse, the threats to her that he would kill her. Ladies and Gentlemen of the jury, you are looking at the defendant at the defense table, who is a wife beater, a drunkard, a liar, a man who cheats on his wife and a cold blooded murderer of two innocent people.

"Do not let his good looks, charm and musical talents fool you. Do not let the acts of innocence fool you, for he is a good actor, but a mean-spirited person. The defense will tell you he is innocent and has an alibi, that he loved Nike. Well, Ladies and Gentlemen of the jury, if he loved her, why did he beat her and tell her he was going to kill her? If he has an alibi, let him bring a witness into this court and take an oath to tell the truth under penalty for perjury. Mr. Samson claims he is innocent. If he is as innocent as a lamb, let him get on the witness stand and be cross examined by the prosecution team.

"He is not innocent and we will prove it. You will see and hear enough evidence to convict Mr. Samson of first degree murder and we will ask for the death penalty. Thank you, Ladies and Gentlemen."

"I have concluded my opening statement to the jury, Your Honor."

"Ladies and Gentlemen, it is 12:45 PM past time for our lunch break. We will, return to this courtroom at 2 PM. Ladies and Gentlemen of the Jury, I caution you not to discuss with any one anyone or each other any thing about this case. You will only discuss it in the jury room during the deliberation of this case. Have a nice lunch and I'll see you at 2 PM.

"Court adjourned," said the bailiff.

The bailiff led the jurors out of the back of the courthouse, around the side and two blocks across the square to Rooster's Cafe.

Rooster's Cafe was in the center of Three Notch, where most of the businessmen, politicians and, on Saturdays, the farmers would gather to dine and socialize. During the elections almost everyone in town would crowd into the cafe for the election returns. As the bailiff led the jurors into the cafe, Possum Stroud and Tater Mathews were still discussing the election returns of the day before.

Possum and Tater both ran for County Commissioner of their District. Possum didn't campaign. He said, "Shucks everybody knows ole Possum." On the afternoon of election day he and his wife Pearlie Mae went by and picked up his mama, Mable Lee, and went to vote. After voting they went to Rooster's Cafe. Rooster cleaned the dinner menu off the blackboard and put up the candidates names to tally the votes. Mable Lee and Pearlie Mae ordered hamburgers, and R.C. Colas, while Possum had pig knuckles and white lightnin' kool-aid.

After all the votes were in and counted, Possum got two votes and Tater got four votes. Possum sat there sucking on his pig knuckles and drinking his white lightnin' kool-aid, looking at Pearlie Mae then at his mama and trying to figure out which one didn't vote for him. As Tater got up to leave, Possum asked Tater where he wuz going. Tater said, "I'm going over to the courthouse.

"To get a recount?" asked Possum.

"No," said Tater. "I'm going to get a gun permit and a gun. Anybody that ain't got no more friends than to get three votes besides his own needs a gun."

As the jurors walked in, Possum was telling Tater. "I don't know if I should disown my Mama, or get a new wife."

Rooster Watkins, the owner, led the jurors to the dining and meeting room in the back. This room is where the Lions Club, Chamber of Commerce luncheons, and other large parties met. The N.A.C.P. postponed their Tuesday 12:30 meeting until 1:30 PM. The N.A.C.P. (National Association of Cotton Pickers) ordered for lunch, in advance, Rooster's famous chicken croquettes. On Monday, Rooster had served roasted chicken, then took the leftovers and roasted more chicken so he would have enough for the jurors. The croquettes had celery, grated onions, eggs, lemon juice, chicken broth, dry mustard, worcestershire sauce and stale bread, which he made into crumbs. He served this with butter beans, okra, cucumbers, corn fritters, with cracklin' corn bread and sweet potato pie. Mr. Haul rose and asked the Reverend John Paul Pope to say the blessing for the food.

The Reverend Pope rose and said, "Oh Lord, we thank thee for this food, and I quote from the Book of Numbers, chapter 11, verse 5. 'We remember the fish which we did eat in Egypt freely; the cucumbers, and the melons, and the leeks, and the onions and the garlic.' As we the jurors go into this trial, let us ask our Lord for guidance and patience. Now bless this chicken, butter beans, okra, cucumbers and other fine cooking by Mr. Rooster for our bodies. Amen."

As they sat down to eat Al K. Haul thought, "I'll ask each of the jurors to say grace so we will not have a long winded preacher, preaching over lunch every day."

The jury members made small talk, trying to get to know each other, for they would have to spend a great deal of time together, and they did not hear what was asked of each other during the selection of the jurors. Kit Carson and Tom Mix talked to each other for they had something in common, ranching and picture making. Mrs. Kitty Kat and Mr. Al K. Haul found that they had similar interests as Mrs. Kat's husband was a business owner of a hardware store, and she knew Mr. Haul's wife, Carrie N. Haul. Mr. Macy and Miss Iola Bridges were teachers and had something in common. Mr. Rhett Cutler, the logging contractor, Mr. LeRoy Rodgers and Mae East got along fine, as Mae East's husband farmed and had sold some timber that Mr. Cutler snaked out of the woods. Also, Mr. Rodgers had a large tract of timber on his farm. Thelma Jitter, the youngest, felt out of place, but Minnie Curl made her laugh so she felt at ease with her. U. R. Short, Hoot Gibson and the Reverend Pope seem to get along well until The Reverend would quote biblical verses. U. R. was good about changing the subject. Shirley Pimple sort of sided off with Iola Bridges, both of them being old maids.

After lunch Dean Autry stood at the entrance to the rest room while the jurors visited the facilities. When they finished Dean led them back across the square, in the back of the courthouse, and up the stairs to the jury room.

The Three Notch County Courthouse, a two-story building, was made of granite shipped from the mountains of North Alabama. The building sits on the east side of the town square. The square is a one block square in the center of Three Notch with sidewalks going from the east to the west and another from the square where the sidewalks crossed, a statue of a confederate soldier facing the courthouse saluting. On the first floor of the courthouse is the Probate Judge, Circuit Clerk, State Attorney's Office, Public Defender's Office, Sheriff's Office with rooms for deputies, clerks, and other space to carry on the duties of the Sheriff's department. Located on the second floor was the courtroom, Judge's Office, an office for the prosecutor and defense attorney, a conference room, a jury room, rest room for the jury, and a rest room for the courtroom personnel.

As the jurors walked behind the courthouse, they saw a covered walkway where the prisoners and the accused were escorted to the courthouse from the jail. The jail was a two-story brick building, housing the prisoners on the top floor with only one stairway from the second floor to the first where it opened into the Jailer's Office, a Mr. Wilbur Anders.

The first floor consisted of a two bedroom apartment with kitchen, living room, dining room, sun porch and the office. Sue Anders, Wilbur's wife, did the cooking for the prisoners. There were three jailers, working eight hours shifts. The sheriff's deputies were available to help when needed. At night when the last deputy left the Sheriff's Office in the courthouse, they would tell the telephone operator to put all calls through to the Jail's Office when anyone needed the sheriff. The jailer who was on night duty, knew who was on duty at the Sheriff's Office and how to reach that person. The telephone of the jail was 1313, the Sheriff's Office was 1312. Sheriff, Clyde Jenkins and Jailer, Wilbur Anders, ran a no-frills no-nonsense jail. The jurors would see this facility a great deal in passing it each day out of the back of the courthouse. The jury room faced east with the jail about 50 yards from the courthouse. The second floor of the courthouse looked into the second floor of the jail house. However, the jurors couldn't see much of the inside of the jail because of the bars and the way the windows were constructed.

The jurors returned to the jury room at 1:50 PM, and about the time they had settled down the bailiff called them into the jury box. As they entered, everyone was standing. After they were in place, the Bailiff Dean Autry spoke, "Be seated. Three Notch 2 1/4 Circuit Court, is now in session, Judge Vance Ego presiding."

The judge looked over at the defense team and asked, "Mr. Kockran will your opening statement be over two hours long? If so, we will have your opening statement tomorrow."

"Your Honor," spoke Mr. Kockran," we should be finished by four o'clock, for sure no later than 4:30 PM."

"Start your opening statement Mr. Kockran."

"Good afternoon. Your Honor, members of the court, Ladies and Gentlemen of the jury, we will prove that Mr. Samson is innocent of the charges placed against him. The prosecutor states that the murder of Nike Samson, occurred at approximate 8:30 PM according to the medical examiner's report. We will prove that Mr. Samson was not near the Mansion on the Hill at that time. We will also show that the Sheriff's Department altered the evidence to frame Mr. Samson.

"The weapon was not and is not owned by Mr. Samson. Mr. Samson is a recording artist, a businessman, a churchgoing Christian, a loving father and, above all, an outstanding citizen. Ladies and Gentlemen of the jury, look at the defendant.

"Does this man look like a killer of two people? One is almost unknown to him, and the other is the mother of his two children. Will you listen to the evidence as we refute and prove each piece that the prosecutor bring forth?

"The prosecutor will say that Mr. Samson had the motive to do this dastardly deed to the mother of his children. Sure there was a difference of opinion on occasions. You are married, have you and your spouse ever disagreed on anything? Of course you have. And what did you do? Did you kill your spouse? Of course not. Did you feel like it at times? Of course you did. Did you ever say I could kill her or (him)? Most of you did or thought that. No, you did not do it or would not do the deed. The point is, that the prosecutor will say that Mr. Samson said this or thought these thoughts. That doesn't mean he did. The prosecutor must prove without a reasonable doubt, that Mr. Samson did this deed.

"Did a jealous boy friend do this ghastly murder? Or was it a jealous lover of Mr. Clem Hooper? Was it a burglar, trying to burglarize the house, and Mr. Hooper happened to be there and tried to stop the burglar. Or was it a hog rustler, knowing Mrs. Samson would be alone and he would take the hogs? Maybe when Mr. Hooper and Mrs. Samson confronted him, and he slashed their throats, right there in the hog pen. Think about this and remember Mr. Samson had left for Shreveport, La. before 9 PM. Could he have done this to the woman, who he still loved, the mother of his children, then go to sleep in his bus, and be prepared to sing at a huge concert? No Ladies and Gentlemen, this man could not control his emotions after doing a deed of this sort and give a great performance. Mr. Samson is a gentle man, loving father, and son, with not a malicious bone in his body. I am confident, after you listen to the testimony, and hear the weak evidence and the strong defense, you will find Mr. Samson not guilty."

"Ladies and Gentlemen, Your Honor, the Defense has concluded it's opening statement. Thank you."

Judge Ego looked at the jury and said, "Ladies and Gentlemen, you may retire to the jury room for a few minutes while I attend to some legal matters with the attorneys."

Bailiff Dean Autry said, "All rise," and led the jury into the jury room."

Judge Ego called the attorneys into his chambers, where he asked that they submit two copies of their witness list in order of appearance, of which he gave the opposing teams a copy. Glancing at the list, Judge Ego looked at the prosecution team and asked, "Miss Kluck, who will be the starting attorney for the prosecution?"

"I will start for the prosecution team, Your Honor," answered Miss Kluck.

"Good, your first witness will be Mr. Nick Webb, then you will follow the list. There will be no showboating in this courtroom, no snide remarks to or about anyone, I expect a no nonsense, professional courtesy to all, and I do not want any arguing, when I overrule or sustain an objection. We will not have the time for any witness to take the stand this afternoon, I will excuse the jury for the night. Have your witnesses prepared to start tomorrow. Let's go back in the courtroom."

"Bailiff, call the jury to the jury box."

After the jury had been seated, Bailiff Autry called the court to order.

"Ladies and Gentlemen of the jury, you will be excused for the night and the court will convene at 10 AM tomorrow. Do not speak to anyone about this case. If you see something that would pertain to this case in the paper, do not read about it. If anything comes on the radio, leave the area or turn the radio off, and I want you to understand me clearly. You will not discuss this case among yourselves, your spouse, family members, or friends. Good day and have a nice evening."

Chapter Nineteen

Big Ben jarred Martha awake with it's loud alarm. It was still dark and as she reached for the light she remembered setting Big Ben to get an early start for court. However, she would snooze for a few minutes. Her thoughts went to Bradford Larson, an old boyfriend she still missed. Oh how she longed for him to be laying beside her and making love. Brad was a great lover, but she and Brad did not get along together in their daily lives, except for love making. Brad said she was too aggressive and she put her work above everything else. They parted but remained good friends and had lunch on occasion.

Brad's family owned a lot of land with timber, a sawmill, and a lumber and window supply company. She could have married Brad and life would have been slower.

Enough of these thoughts as she got up and stumbled in the bathroom. Her head had a dull ache and her stomach was cramping. Oh hell, she thought, as she reached in the linen closet for her sanitary belt and napkin pads, I should have known when I get horny I would have a bitchy day. After bathing she walked in the dressing area and saw herself in the mirror. Gad am I ugly. How Brad ever thought I was beautiful I don't know, my eyes are bloodshot and look like a rabbit with wrinkled eyes peeking out of an outhouse. My hair is stringy, my skin is pale and has pimples all over it, if my nose was a guitar I'd be the worlds best picker. Martha started brushing her hair, and after she finished, her thick brunette wavy hair cascaded around her shoulders. Her light brown eyes, the color of specially blended Colombian coffee with a touch of cream, looked open and cheerful. The light rouge and powder covered her pale skin and the two pimples, the dark red lipstick made her mouth look sensual with generous lips. She reached in the clothes closet and took out a light blue long-sleeved blouse with a V front of white serge, trimmed with lace. She added a full skirt that reached two inches below the knee and a half slip made of white Egyptian cotton, slightly starched. Just as she pulled her light beige mercerized silk hose up, she realized that she had put on a sanitary belt that did not have a hose supporter. Damn, she would have to take the skirt, panties, sanitary belt, and napkin off and redo the dressing with the sanitary belt with the hose supporters. What a bitchy day this has started out to be. When she finally finished dressing and looked in the full length mirror, she saw a neatly dressed woman five feet seven inches tall, weighing 115 pounds, on a curved body with shapely legs.

She started for the door and remembered that she had sent away for some pills from an advertisement that was in a magazine. It was for Dr. Rose's Female Pills, "the unfailing remedy for all forms of the female weakness such as tardy or irregular periods and suppression of the menses. It will give tone to the entire female system, making the eyes bright, the cheeks rosy, and give strength and buoyancy to the step." Martha turned around and went into the kitchen and got the bottle of Dr. Rose's Female Pills, took two and put a couple more in her purse as she thought, "O.K. Mr. OJ Samson here I come."

On the other side of Three Notch, Donny Kockran woke up at six-thirty, and made a cup of coffee. Donny had stayed in the study well past 1 AM pursuing his strategy for the defense of OJ. When he stumbled into the bathroom and put the coffee cup on the dressing counter, he saw himself in the mirror. He didn't like what he saw, two eyes that were red, as if he had not slept for two weeks, his jowls, normally taut, were now slack, and his face looked as if it had a three day growth of beard, although he had shaved the day before.

Not only did he look bad, he felt as if he had a big hangover. He had not touched any alcoholic beverage since he started this case, but he still remembered how the hangovers felt. A good stiff drink of White Ribbon Vitae-Likker of Life would make him perk up in a jiffy. Hell what am I thinking of, I can't let this case get me on the booze. Donny gulped the coffee down and headed to the kitchen where he prepared his breakfast. He refilled his cup and sat in a chair at the breakfast nook sipping his coffee, and trying to get his mind to work in the order of the day when Nick Webb, the first witness takes the stand. He finished the coffee and headed for a hot shower, hoping this would snap him back to his old self. After the shower and shave he put on some Old Spice after shave and began to feel better. In the kitchen he had two eggs, hot grits, buttermilk biscuits, and country sausage from the farm of Old Joe Clark. Donny ate the breakfast, had another cup of coffee and was ready to take on the world, or at the least Martha Kluck. He opened his brief case and began putting the papers in order, when the telephone rang. It was Barry Kall who would start the cross-examination of the first witness. Barry was excellent in cross-examination of a witness and Donny had given the go ahead to Barry on opening day.

"Donny, I am in Montgomery and leaving now, however, it will take me two hours to get there, which would make it about 10:30. Can you stall the court for 30 to 45 minutes?"

Barry didn't give an excuse as to why he was in Montgomery or why he was just leaving. Barry was single, 29 years old, well built, six feet tall weighing in at 185 pounds, with fine blond wavy hair, a light complexion, with outdoor he-man rugged good looks, liquid blue eyes, turning to cold steel on direct or cross-examination. He had the mannerisms that attracted females, similar to a male elk when a cow was in heat. Three Notch being a small town where everyone knew what went on, Barry and others would take their female friends that they wanted to be discreet with, to

Montgomery where there were nice restaurants, night clubs and hotels.

"Barry," screamed Donny, "Who in the hell is so frigging good to get your mind off this case, you know we have a 10 AM court time. Get your ass here by ten o'clock and leave that twerp in the sack. Now move!"

Donny slammed the phone down and darted for the door hoping to find an excuse to delay the opening of the court and the State's first witness. He hoped to God Barry was not hung over and too fucked out so he could drive at a high rate of speed without having an accident, or get stopped for speeding.

Donny headed for his automobile for the short drive to the courthouse. It was beautiful fall day. The leaves were turning slightly, the sun was out as he drove down Church Street. The thing marring the day was Barry and his frigging women, well he had to think of sometime. Maybe he could say Berry has an upset stomach and has taken some Blackdrough Balsam to quickly stop the diarrhea and soothe his nervous stomach, and would be a few minutes late, then pray that he would not be more than 30 minutes late and Judge Ego would not call his house. "Hell," he thought, "I'll have a nervous stomach and diarrhea before this day is over."

Chapter Twenty

As Donny drove past the courthouse to the parking lot behind it, he looked at his watch, which read 8:45 AM. Maybe in about an hour he could go to the judge's chambers and engage him in some court procedure that would delay the time.

He entered the office and all of his staff was there, except Barry. Kay Lane, the receptionist, had a message from Barry. He stopped at the Coffee Pot Diner in Wing and should be here by 10:00 to 10:15.

Donny was busy getting everything in order when Kay called and reminded him by the time he got to court it would be 9:55. "Oh hell, I forgot to see Judge Ego to see if I could delay the court," he thought. "Oh, well I'll wing it."

Bailiff Dean Autry announced, "All Rise."

Judge Ego took his chair and asked Bailiff Autry to bring the jurors in. After the jurors were seated, Judge Ego looked around and asked if everyone was here. Donny stood up and answered, "No Your Honor, Mr. Kall has diarrhea and has taken some Blackdrough Balsam. He called and said he was better and would be here not later than 10:15, I ask the court's indulgence. I'll call to see if he has left yet."

Judge Ego turned to the jury and as he turned he began sniffing the air, looking at the jurors he said, "What is that?" Kitty Kat, juror number three, gave the expression that told the Judge, "It's not me." Bailiff Autry walked over and looked down the jury pool and saw that Rhett Cutler, juror number four, had something on his shoes. Mr. Cutler is the logger, that snakes logs out of the woods.

This day Mr. Cutler was dressed in an almost new overall and jumper, a white shirt, frayed at the collar, all freshly washed, lightly starched and ironed. He had on a pair of almost new high-top brogan shoes and white socks, and on the bottom of one of the brogans was a dark substance.

Mr. Tom Mix, the number two juror, a cowboy rancher, looked over and said, "Hey Rhett, you should have wiped the horse crap off of your shoes before coming to court."

Cutler gave Mr. Mix a shrug and said to him, "You phony asshole of a cowboy, go back to making dem pitcher shows. You wouldn't know hoss shit from bull shit. I wus feeding old Blue, Red, Whitie and Marbelle before coming to court, and I could have stepped in the bull shit."

Tom Mix jumped as the Bailiff ran over and Judge Ego was banging his gavel and hollering, "ORDER IN THE COURTROOM."

After Bailiff Dean Autry and Judge Vance Ego restored order, Judge Ego said, "Ladies and Gentlemen of the jury, we will recess for 30 minutes. I want you to go to the jury room, and we will have the Bailiff accompany you and you will remain in the jury room until the recess is over. You may use the rest room one at a time. I will not, understand, will not allow any more outbursts from the jury. If you do you will be held in contempt of court. Mr. Cutler, you will be given a brush and towel so you can clean your shoes. In the future, I suggest each of you check your shoes before entering the courthouse. Will the jury rise and face me and look me in the eyes. Do you understand my instructions, if not raise your hands?" None of the jury raised a hand and the judge called the recess.

Donny gave a sigh of relief. He now had 30 minutes for Barry to show up. He went to his office and had a note from Kay that Barry called from just outside of town and would be there in 10 minutes. Just as Donny finished reading the note, Barry came in looking fresh and rested. Donny filled Barry in on the diarrhera and

Blackdrough story, and the fracas in court to delay the witness. They sat down to plan their strategy. Barry did not elaborate on his overnight escapade, nor did Donny ask at this time.

Chapter Twenty-One

At 10:30 Judge Ego entered the courtroom and the bailiff said "All rise, court is now in session, Judge Vance Ego, presiding, be seated please."

"Is the prosecution ready?" asked Judge Ego.

"We are ready, Your Honor," answered Miss Martha Kluck.

"Is the defense ready?" asked Judge Ego.

"The defense is ready," answered Mr. Donny Kockran.

"Bailiff, call the first witness, Mr. Nick Webb, to the stand," Judge Ego said and nodded to the Bailiff.

Nick Webb, a farmer and the neighbor who found the bodies of Nike Samson and Clem Hooper, walked down the center of the courtroom from the witness room. As he walked he had the gait of a farmer plowing his mule, long slow strides with shoulders slightly humped over at the angle he would be, if holding the plow handles. Nick was about six feet two inches tall, slender built, with dark hair streaked with gray. His face was weather beaten, with horizontal wrinkles on his face, thin lips and deep set brown eyes. His hands were noticeable due to their size. They were extra large, bony with long fingers, coarse and callused. Nick was about 35 years old and looked and carried himself as a person of 45. He had on his dress overalls and jumper, that he wore to town on Saturdays. They were freshly washed, with a little too much starch. Today he had on his Sunday white shirt and black leather low cut shoes with new white socks, He carried a white Panama hat in his left hand. He seemed uncomfortable and ill at ease as he took the witness stand. However, you could look at Mr. Nick Webb and see that he was a no nonsense fellow.

The court clerk, Mrs. Shirley Nation, stood in front of Clem and asked him to raise his hand.

"Do you swear to tell the truth, the whole truth, and nothing but the truth so help you God?"

"Yes Mam," answered Mr. Webb in a loud clear voice, looking Mrs. Nation straight in the eyes.

"All right Miss Kluck, you may start your direct examination."

"Thank you Your Honor," and she thought, "I must get this man on my side, as he looks and talk as if he can't be pushed or rattled."

"Mr. Webb, will you please tell the jury, as you look at them what you were doing on the morning of June 13 and the time."

"Well, Mam, I got up at three that morning, put some wood in the cook stove, lighted it and put some water on to make coffee, while I went out to the barn to feed my mules. I went back in the house had my coffee with two aigs and some sausage and grits with ham gravy, that my wife, Velma, had made. After breakfast I put some cawn in the wagon, hitched up Maude and left for Mathews Grocery and Cawn Mill on the edge of Three Notch, where I wus going to git some groceries and have my cawn ground into meal.

"I live a mile from the Samson's and I wus near the Mansion on the Hill, when it wus getting daylight. I heard all this noise coming from the pig pen at the side of the barn. I didn't pay too much attention, as I have lots of hogs, and I know they make a lot of noise this time of morning."

"Mr. Webb, do you know the time of day, when you heard this noise?"

"About this time of the year daylight is about four o'clock or a little after. I didn't look at my watch caus as the road turned east, I saw the sky wus getting light, and about five minutes later I wus at The Mansion on the Hill."

"Mr., Webb, how far is the barn and pig pen from the road where your wagon was, when you first heard the noise."

"Oh, I think about a 100 yards, more or less."

"Mr. Webb, how can you be sure about the distance?"

"My barn is 100 yards from the road, about the same distance as Mrs. Samson."

Miss Kluck walked over in front of the jury at the corner of the jury box, turned toward Mr. Webb, smiled and said, "Mr. Webb, I know that the memory of this particular morning is not a pleasant one and I feel bad for bringing this up, but would you describe to this court what made you investigate the noise?"

"As I said, I have lots of hogs and know they make lots of noise about this time of the morning, as it's close to feeding time. But this noise was different than the noise they make about feeding time and I went to see what the matter was, thinking maybe one or more was hung in a barbed wire fence."

"What was different about the noise that made you suspicious enough to investigate the pig pen?"

"Well instead of them grunting like they do for food, they were loud, and shrill, then low moans like they wus in pain. I never heard that type of grunts and groans before."

"Did you go up to the pig pen to investigate that strange noise?"

"Yes Mam, I did."

"What was the first thing that you saw when you looked into the pig pen?"

"Well the hogs wus standing over to one side, except the two pet pigs, Root and Snoot, and they wus near a big pile of bloody clothes. When I got closer I saw the body of a woman, with blood all over her. Her throat wus cut and there wus cuts all over the upper body with blood everywhere. It wus awful, I butcher hogs and cattle every winter, but I ain't seen nothing cut like this, I got sick to my stomach and had to throw up."

" Mr. Webb are you all right?"

"Yes Mam, but I would like to have some water."

"Your Honor, may we take a few minutes recess for the witness to compose himself?"

"We will take 10 minutes, so that the witness and jurors can go the rest room and get some water."

"All rise," said Mr. Autry, "court is in recess."

Miss Kluck took Mr. Webb's arm and led him to a hall in back of the courtroom and went to get some water for him. While she was gone for the water, Mr. Webb reached in the pocket in the center of his overall bib and took out a can of Prince Albert smoking tobacco and a packet of Ace cigarette papers, rolled a cigarette and lit up a smoke. Miss Kluck brought the water back and asked if he was all right.

"Yes Mam, but I want to go to the toilet."

Martha showed him where the rest rooms were and as he went into the toilet, he thought, "What a nice woman she is and as purty as a puppy in the sunshine."

Court was called to order after 10 minutes, and when the jury was seated, Judge Ego asked Mr. Webb to return to the witness chair.

"Can you continue now, Mr. Webb?"

"Yes Sir, I am fine."

"You said before the break that you saw a woman. How could you tell it was a woman, did you recognize her?" asked Martha Kluck.

"No Mam, I would never recognize her, but the body had hair like a woman, and the dress was torn and pulled down below the hips."

"Did you know Mrs. Samson?"

"Yes Mam, I did a little work for her once in a while and Velma would take care of the young'ns from time to time."

"What did you do next?"

"I started to the house to see about the young'ns, and I seen this other body with his throat cut, and his stomach wus slit from hip to hip. I know it was a man caus' he had on long pants and a man's haircut. I ran up to the house scared I wus goin' to find the young'ns all cut up, but when I got thar, they wus asleep in bed."

"Did you wake them up to be sure they were alive?"

"Yes Mam, I did."

"What did you do next?"

"I told them their Mama wus sick and I wus taking them with me. Knowing me and being sleepy they came with me. I took a quilt and put in it the wagon and we took off lickety split to the Mathew's store."

"When you reached Mathew's Grocery, did you call the Sheriff's Office?"

"Yes Mam, I told them what I saw and they told me to stay at the Mathew's store until they got there. When the Sheriff got there I left the young'ns with Mrs. Mathew to take care of, and I went with the Sheriff to the Mansion on the Hill."

"What happened when you reached the pig pen?"

"Showed the Sheriff the bodies and I got sick again and threw up, I ain't never seen a mess like that. I took the hogs and put them in the pasture and fed them. Then answered all the question the Sheriff ast."

"Did you see any type of knife or weapon?"

"No Mam, I didn't."

"How long did you stay at the scene of the crime?"

"I left just after I fed the hogs, walked back to Mathew's Grocery, to get my mule and wagon and take the young'ns back to Velma to care for them."

"What time did you start walking back to Mathew's Grocery Store, Mr. Webb?"

"Right near as I can figure it wus nigh on to 7:30."

"Thank you, Mr. Webb."

"Your Honor, the Prosecution has finished with Mr. Webb, subject to recall."

It was 12:30, past lunch and Judge Ego recessed the court until two o'clock, cautioning the jurors not to discuss with anyone or each other anything relating to the case.

The bailiff took the jurors out of the courthouse, past the jail and across the square to Rooster's Cafe.

Chapter Twenty Two

After the jurors were seated, Al K. Haul announced that he would say grace today, and each day the juror to his right would say grace. He did this so the Reverend John Paul Pope would not get on his winded prayer. It would be a while before it got back to the Reverend, as he sat on the left side of Al K. Haul.

"Let us bow our heads. Oh Lord, give us our daily bread, thank you in thy name, Amen."

As the jurors began their meal, Tom Mix sitting next to Rhett Cutler said to him, "Rhett I apologize for what I said to you this morning about the horse crap, I was only joking to sort of relieve the tension, because it looks as if we have a long grind ahead of us."

"Tom, I'm sorry I called you a phony asshole of a cowboy, I wus out feeding the oxen and ole Blue wus feeling porely and I'm have concerns 'bout him, and I didn't notice I had bull shit on my brogans. Yur a right nice feller and a good cowboy in the picther shows."

There was other small talk during the lunch break, and when they finished lunch, Bailiff Autry led them back across the square to the courthouse. As they went behind the courthouse and in front of the jail, Thelma Jitter saw Barbé, OJ's girl friend, going into the jail. She tried to imagine what it would be like to date OJ if this had not happened. "Gee I can't have thoughts like this," she thought, "but he doesn't seem like a murderer."

A few minutes after the jurors had returned to the jury room, Bailiff Autry called them into the courtroom earlier than the expected starting time.

After being seated Judge Ego announced that court would be adjoined until Monday at 10 AM.

That afternoon when Barbé visited OJ at the jail, he seemed upset with her.

"Someone told me that you went to Pensacola with Ted Bear, and it was not for a gig. What is going on?" he asked her.

"We went down to talk to a promoter about a concert in Ocala, Fla. We had a hard time getting to see him, but this is a large concert, so we stayed overnight, in separate rooms."

OJ got upset and started screaming at the top of his voice, "Don't give me that bull shit you frigging whore. I know better. You and that peckerhead was shacked up in some hotel on the beach."

The guard heard the commotion and came running down the cell block. OJ was red in the face trying to reach Barbé through the bars. The guards escorted Barbé out of the jail, and told him if he didn't settle down they would put him in the padded cell in the basement. OJ tried to settle down, but he knew he was being taken for a ride. Well, he would put a stop to this. He asked his guard to call Donny Kockran for him.

Donny arrived in about 45 minutes. The guard had told him on the telephone what had occurred. As Donny walked down the cell block and got nearer to OJ's cell he could see him pacing back and forth, cursing at the top of his voice.

After the guard let him in the cell, Donny said, "OJ you must calm down. All the prosecution has to do, if they find out, and they will find out about this, is to prove what a violent temper you have. Just calm down and let's talk about it in a rational manner."

OJ told Donny about Barbé and Ted Bear and said "Cancel her contract she's not that good of a singer, only a good piece of ass, and when I get out of here I can find plenty of others."

"OK, I'll work on it, but in the mean time I am canceling her visiting privileges. You stay cool man, we can work this thing out.

I need to go and get some work done. Your Pa and Ma will be coming to see you in the morning, so for their sakes stay calm."

"Thanks for coming Donny, I'll be OK."

Donny rushed back to his office to call Barbé, damn that twerp to screw up the good thing they had. But, when he arrived at the office, Barbé was waiting for him.

"What can I do, Donny, to get OJ calmed down?" asked Barbé.

"I am afraid that it is to late now, Barbé, OJ has told me to cancel the contract. He doesn't know that it is a partnership. When he finds out he will get another attorney to represent him in this matter, and the way it was put together, they can surely win."

"What can we do to stop the flow of water, buy him out or sell to him?"

"You have made OJ so mad that he would not sell to you at any price. This comes at a bad time, just when the trial started. I have two great concerns, first to protect my client, I should not have gone into this deal with you. The second problem is to gracefully get us out without me being disbarred and you going to jail."

"You mean I could go to jail?" moaned Barbé.

"You bet your sweet ass you could, let me think about this tonight. Call me at 10 in the morning."

Barbé, left Donny's office, thinking, "I can't go to jail. If I can walk away from this mess, I can sing with Teddy Bear".

After Barbé left Donny thought, "I hope to hell I scared the shit out of that twerp. I'll see if she will take $2,000 and sign a release and outright sale. OJ is too torn up and worried about the trial to go over the papers in detail". Donny sat back in his chair, lit a cigarette and went over the details of the sale of the partnership. He thought about what he would tell, Barbé and OJ, and got his mind back on the trial for Monday morning.

The next morning at 10 sharp Barbé was at Donny's office.

"Were you able to talk to OJ about our problem?" Barbé asked meekly.

Donny knew he had struck a home run yesterday afternoon about scaring her.

"Well, Barbé, we have a real tough problem. He is still mad and wants revenge, but I have the problem well in hand. OJ will give you $2,000, if you will sign over the partnership, release all assets, and go through his agent on any of his songs before singing them. I doubt if the agent will give permission for you to use them at any price. I wouldn't approach that angle if I were you. My suggestion is for you to take the money and run."

"But, Donny, I have put in a lot of hard work and expense into this partnership and all he wants to give me is $2,000?"

"Shit", thought Donny, "this twerp is hard headed. I guess I will have to throw the fear of God in her".

"Barbé I didn't want to tell you this, but I have been unable to convince OJ not to prosecute you for fraud. He only let me make this offer to you.

"Do you have any idea whatsoever is involved in the mess that you got into? Well, let me tell you. First, you told, and led OJ to believe that this was an ordinary contract, where he would finance you and write songs to get you stardom, and split the profits. Remember, he put up the front money and paid you a handsome salary with all expenses, where, by the way you lived high on the hog. You were an average singer who made an average living singing. OJ has not realized any money in this deal, in fact, when he pays you the $2,000, he will lose money. If you don't quietly accept the money and sign the papers, you can be prosecuted. Under Alabama Statute 3615 chapter 23, subchapter 11, citing the case of Notizzy Talent Agency, Morning Starr was prosecuted for misleading the agency, for fraud, lying about the expense account, signing the partnership papers, and for making the client believe, (by sexual behavior), he would be signing a work contract. Morning Starr received two years in the state prison, plus a $1,000 fine that had to be paid before a parole hearing or release from prison. If you take the money, I think I can talk OJ into accepting the deal. If not, get yourself a lawyer, because shit is going to hit the fan and blow up right in your face."

"OK Donny, I will sign the papers. Lets end this mess, I don't want to go to prison."

Donny sighed a big sigh of relief, the bull shit worked. He whipped out the papers, he had prepared early that morning and called in his secretary to notarize the signature.

After the signing, ending the partnership between Barbé' and OJ, Barbé headed for the door, looking as if she had lost her last friend. As she walked Donny thought, "she won't be without any friends, all they need to look at is that cute ass and the way each side wiggles up and down as she walks. Oh hell, back to getting OJ out of his problem."

Chapter Twenty-Three

About the time Barbé was leaving Donny's office, Jim Paul and Delilah Samson were arriving at the jail to see their son, Oscar James Samson.

After arriving in the visitor's room he hugged his Pa and after hugging his Ma, broke down and began crying. Delilah cradled OJ's head in her lap and as she stroked his hair, it seemed as if all of this trouble had never happened, as if OJ were still a little boy needing his Ma and she was loving and giving him comfort. "Oh God", she prayed, "get my baby out of this mess". She had to be strong for OJ and she ran her hand along the side of his face and said,"Honey, Jesus will take care of us, pray often for Him to give us guidance. Lets pray together now and get on with our visiting."

She thought as she started praying, she had to be the strong one, as he was her baby and Jim Paul was so torn up he couldn't think straight. "Oh Lord, our saviour, we would ask that you forgive us our sins, which as mortal people we have many. Help us to overcome our enemies. Bless them as they do not know what they are doing. Help us in our trials and tribulations. Keep us safe and as for the trouble of OJ, please, oh dear Jesus, keep and see him safely through this turmoil, as we know he did not do this deed that he is charged with. Thank you for the many blessings you have bestowed upon us, our crops, for the food you have given us and our health. We count every blessing and thank you for them. Keep us safe as we travel the hard road ahead in the coming weeks. Amen."

After the prayer Pa, told OJ about the crops and still.

"Son we ain't doing too good at the still. The Sad and Happy Drive-In is not using as much likker as they did. We have acres of cawn that we can't use or sell at a price to make a profit. We can't plant cotton again, cauz the bole weevil is eating the cotton crops up. Lots of the farmers are planting goobers, that is peanuts, in place of cotton. Most of the farmers over in Coffee County and Southeast Alabama is planting peanuts instead of cotton. A company has put up a peanut oil mill in Dothan. The farmers in Coffee County are so grateful that they found out peanuts are a better cash crop, and they thank the bole weevil for eating their cotton. They are getting up donations to put up a statue of the bole weevil in the middle of Enterprise. A black man, a Dr. George Washington Carver, up at Tuskegee invented peanut oil for cooking. He made an improved peanut butter. He made shoe polish out of peanuts and some type of cleaner for wood floors. They say he has invented over 25 things from the peanut. I think we should plant peanuts instead of cawn."

"Pa, it seems to me you are sold on this peanut harvesting as a business. You know we grew them to fatten the hogs and for eating and candy making."

"I am sold on the idea, son, the county agent thinks we should get in on the planting of peanuts, but I worry about one thing."

"What is that Pa, money?"

"Well, yes and no. You see, if we plant a lot of peanuts, it will cost too much to pick them, plus the time for the field hands to pick them."

"But Pa, don't they have peanut picking machines that can come to the field and pick them ?"

"Yes, son, but there is only one peanut picker in the county. Besides taking a long time to get to you, he keeps a third of the peanuts for picking them."

"An idea just struck me. See what a peanut picker would cost, with a gasoline engine to run it, and find out from the county agent how many pounds or tons of peanuts per acre is the average. Also, how many farmers there are in Three Notch, Chocktahathic, Coffee and Conecuh County that is growing peanuts and about how many pounds they will produce?"

"Son, what in the world do you have in mind?"

"Well, you see, Pa, Ma wants us to get out of the likker business, and I would like to sell the Sad and Happy Drive-In and get out of that business. With my singing, and you and me together in the peanut business, growing, picking for us and others, and maybe a warehouse, buying and selling peanuts, we could do well. I should be out of here in a month or less cause I can't see them doing anything but turning me loose as I ain't hurt nobody."

"Bless you. Son, I know my boy has a good heart, and you would do the right thing, the good Lord will see us over this bad dream, and before long you and Pa can be working together again," said Ma.

"Thanks Ma, now you and Pa go home, cause Pa has some errands to do. I will get Donny to get me a civil lawyer so I can sell the Sad and Happy Drive-In. Cholly Spinks has always wanted the business. Pa, go by the Cholly Hoss Honky Tonk and Country Club and ask Cholly to come see me."

After Pa and Ma left, OJ lay down on the bunk bed. He felt in better spirits than he had since he was arrested. Feeling he would be out soon, starting in a new business, peanuts, where he started while in school, and singing and writing songs and hearing his fans shout his name. Life is good.

He day dreamed of the future until he went into a deep restful sleep.

Chapter Twenty-Four

On Monday at 10 AM sharp Bailiff Dean Autry, called the court to order.

Judge Ego asked Mr. Kockran if he was ready to cross examine the witness, Mr. Nick Webb.

"Yes, Your Honor," answered Mr. Kockran.

Mr. Webb was called to the stand. As he took the chair Judge Ego turned to Mr. Webb and said, "Mr. Webb, you are still under oath. Proceed Mr. Kockran."

"Good morning, Mr. Webb."

"Morning to you sir," answered Mr. Webb.

"Mr. Webb, we want to be sure of the time you found the two bodies. You stated it was four o'clock when you found the bodies, How can you be so sure it was four o'clock?"

"I didn't say I was sure it was four o'clock. I said, it wuz getting daylight, and this time of the year daylight is about four or a little after."

"Then it could have been 4:30 when you found the bodies, Mr. Webb?"

"Mr. Lawyer," answered Mr. Webb, "It wuz before 4:30. I saw the light from the sun, which wuz below the trees in the east while I wus about five minutes from The Mansion on the Hill. According to the Old Farmer's Almanac, the sun would rise at 4:37. I had already found the bodies and wuz coming out of the house with the two chillun when I saw the sun peep up in the east."

"Mr. Webb, how is it that you read the Farmer's Almanac on this particular day, and how do you remember that it was on June 13 that you read it?"

"First, Mr. Lawyer."

"The name is Mr. Kockran," Donny informed Mr. Webb.

"Mr. Kockran or Mr. Lawyer, if you have ever lived on a farm, you otta know that the farmer lives by the old Farmer's Almanac to know when it will rain, when to plant seed and all sorts of information. I did not read the Almanac as I recall on June 13, but I did read it on June 12. I wanted to go to Mathew's Grocery and Cawn Mill, and needed to get an early start. I didn't want to be on the road before daybreak cauz the shirt factory workers sometimes go to work early and I didn't have a light for the wagon. To keep from being run over by the shirt factory workers, I looked up in the Old Farmers Almanac the time the sun would rise. It said 4:37, so I wuz coming out of the house with the chillun when the sun was rising."

"Mr. Webb, will you tell the jury why you went up to barn, where you found the bodies?"

"Well suh, I wus riding down the road, and as I got near the Mansion on the Hill, I heard hogs grunting real loud and awful shrill. I thought maybe they were hung up in a fence. Knowing Mrs. Samson lived alone and there wuz no light in the house, I decided I would do her a favor and help the hogs get out of the fence. But when I got close enough to see, I found the hogs were standing over to one side. Cauz the light was dim, I saw some clothes piled up on one side. That is when I went over and found out that they wuz bodies."

"And, Mr. Webb, you said this was 4:30 in the morning?"

"No Sir, I didn't say what time it wuz, I said about five minutes before I got there it wus getting light. The sun came up at 4:37 when I wuz bringing the chillun out of the house. It musta been between 4:35 and 4:45."

"Could it have been 4:15?"

"No Sir!"

"Are you sure that it wasn't 4:10?"

"I am as sure that the sunrise wus 4:37, as I am sure when I hear ole Mullet barking and know that he has a possum treed, Mr. Kockran. I ain't going to change the truth if you keep asking me til the cows come home."

"Your Honor," Miss Kluck said as she stood up, "the defense is badgering the witness."

"Mr. Kockran," said Judge Ego, "move along to another question and do not badger the witness."

"I apologize, Your Honor."

"Mr. Webb, did you see any weapon or instrument, while you were there or on your return with the Sheriff, that could have caused the death of these two people?"

"No Sir, I did not."

"Your Honor, I have no further questions of this witness," stated Mr. Kockran.

The judge looked at Miss Kluck and asked, "Any recross Miss Kluck?"

"No, Your Honor," she answered.

"Miss Kluck, call your next witness," the Judge said.

"The State calls Sheriff Clyde Jenkins, Sheriff of Three Notch County to the stand."

Sheriff Clyde Jenkins strolled to the witness stand, as the jurors looked on. They saw a man about six feet two inches tall, muscular, with broad shoulders, black hair, prominent check bones, dark brown eyes, with a dark reddish complexion. The way he carried himself and his complexion gave bearing to his part Indian heritage. He walked up to the stand, held up his right hand, and after the oath was read to him by Shirley Nation, he said, "I do."

"Sheriff Jenkins," asked Miss Kluck, "How long have you been Sheriff of Three Notch County?"

"I am in my ninth year as Sheriff," answered Sheriff Jenkins.

"Before you were elected Sheriff were you involved with law enforcement?"

"Yes Mam, I was on the Three Notch police force for two years, then a deputy Sheriff for three years, then I ran for Sheriff and have been elected every election since."

"Sheriff, tell the jurors the events leading up to and ending with the Coroner removing the bodies of Mrs. Nike Samson and Mr. Clem Hooper."

"I object, Your Honor, this question is too involved and the answer may include some inappropriate answers," stated Mr. Kockran.

The Judge thought for a second and called a side bar, where he informed the attorneys that the questions should be short enough that the answer would cover the one subject.

Miss Kluck looked at the jurors and then to the Sheriff and smiled.

"Tell us what time you received the message that there was a murder."

"The jailer at the jail called my home at 6:21 AM the morning of June 13. He informed me that a Mr. Nick Webb was at the Mathew's Grocery and Corn Mill and said there was two people killed at The Mansion on the Hill," answered Sheriff Jenkins.

"Did you proceed to the Mathew's Grocery Store?"

"First I called Deputy Van Otter, who is a detective and another deputy who is also a detective, Mark Burman, and told them to meet me at the Mansion on the Hill, Rural Route Three in the Slap Out Community. I then went to Mathew's Grocery and met Mr. Webb and we proceeded to The Mansion on the Hill. On the way, Mr. Webb, filled me in on what he knew from the time he found the bodies until I picked him up."

"What did you observe upon your arrival at the crime scene, Sheriff Jenkins?"

Deputy Detectives Otter and Burman who arrived before I did, had secured the crime scene and were waiting for me. I saw two bodies in a hog pen. The hog pen was wet and sloppy, the bodies were muddy, bloody and broken. It was the worst crime scene I have seen in all my years of law enforcement, in fact, this was the first time I got sick to my stomach. I was still heaving when the coroner arrived. I had also called him. The coroner, Dr. Mack Davis, gave me a whiff of smelling salts."

"Did you identify the bodies?" asked Miss Kluck.

"No. Mam I couldn't. I did not know the victims, but we knew Mrs. Samson lived there. Mr. Webb said he couldn't look at the bodies again, but the female looked like Mrs. Samson. I sent Detectives Van Otter and Mark Burman to The Sad and Happy Drive-In to get Mr. Samson to identify or try to identify the body of the female. We checked the wallet of the male and found a pay stub from Shorty's Barbecue restaurant, and one of the detectives went to Shorty's Barbecue to get someone to come out and identify the male."

Judge Ego interrupted and announced that it was time for the lunch break and said, "Court is adjoined until one-thirty."

The jurors left the court and made the familiar march around the courthouse, in front of the jail, across the square to Rooster's Cafe.

Today Rooster had boiled butter beans with a slab of white meat, okra with some finger peas, hot baked sweet potatoes, fresh corn, turnips, corn bread and roast beef, roasted with small white potatoes and onions for lunch. If anyone wanted deep fried pork chops, they could substitute the chops in place of the roast beef. Ice tea or coffee was served. Rhett Cutler said, "After hearing about them hogs I don't think I will have any pork chops."

Everyone agreed, and Mrs. Mae East was asked to say the blessing.

"Thank you, Lord, for the many blessings you have bestowed on us. Grant us the wisdom to make the right decision in our quest for fairness and I will close with Genesis Chapter 27, verse 4. 'And make me savor meat such as I love, and bring it to me that I may eat'. Amen."

Al K. Haul, thought, Well another long winded wanta be preacher. I'll be glad when this is over. I may say the blessing from now on and just say, 'Lord bless this food'."

After every one had eaten, the waitress, Sue Kitchen, served everyone peach cobbler and more ice tea or coffee. Then, after everyone had their turn in the rest rooms, they started their trip back to the courthouse.

One-thirty found the jurors in place and Judge Ego told Miss Kluck to resume the direct examination of Sheriff Jenkins.

"Sheriff Jenkins, did you or your deputies find the murder weapon?"

"No, Mam we have not," answered Sheriff Jenkins.

"Do you know what type of weapon was used in these terrible murders?"

"No, Mam, the only thing we are sure of is that a knife was used."

"What type of knife was used on the victims Sheriff Jenkins?" asked Miss Kluck.

"It was a very sharp knife, and, from the looks of the wounds, the blade must of been about four inches long. I am not sure, Dr. Mack Davis, the coroner, could give you a better answer."

"Did you find any knives in the barn?"

"Yes, we found a skinning knife, fish scaling knife, a rusty butcher knife and a barlow knife that had one broken blade."

"Sheriff, did you observe any blood or blood stain on any of the knives?"

"No, but we sent them to the State lab in Montgomery for testing."

"What was the outcome of the testing, any blood found on any of the knives?"

"Only animal blood on the skinning knife and the rusty barlow knife, no human blood was found on any of the knives."

"Could you tell if any knives were missing, Sheriff Jenkins?"

"Like all farms there is a knife for most any job, so I couldn't tell."

"Thank you Sheriff Jenkins."

"Mr. Kockran you may cross examine the witness," said Judge Ego.

"Your Honor, Mr. Barry Kall will cross examine this witness," stated Mr. Kockran.

"Proceed, Mr. Kall."

"Sheriff Jenkins, did you examine the bodies yourself?"

"Yes, I attempted to do that, but got sick to my stomach. Dr. Davis arrived and gave me some smelling salts and after a few minutes, he and I did a plenary exam."

"Could you tell the jurors the time of death?"

"From the dried blood and the temperature of the bodies, rigor mortis had set in, and as a layman on the subject I mentioned to Dr. Davis that it looked as if they had been dead for about 11 hours. He would not say until he had the bodies back at the hospital lab. He later confirmed that death had occurred about 8:30 on the night of June the 12."

"Your Honor, I object, the answer is hearsay," stated Miss Kluck.

"Sustained, ignore the answer about Dr. Davis," said Judge Ego.

"Sheriff Jenkins, what time was it when you and the coroner examined the bodies?"

"I would say between 7:00 and 7:30 AM on the morning of June 13."

"How did the coroner determine the time of death to be about 8.30?"

"Mr. Kall, you would have to ask the coroner this question."

"Sheriff, what qualifications do you have for estimating the time of death on bodies?"

"Approximately 14 years in law enforcement, where I have seen and investigated quite a number of deaths, due to natural causes, accidents, and foul play. After the coroner had finished with his investigations, I would compare my estimates with his report, and, in the last few years, they have been very close."

"Sheriff Jenkins, could the deaths have occurred at 10 PM on the 12th?"

"From my professional experience, I would say no."

"Can you tell us how you arrived at this opinion?"

"June is a warm month with very little breeze, and if the bodies had been shot or stabbed with a small amount of blood loss it would take about 13 hours for rigor mortis to be complete, but we have two bodies horribly slashed with multiple cuts, and this caused almost all of the blood to drain out in a matter of minutes, and I estimate about 11 hours for rigor mortis to be fully complete. In the case of Samson and Hooper, rigor mortis was complete. If you subtracted 11 hours from the 7:30 AM examination of the bodies, the time would be about 8:30 PM the night before."

"Thank you, Sheriff Jenkins, that concludes my direct of the Sheriff, Your Honor."

There was no redirect of the witness and as the Sheriff stepped down Judge Ego said, "Miss Kluck who will be your first witness tomorrow?"

Your Honor, I will call the coroner, Dr. Mack Davis."

Judge Ego cautioned the jurors not to talk about the case and said, "Court is adjourned for the day and will covene tomorrow at 10 AM."

Chapter Twenty-Five

When OJ returned to his cell, a visitor was waiting for him in the visiting room. It was Charlie Spink, the owner of Cholly Hoss Honky Tonk and Country Club.

"Hi OJ," said Cholly, "I hate to have to do business with you when you are in this position, but I will be as fair as my wallet will let me. What do you have in mind?"

"Well, Cholly, Pa wants to get out of the likker business and put everything in the peanut business."

"Don't you think you will be putting all of your eggs in one basket, OJ?"

"No, cause Pa will plant and harvest most of the land we have cawn planted on, and get a peanut picker to pick peanuts for the other farmers, also. If he can find a good manager who knows peanuts, he will buy and sell peanuts. When I get out I can take over some of the operations. All I am asking is a fair price for the Sad and Happy Drive-In and the still. Of course, the still will have to be moved."

"We can do that."

After discussing the price and other details OJ and Cholly came to an agreement on the transfer of the business.

He looked at Cholly and said, "I will have my attorney on civil matters draw up the papers. We can close out shortly. I want to thank you Cholly.

"When the trial is over and I am released, we will go out for a good stiff drink and dinner. I wish you the best of luck, but you know the business. As Pa says, 'It is hard to learn a business from the top down'."

"Thank you, OJ. I know you will be out of all this crap and, when the trial is over, sure we can go out. In fact, let's plan on several days in Fort Walton Beach, Florida, and pick up some hot chicks, hit the honky tonks, eat oysters and drink beer."

"It's a deal. We will stop down at Sasser, and have a mess of pecan crusted possum baked in corn bread dressing and sweet taters. See you later Cholly."

After Cholly left, OJ had the jailer, Wilbur, call his civil attorney, Ole Joe Clark, to ask him to come over as soon as possible. Wilbur came back and told him, "Ole Joe Clark will be here in 30 minutes, but he can only stay to seven-thirty."

Ole Joe Clark arrived at the jail at 6:45 and OJ gave him the details, with the price and takeover date of the Sad and Happy Drive-In and moving of the still. As Ole Joe Clark was leaving, OJ said, "Joe go out to see Pa when you have the papers ready and explain the details to him. Thanks, Joe."

After getting back to his cell and realized he had missed chow. He lay down on his bunk and thought, "You never know how long a day is until you get in jail. Oh, well, it won't be too long now."

Before court convened the next morning, Ole Joe Clark came over to the jail. He met with OJ as he was waiting in the holding cell to be escorted to the courthouse.

I have spent a good part of the night writing up the sales contract on the properties you wanted sold to Charlie Spinks. The price and terms are in this sales agreement. Read it and if is to your satisfaction, sign and date it. I will get the guard or someone to witness the signature."

After reading the sales agreement twice, he could not find anything he disagreed with.

"That looks good Joe, call Mr. Wilbur Anders to witness my signature."

Just as he and the witnesses had signed the sales agreement, the guard came for him to appear in the courtroom.

Chapter Twenty-Six

It was 10 AM when the bailiff called the court to order.

Judge Ego looked over at Miss Kluck and said, "Miss Kluck, are you and your witness, Dr. Mack Davis, ready to began the testimony?"

"Yes, Your Honor."

"Mrs. Nation, call Dr. Davis to the stand and swear in the witness."

After the witness, was sworn in Miss Kluck addressed him and said, "Dr. Davis, state your full name and title."

"My name is Mackinley C. Davis. My title is Chief Coroner for the County of Three Notch, Alabama."

"What are your qualifications for Chief Coroner Dr. Davis?" asked Miss Kluck.

"I attended the University of Alabama Medical School, interned at the Baptist Hospital in Birmingham, and, afterwards, I went into private practice with a Dr. Lott for two years. While with Dr. Lott, I worked at night at the County Morgue. While at the morgue, I studied pathology and made notes on how death occurred. If the death was unnatural such as by shooting, knifing or cutting, I would try to establish how long the person had been dead and just exactly how the person was killed. I also studied autopsy. I did postmortem examinations, dissecting the bodies, doing necropsy and pathological examinations of the dead. After two years, I moved to Three Notch. That was 11 years ago, and opened a private practice. A year later I was appointed Coroner for the County of Three Notch.

"After I was appointed Coroner, I took a course in criminology. I am a member of the American Medical Association, American Association of Coroners, and at present, the President of the Alabama Chapter of that organization, and the American Association of Criminologists."

"Dr. Davis, what time did you arrive at the scene of the crime?"

"Seven-fifteen AM."

"Doctor, tell the jurors what you observed upon your arrival at the scene of the crime."

"Before I saw anything clearly, the odor was the first thing I noticed. The odor was of hog dung, hog slop, sour mud, human feces and rotting flesh and blood. As I got nearer to the area of the crime scene, I saw what looked like two bundles of clothes that had been piled up in a heap. As I walked through the muddy hog pen, I saw a human body, or what was left of it. About six feet from the first body was another one. On a closer inspection, I saw that the first body was a female and the second body was a male. When I looked around I saw Sheriff Jenkins looking as if he was going to faint. I opened my bag, took out the smelling salts and gave him a couple of whiffs."

"What about the bodies, Dr. Davis, would you describe the bodies as they lay there in the muddy hog pen?"

"The first body, later identified as Mrs. Nike Samson, was laying on her right side with her head back almost touching her shoulder blades. Her throat was cut starting just under the left ear, cutting her sternohyoid and sternocleidomastoid ending at the platysma, directly below the right side of her neck. Another slash was made on the right side starting at the anterior serratus going across the body under the breast, almost severing her breast and ending at the greater pectoralis. The brachialis of her right arm was slashed as were the triceps of her left arm. Cut marks were on the back of both her hands. A stab wound was in the linea alba area, but little blood, because the cutting of the throat, the jugular vein was severed and the blood spurted out of this cut. This was what I saw before moving the body to the morgue and cleaning it up for a thorough examination."

The second body was a male, later identified as Clem Hooper. Mr. Hooper's body was laying on his back with blood all over the front of him. He had a deep and long wound starting at the abdominal aponeurosis, this is the stomach area, and going up to the rectus abdominis area about six inches. The wound was deep enough and the killer was strong enough to lift the victim off the ground and death was instantaneous. The blood and mud were so bad I could not see any other visible wounds."

"Dr. Davis, could you tell the jurors in nonmedical terms about Mrs. Samson's neck wound?"

"Yes, Miss Kluck, the wound started on the left side of her neck, right here." Dr. Davis pointed to a spot on his neck below the ear about three inches. "The weapon was pulled across the neck in this fashion." Dr. Davis put his right hand with the forefinger on his neck, pulling the finger across the neck and stopped below the right ear. "The wound was deep enough that it cut the jugular vein," he said as he pointed to the area of the vein.

"What about the wound, I believe you said the anterior serratus area and the greater pectoralis area?" asked Miss Kluck.

"The anterior serratus is the area slightly under, in this case the right arm, and across to the greater pectoralis area, which is over the left breast." Dr. Davis took his right forefinger and placed it on his right side just below the breast, drew it underneath the breast, across his chest to the upper part of his chest near the left arm and rib cage. He took his finger and went back to the right breast and moved it slowly under his breast and said, "This is where the weapon went, under the breast almost severing the breast," drawing his finger to the upper right side of his chest over the breast. "The cut on the triceps of her left arm ran from here, pointing to the left arm at the top of the muscle and then into the anterior serratus, again pointing to the breast area. The brachialis of the right arm is just above the elbow of the right arm, as he pointed his finger to the spot."

"Doctor, the other cuts and scratches you found after you cleaned the body, were they life threatening?"

"No."

"Which were the wounds that took the victim's life Dr. Davis?"

"Either the neck or the breast wound would be sufficient to kill her. However, I believe the throat wound was the second one and she was more than likely dead by the time her body hit the ground. The breast wound would have killed her, but it would take longer for her to die. Mr. Hooper was killed first. The killer then turned and slashed Mrs. Samson across the front, grabbed her head under his left arm and pulled the weapon across her throat from left to right, cutting her jugular vein. She died in seconds."

"Dr. Davis, with all of the blood, did you find any blood other than the two victims blood?"

"Yes, Miss Kluck, we found that Mrs. Samson's blood type was O positive, Mr. Hooper's blood was type O negative. We found type A negative blood on both bodies and on the gate and fence post."

"Dr. Davis did you ever get a sample of Mr. Oscar James Samson's blood?"

"Yes we did, Miss Kluck."

"What is Mr. Oscar James Samson's blood type, Dr. Davis?"

Dr. Davis looked at a sheet of paper and said, "The lab report of blood taken from Mr. Samson on the day of his arrest, as he was booked into the county jail, shows that Mr. Samson's blood type is A negative."

"Dr. Davis did you find any other type A negative blood on the bodies in the morgue while you were doing your postmortems, and, if so, which body?"

"Yes, Miss Kluck, I found type A negative blood on both bodies. The killer was vicious, and from the evidence, Mr. Hooper was killed first. It was a quick thrust. In layman's words, the lower part of the stomach, or bowels. The killer struck so hard that the knife handle went into the flesh about one-half inch.

While the knife was in the bowels, the killer, with a quick and strong upper movement of his or her arm, slashing about six inches upwards, almost disemboeled the victim. At this point, blood spattered everywhere. The killer would have been covered with blood." Dr. Davis stood up pointed his right forefinger just below his navel, and jabbed his finger into his belly and, with a quick movement, moved his finger up to a point about six or seven inches.

"Your Honor," Miss Kluck addressed Judge Ego, "I would like to submit as evidence, 14 photographs, one each showing where the victims were found and the surrounding area, two showing a close up of each victim, 10 photographs of the victims and their wounds in the morgue in various positions."

Judge Ego replied, "Submit a copy of each photograph to the defense, and let Mrs. Nation assign an evidence number to each of them. Continue, Miss Kluck."

"Your Honor it is now 11:40. I would like to call a recess for lunch as, we will show the photographs to the jurors, and I don't think it would be appropriate to show these before lunch."

"Court is recessed until one PM," announced Judge Ego.

Bailiff Autry led the jurors across the square to Rooster's Cafe, into the back room. The group was somber with very little talking. Al K. Haul asked Thelma Jitter to say the blessing, hoping it would be short.

"Give us day by day our daily bread. Thank you, Lord. Amen," prayed Miss Jitter.

"Thank God for a short one," thought Mr. Haul.

For lunch, Rooster served country fried steak, carrots, butter beans and boiled corn with ice tea and banana pudding for desert.

Everyone was quiet during lunch. Rhett Cutler tried to inject a little humor in the group by saying, "The vittles are good, better than what I git at home. Sometimes I'd rather have a moon pie and parched peanuts in a RC cola, than all this rich folks vittles."

No one cracked a smile or answered. There was a little talk about the weather, and, when they finished, they went to the rest rooms, crossed the square behind the courthouse, and in front of the jail. Miss Jitter looked up at the top floor, but saw no one.

The court convened at one o'clock, and Dr. Davis again took the stand.

Judge Ego reminded the coroner that he was still under oath.

Miss Kluck asked Dr. Davis to take the photographs, starting with the photograph number one of Mr. Hooper, who was the first victim. Then she asked him to show photo number two of Mrs. Samson, then the 10 photographs taken in the morgue. She asked Dr. Davis to face the jurors and go over, in laymans terms, each photograph, explaining the testimony he gave earlier in the morning.

As Dr. Davis did this, some of the jurors got pale, some looked away. The court had to take a 10 minute recess after Miss Iola Bridges vomited in the jury box. While the jurors were out, a janitor cleaned the jury box.

When the recess was over, Miss Kluck apologized for the gruesome photographs, but said it was necessary so that they could see how vicious the killer was.

She turned to Dr. Davis and asked, "Can you tell the jurors what type of weapon was used?"

"It was some sort of knife with a folding blade. The blade was four inches long, sharp on one edge only. From the looks of the wounds, I would think that the blade had a slight curve on the end."

"Thank you, Dr. Davis. This concludes my direct, Your Honor," stated Miss Kluck.

The judge looked at Mr. Kockran and asked, "Who will do the cross examination?"

"I will, Your Honor," answered Donny.

"You may start your cross after a 10 minute recess," spoke Judge Ego.

After the recess, Dr. Davis took the stand. Judge Ego again reminded him he was still under oath and told Donny Kockran to start with his cross.

"Good afternoon, Dr. Davis, and Ladies and Gentlemen of the jury. I know that this has been an ordeal for you. It is not a pleasant sight to see all of the horrible photographs, and it was a terrible murder of the two victims, however, justice must be done."

"Dr. Davis, we will accept your theory that the horrible deaths were as you relate them, however, we are here today to find out who did these dastardly deeds. Can you tell us, Dr. Davis, how much blood was on the perpetrator?"

"With the first victim, Mr. Hooper, the blood would have squirted straight out, about a half pint that would have hit the perpetrator in the center of his body. On the second victim, Mrs. Samson, the head was grasped under the left arm of the perpetrator, and at the same time reaching around cutting her throat, which in turn cut her jugular vein. This would let the blood gush out at a high pressure, letting about one third of her blood spray the perpetrator all over the left arm, left side, down the side and front of his pants leg."

"How do you know the perpetrator was a male, Dr. Davis?"

"By the size and strength it would take to commit the murders in the fashion they were done. A woman would have to be larger than the average woman, taller and be very muscular. There are other clues that can be answered by the detectives."

"Dr. Davis, the person that did this crime, would have blood under his nails, soaked though his clothes to the skin, and possibly in his hair. Would this be easy to clean and how long would it remain on the perpetrator, after an ordinary bath with some scrubbing?"

"It would take some time to wear it off after a good scrubbing."

"Dr. Davis, a week after the crime, could blood be found in the hair, on the skin and under the nails, from scratching, and put under a microscope?"

"Yes, Mr. Kockran, they could."

"Was a sample of skin scratching from the arm, from under the finger nails, skin from the belly, from the head and hair samples, of Mr. OJ Samson, submitted to you for testing on June 19?"

"Yes Sir, they were."

"Did you find any blood samples that was O negative or O positive in the test you conducted of Mr. Samson's skin, head, hair or scaping from under the finger nails taken on June 19, Dr. Davis?"

"No, I did not."

"Why, Dr. Davis, was a man arrested for a double murder when you have no evidence of the victims blood, no weapon connected to him, no witness placing him being at the scene? That is all Dr. Davis."

"Your Honor, this is all I have for this witness today. It is getting late and I would like to continue the cross in the morning."

"Court is adjoined until ten tomorrow morning."

After returning to his cell, OJ's Pa came to see him. They both were very happy with the cross examination that Donny had done.

Pa told him about the visit from the attorney and that everything was going well.

"You will soon be out, son and we can get on with our lives. Ma sends her love."

After Pa left, he lay back on his bunk and for the first time felt that a ton had been lifted off of him. He was sure he would be out of jail in a matter of days, and he drifted off in a restful sleep.

As OJ was led into the courtroom the next day, he was his old self, smiling, self-assured and jaunty. As he watched the jurors file in, he noticed juror number eight, Miss Thelma Jitter, the beautiful blond with the blue eyes. Maybe after the trial was over and things settled down they could meet. As his eyes followed her, their eyes met as she turned to sit down in the jury box. Her eyes seemed to say, "I believe in you". He knew that he would be with this beautiful creature in the near future. He decided that he wouldn't make eye contact with her again, for he would give himself away, but just wait for that day when the trial was over.

Judge Ego entered the courtroom and the bailiff called out, "Court is in session, the Honorable Judge Vance Ego presiding. All be seated."

"Mr. Kockran, continue with your cross examination of Dr. Davis. Dr. Davis to the stand. You are still under oath, Sir."

"Dr. Davis how many people in Three Notch County have blood type A negative?"

"There are maybe approximately 15,000 people in Three Notch County. The average number of people with blood type A negative is about 8 percent, or thereabout 1,200 people in Three Notch County."

"What about the United States Dr. Davis?"

"Using the same percentage, I would estimate about 13 million people would have blood type A negative."

"Dr. Davis did you take blood samples, head and hair samples, skin scratching from under the finger nails or belly from the 13 million people to determine if they had blood type O in the sampling?"

"I did not, Sir."

"The real killer would have type O in the scratching and other samples would he not? Yet you pick one person out of 13 million with type A negative to test and you found nothing. Are you planning on testing other type A negative people who may be suspects in this crime?"

"No Sir, Sheriff Jenkins has no other suspects at this time."

"Dr. Davis, Sheriff Jenkins could not say with certainty the time of death. Could you tell the jurors the time of death?"

"Yes Sir. The time of death was 8:30 PM, give or take 15 minutes."

"Can you be more certain of the time, was it 8:15, 8:30 or 8:45?"

"I would say 8:15 to 8:30."

"Dr. Davis, think, could it have been 8:40 or even 8:50?"

"No Mr. Kockran, 8:30 is the latest that death occurred and I stake my reputation on the time frame of 8:15 to 8:30."

"How can you be so sure, Dr. Davis?"

"At the scene, rigor mortis had been almost completed at 7:30 am. It normally takes about 12 hours to complete the rigor mortis on an average summer night, when the temperature average is 65 degrees at this time of year. From June 11 through June 15, the night and day temperature were four or five degrees higher than average. On June 12, the night temperature was 69. Therefore, it took longer for rigor mortis to be completed, as the sun was four degrees higher. It heated the wallowing hole for the hogs warmer than normal. The body of Mrs. Samson was partly in the wallowing hole, from the lower part of the hips down. We found at the morgue the trunk and upper extremity had completed the rigor mortis, as the muscles were stiff, rigid, and free from deviation. Our autopsy at 9:45 showed that with the loss of blood, depriving the body of oxygen, the temperature and the rigidity of muscles occurring after death, that death was 13 hours and 45 minutes from that point, making the death at 8:30 PM. Due to the lower extremity being in the hog wallow and the mud holding the heat, rigor was 95 percent complete, as the annular ligament of ankle had a slight flex and would be about 20 or 30 minutes to complete rigor mortis, whereas, we add time for the heat of the mud in the hog wallow, we arrived at 8:30 for the time of death."

"One last question, Dr. Davis. Could the heat from the hog wallow on the lower extremity, cause the upper extremity to slow down the time of rigor mortis?"

"No, Mr. Kockran, maybe at the point of contact of the mud from the wallow, but no more than one or two inches above contact."

"No further questions, Your Honor."

Judge Ego looked at the clock and asked Miss Kluck who her next witness would be.

"It will Detective Van Otter," answered Miss Kluck.

"It is time for the court to adjourn for the day. Court will reconvene at ten am.," Judge Ego announced.

After OJ reached his cell, he lay down on the bunk, closed his eyes and tried to analyze the days proceedings. "How in the hell," he thought, "can the tables turn as they did. When I thought I would be free one day and convicted the next. I left the Sad and Happy Drive-In on my tour bus at nine o'clock, and I have the witnesses to prove it. How could anyone drive four miles do what they say I did, drive back and be clean of all the blood that the coroner said would be on the killer? This can't be done. Donny just has to prove I didn't do it," he thought. He had a very restless night.

The next morning OJ awoke, waited for the guard to take him down the hall for a shower, and afterward was served breakfast. He took the suit, shirt and tie that the guard gave him, which had been left by Donny. He opened the bag and saw his favorite suit, an all worsted medium gray suit, with a white shirt and a red tie. After dressing he felt much better, his mood was improving, he thought even the darkest night ends when the sun comes up. He was ready when the guards came to escort him to court.

Chapter Twenty-Seven

As OJ entered the courtroom, everyone was in place, except the judge and jurors. It would be nice to see juror number eight come in. "Hell," he thought, "I've got to get my mind off of the females and onto my trial. I am fighting for my life." At this time the judge came in and spoke.

"Bailiff bring in the jurors, please."

After the jurors and the spectators were seated, Judge Ego looked at Miss Kluck and told her to call her first witness, Detective Van Otter.

"Your Honor, Mr. Flip Moore will do the direct examination of Detective Van Otter," answered Miss Kluck.

"Mrs. Nation give the oath to Detective Van Otter. You may start the examination Mr. Moore."

Detective Van Otter took the stand and the oath.

"Detective Otter, what time did you arrive at the scene of the crime on the morning of June 13?" asked Mr. Moore.

"I arrived at 6:55, with my partner, Detective Mack Burman."

"What duties did you and your partner perform on your arrival?"

"We checked to see if anyone was in or around the barn or the house. Finding no one, we took some rope out of the car and put it around the perimeter of the crime scene. We looked for a weapon or weapons as we walked over to the bodies. As I got close to the female, who was later identified as Mrs. Samson, I noticed a rubber glove laying about three feet from her body. I could see from that point, no one could help Mrs. Samson, so I picked up the glove with a stick, took it over near the fence and laid it on a rubber sheet we had put down. I then went back to the body.

My partner Detective Burman was by the body of the male, who was later identified as Mr. Clem Hooper. We looked for clues around the bodies but at that time found nothing else."

"What did you do after you searched around the two bodies?" asked Mr. Moore

"About this time Sheriff Jenkins and Mr. Nick Webb arrived and the two of them filled Detective Burman and myself in on what had taken place before. The coroner arrived so Detective Burman and I started looking around. We went into the barn where we found some knives, a skinning knife, a barlow knife, a fish scaling knife, and a rusty butcher knife. The barlow knife had a broken blade.

"Your Honor, I would like to put four knives in evidence," stated Mr. Moore.

"I object," Mr. Kockran said.

"On what basis do you object?" asked Judge Ego.

"They are not relative, Your Honor."

"Your Honor," said Mr. Moore, "They are relative. We will connect them to other evidence."

"Overruled. Continue Mr. Moore."

"Detective Otter, the knives, did they have any type of identification?"

"Yes Sir, three of the knives had the name Sears, Roebuck on them. We wrote to Sears, Roebuck in Chicago, giving the serial number that was on one of the knives."

"Did you receive a reply to your inquiry?"

"Yes sir, an order was placed through the mail for a skinning knife, a butcher knife, a barlow knife that matches the serial number, and a castrating knife with the serial number 8R1883 and S.R. & Co., Inc. stamped on the handle."

"Did anyone find a castrating knife with the serial number 8R1883?"

"No Sir, but the knife was received by Mr. Samson. Our investigation found that the knife was used on a bull calf. The witness who gave us this information was hired by Mr. Samson to do the castrating and is willing to testify."

"Dr. Davis testified that the wound to the stomach of Mr. Hooper was four inches deep, plus a half inch of the knife penetrated the body. Would a knife of the description of the castrating knife fit this description?"

"Yes, Mr. Moore. The blade, according the catalog description, is four inches long, with a slight curve at the tip of the blade."

"Your Honor, I would like to enter into evidence an invoice showing the knives purchased, with the serial numbers and a catalog sheet from Sears, Roebuck catalog, page 470, showing and describing the castrating knife," stated Mr. Moore.

"Mrs. Nation, number and place those item into evidence."

"Mr. Otter, was there any other evidence you found at the scene of the crime?"

"Yes Sir, we found a left hand rubber glove, with four inch cuffs, and on the middle finger a hole, torn or cut. The glove had type O negative and type O positive blood all over it. At the hole on the outside was type A negative blood. The lab turned the glove inside out and found quite a bit of type A negative blood on inside of the glove."

"Did you gather any other evidence at the crime scene Detective Otter?"

"Yes Sir, we set up a screen and scooped up the mud and washed it through the screen. We found a small gold emblem, a gold cross, with a short gold chain of about three inches. It looked like a watch fob."

"Detective Otter, have you made identification on the gold cross?"

"No Sir, we have not at this state of the investigation."

"What was your next step in the investigation, Detective?"

"We left a deputy to watch the crime scene. The Sheriff and the coroner and his people were still there. We went to Mr. Samson's apartment at the Sad and Happy Drive-In to notify him what had happened and tell him that his children were at the Mathew's Grocery and Corn Mill."

Judge Ego interrupted, "Ladies and Gentlemen it is time for our morning break. Court is in recess for 10 minutes."

When court resumed, Mr. Moore continued with the direct examination.

"Detective Otter, tell the jurors what happened when you arrived at the Sad and Happy Drive-In."

"When Detective Burman and I arrived, there was no activity at the business. One automobile, an old model B Ford, was parked behind the store. We assumed this was the manager's car. We knocked on the front door and received no answer, so we went to the back. Nobody answered at that door either. A window on the side of the building was partly open, so we knocked on it. A sleepy voice answered. It was Kaylow Kala, the manager. He let us in and we asked for Mr. Samson. He stated Mr. Samson left the night before to go to Shreveport, La., to hold a concert on the night of June 13. We asked the time he left. He stated Sampson left at five minutes after nine with the drummer doing the driving, I asked him how he knew it was five minutes after nine. He said, 'I close the drive-in at 8:30 and clean up. While I was cleaning, I heard a loud thump on the side of the building, almost like a cow hitting the side of a barn. I had the drive through window open to let the cool air in. I looked out and saw the tour bus leaving. As I closed the window I saw the Jax Beer sign and clock and it was five minutes after nine.' I asked can you be sure the clock had the correct time. 'I guess so,' he said, 'cause Mr. Samson set it at six o'clock, when the drummer came by with the bus to put Mr. Samson's clothes on the bus.' "

"Did you leave the premises and return to Mansion on the Hill?" asked Mr. Moore.

"No Sir, not at that time, Mr. Kala seemed to be afraid of something and he asked us if we would take a look at the side of the building where he heard the thump.

"We escorted Mr. Kala to the side of the building. The only thing we found was a rubber glove similar to the one we found at the crime scene. At the time, we did not inspect the glove, but put it into an evidence bag, and tagged it. We then returned to the crime scene. We put our mileage down and the time we left the drive-in and marked the mileage down when we arrived at the crime scene and also the time of arrival."

"Detective Otter, what was the mileage from the drive-in to the crime scene?"

"Mr. Moore, it was three miles and four tenths."

"Detective, what was the road condition and how long did you take to get to the crime scene and how fast were you driving?"

"First, the roads on Route Three, after you leave the city limits, are sandy with ruts in some places, except when you cross Snit Creek. The hills there are clay. Other than the few ruts, it is a fairly good sandy country road. Our time from the time we left the drive-in until we arrived at the Mansion on the Hill was eight minutes. We did not encounter any traffic on the way. We made good time. If we had pushed, we could have made it in six and a half minutes."

"Detective Otter, if someone from the town of Three Notch, left town and went to the Mansion on the Hill murdered two people and returned to Three Notch, could this have been done in 30 minutes?"

"Yes Sir, the quickest you could get from here to the Mansion on the Hill would be six and a half minutes going and six and a half minutes returning. Parking the car, walking to the house or hog pen, encountering the two people, and murdering them could be done in about 10 to 12 minutes. My estimate of the time it took to do this would be in the least amount of time, 25 minutes. At 25 minutes, a person would be able to kill two people in the manner in which they were murdered. It would take about 10 minutes or more to change clothes and wash up, according to the blood that would have gotten on a person."

"Detective Otter, did you find out anything on the gold cross?"

"Not much. We determined that the cross was part of a watch fob. It had a three inch broken chain, below where a clasp would have been. The cross is 14 karat gold fill. The chain is ten karat gold. We have been unable to establish where the fob was purchased or the owner of the fob."

"At this time, I have no further questions for Mr. Otter, but I would like the option to recall him later," Mr. Moore said to Judge Ego.

"Ladies and Gentlemen, as it is near the time for our lunch break, we will recess until 1:15. Court is adjourned," Judge Ego said.

The jurors took their walk behind the courthouse, in front of the jail, across the square to Rooster's Cafe, where they were let into the back room. Al K. Haul asked Mr. U. R. Short to say the blessing. Mr. Short did not want to, but said, "I'll say a verse from John, chapter 21 verse 12, 'Jesus sayeth unto them, come and dine.' Amen."

The jurors were a little more relaxed and upbeat than they had been the day before. They made small talk, and Rhett Cutler, who snakes logs with bulls, asked, "Who knows the difference between a bull and a cow?"

They looked around at each other, but Miss Jitter, in her gingham blue and white dress looking every bit of her 21 years, smiled sweetly and said, "One is a he and one is a she," and gave a little laugh.

"Rhett looked at the sweet young thing and said, "Close, but no apple, you can tell a bull cauz when you milk him he always smiles."

This got a laugh, so Leroy Rogers, the cotton farmer from the southern end of Three Notch County, said, "I found the first Rebel Bible in a cave and lots of our customs were taken from it. For instance, from the book of PMS chapter 13, verse four reads, 'Then Mary rode Joseph's ass all the way back to Bethlehem, and bitching was herein created.' "

Most of the jurors laughed, except Mrs. Iola Bridges and the Reverend John Paul Pope, who said, "Thou shalt not take the Lord's name in vain."

"I'm not taking the Lord's name in vain. I ain't even mentioned his name yet, but in the Rebel Bible, book of Feasting, chapter 13, verse five, it does mention the Lord. It says, 'On the fifth day the Lord said, let there be turnip greens and okra, so it came to pass, that the South was filled with turnip greens and okra.' "

There were few laughs, but it was time to go back to jury room. Almost everyone, enjoyed this lunch. They were now getting to know each other.

On the way to the courthouse, Leroy skipped a step and came along side of Minnie Curl, the beautician and part-time comedian, and asked her, "Did you know the Rebel Bible had 12 commandments?

"No," she answered, "What are they?"

"Number eleven is, 'Thou shalt not covet thy neighbors possum and taters.' "

Minnie thought, "I'll use that in my routine."

About this time they arrived at the courthouse, so Minnie didn't get to hear commandment number 12.

After being seated, Judge Ego called the court to order and asked Mr. Kockran, "Who will do the cross of Detective Van Otter?"

"Mr. Rufus Cobb will do the cross, Your Honor," answered Mr. Kockran.

Detective Van Otter took the stand and was reminded by Judge Ego that he was still under oath.

"Detective Otter, the knives you found, was there any blood on any of them?"

"No Sir."

"About the missing knife, the castrating knife, did you determine whether Mr. Samson left the knife in the barn or carried it with him when he moved out of the Mansion on the Hill?"

"No Sir."

Detective Otter, did you find anyone who has seen the knife in Mr. Samson's possession after the castration of the bull?"

"No sir."

"Detective Otter, the castrating knife was in the barn, with no lock, accessible to anyone coming to the farm. In fact, Detective Otter, anyone passing the farm could have gone into the barn and removed the knives, couldn't they?"

"Yes Sir."

"Have you seen any gloves similar to the ones you found at the scene of the crime and at the Sad and Happy Drive-In, any other place, such as at homes, hardware stores, farms, packing plants?"

"Yes Sir."

"Where have you seen similar gloves?"

"Well, I have seen them in hardware stores and on a farm."

"In fact, Detective Otter, most all farms have gloves of this sort, do they not, for use in butchering hogs and cattle, for scrapping the hair off the hogs, after butchering them and dipping them in scalding water, and cattle farmers may use them to help in delivering calves?"

"Yes Sir, these gloves are common on farms."

"You stated you picked up a glove at the scene. Did you notice anything unusual on or about it, such as a cut, blood or anything not a part of the glove?"

"Yes Sir, there was a hole was in the left glove, and blood on the outside, and some on the inside."

"Do you know the blood type of the blood on the inside of the glove?"

"Yes Sir, type A negative."

"What is the blood type of Mr. Samson?"

"Mr. Cobb, his blood type is A negative."

"Detective Otter, how many people in Three Notch County have type A negative blood?"

"I don't know."

"Detective Otter, do you know the blood type of the person who castrated the bull for Mr. Samson?"

"No Sir."

"Could he have type A negative blood? Could some of the enemies of Mr. Samson in the moonshine business have type A negative blood? Have you had them tested?"

"I don't know the blood type of any of the people you mentioned and no we have not taken blood samples from them."

"Detective Otter, we will move on to the time it took you to drive from the Sad and Happy Drive-In to the Mansion on the Hill. Detective Otter, are you an expert driver?"

"I think I am, Mr. Cobb."

"If you was in a big hurry to go from the Mansion the Hill to the Sad and Happy Drive-In, could you do it in less than seven minutes?"

"I think so."

"Detective Otter, how far is it to the crime scene from the drive-in?"

"It was three miles and four tenths.'

"Then detective Otter, someone must be an excellent driver and a strong person to go there and back and commit the murders, in 30 minutes."

"Yes."

"Detective Otter, the Jax Beer clock in the bar was at five minutes after nine, according to Mr. Kala, wasn't it?"

"Yes Sir."

"Thank you, Detective Otter. Your Honor, I have no further questions for this witness."

Judge Ego recessed the court for 10 minutes.

"Mr. Moore, do you have any redirect?" asked Judge Ego.

"Yes Sir, I do."

Judge Ego asked the detective to take the stand, and reminded him that he was still under oath.

"Detective Otter, where were the knives located in the barn?"

"They were in an old kitchen safe where they used to put the dishes, above the counter top."

"Then the knives were not in the open, where anyone walking through the barn would see them?"

"No, they were not."

"Detective Otter, is the castrating knife a popular knife with farmers?"

"No Sir. Only a large farm would find it useful, because of the expense of the knife, for the very few times they would use it."

"Why would someone like Mr. Samson purchase a castrating knife?"

"My opinion and what I found out in my investigation is that before Mr. and Mrs. Samson separated, Mr. Samson had plans to raise bulls, castrate them and when grown, sell the oxen. But the separation and divorce interrupted his plans."

"Detective Otter, on the time it takes to go to the Mansion on the Hill from the drive-in, could someone drive out there and murder two people in the fashion they were murdered in 30 minutes or less?"

"Yes Sir, the killer could do it in 30 minutes or less, driving very fast. And, if in a rage, the killer caught the victims by surprise, he could do the murders very quickly."

"Detective Otter, can you tell us, if the gloves belong to Mr. Samson, and were left at the Mansion on The Hill, or were brought to the crime scene?"

"In our investigation we found that the gloves were not at the Mansion on the Hill, but brought to the crime scene."

"How did you arrive at this conclusion?"

"Well, Mr. Evans Lee, the gentlemen who did the castrating of the bull calf, stated that after the job was done, he asked to borrow the gloves for a couple days. Mr. Samson let him have them, and said to drop them off at the Sad and Happy Drive-In.

About three days later Mr. Lee stated he dropped the gloves off at the Sad and Happy Drive-In."

"Was this before the separation and divorce or after?"

"This was a few days before the separation, Mr. Moore."

"Your Honor, I have no further questions of this witness."

"Court is adjourned until tomorrow at ten o'clock," announced Judge Ego.

Chapter Twenty-Eight

After OJ returned to his cell, he asked to speak with Mr. Kockran, at once.

In about 30 minutes Donny came to the cell, and asked, "What's troubling you now, OJ?"

"Well, Donny, the whole case went to hell in a hand basket this afternoon. We seem to be losing the case."

"No, OJ, at this time we are in a fair position. Why do you ask?"

"The witness Van Otter, you led him into putting the time line too close, then you led him into the glove being left at the Sad and Happy Drive-In."

"In the deposition, Kaylow Kala gave the time that the tour bus left, Detective Van Otter gave the time it took to drive to the Mansion on the Hill, Mr. Evans Lee gave the deposition about the glove. I wanted to introduce the two items in a low key way, so that it would not be a big deal. We will have to overcome these things plus a number of other items. We need to deal with them as they come up, and try to overcome them with defense witnesses. Just be calm. Look calm in the courtroom, and, by all means, don't show anger."

On the drive home, Donny's mind went over the case. He realized he was in a tough situation. He would have to go the circumstantial evidence and reasonable doubt routine. He had to find a witness to refute the time frame.

"Court is now in session," announced Bailiff Autry, after the judge and jurors were seated.

"Miss Kluck, who is your witness this morning?"

"The witness is Detective Mack Burman, Your Honor," answered Miss Kluck.

"Mrs. Nation have Detective Burman take the oath, and start your direct Miss Kluck."

After taking the oath, Detective Burman gave the same answers as Detective Otter, except, he stated, just before leaving the crime scene at the Mansion on the Hill, he had helped Dr. Davis' assistant, make plaster of Paris casts of the foot prints and the tire tracks.

"Detective Burman, did you see any tire tracks at the Sad and Happy Drive-In that looked like the ones at the Mansion on the Hill?"

"Well, Miss Kluck, to me it looked like it was a match, but I am not an expert on tire tracks."

"Did you make a plaster of Paris cast of those tire tracks, Detective Burman?"

"No Mam, I only assisted at the crime scene. I put some old two by fours around the tracks, and a blanket over the top, so Dr. Davis could tell where they were."

This completed the direct of Detective Burman, and Judge Ego called a recess of 10 minutes.

After the court was called to order, the judge asked Mr. Kockran who would cross examine Detective Burman, and Mr. Kockran answered that he would.

After Detective Burman took the stand, Mr. Kockran asked, "Who's watch did you use to time the run from the Sad & Happy Drive-In to the Mansion on the Hill?"

"We used Detective Otter's watch," he answered.

"Was the watch checked either before or after the run to see if it was accurate?"

"No Sir."

"The watch could have been running fast, as far as you know, Detective Burman. Yes or no?"

"Yes Sir, It could have or it could not have been."

Mr. Kockran interrupted in a loud voice, "Your Honor, instruct the witness to answer the question with a yes or no, not two answers?"

"Detective Burman, answer the question, when asked, with a yes or no."

Judge Ego looked at the jurors and said the detective answered the question with a yes, and to disregard any answer after that.

"Detective Burman, when where you promoted to detective?"

"I am an acting detective. My rank is Deputy Sheriff, Sir."

"Then you have never been to school, or had any training on detective procedures, only on the job training. Is that a fair statement Deputy Burman?"

"Yes Sir."

"That is all Deputy Burman."

"Any redirect, Miss Kluck?" asked Judge Ego.

"Detective Burman, were you officially promoted to acting detective?"

"Yes Mam."

"How many cases have you been on that have required detective work?"

"Six, Mam."

"Thank you Detective Burman."

"Any recross, Mr. Kockran?" asked Judge Ego.

"Yes," answered Donny Kockran.

"Deputy Burman, how many of the six cases was for murder?"

"Not any, Sir."

"Weren't they for petit or petty crimes, Detective Burman? Answer yes or no."

"Yes, Mr. Kockran."

"It is my understanding Deputy Burman, that you have not assisted or investigated any murders. Yes or no?"

"No Sir."

"That is all for the defense, Your Honor."

After Mack Burman had finished, a lunch recess was called, and the jurors took their daily walk to Rooster's Cafe.

After being seated, Al K. Haul asked Leroy Rogers to say the blessing.

"Thank you, Lord, for this food as there is nothing better for a man, than that he should eat and drink. Amen."

As the meal of meat loaf, baked beans and boiled corn was being served, Minnie Curl asked Leroy Rodgers, "Leroy, I have been thinking all night about what you said about the 12 commandments. What in the world is number 12?"

"My dear, Minnie, the twelfth commandment is, "Thou shalt not admit adultery."

This put a little laughter in the meal and everyone started talking, and soon it was time to return to the courtroom.

The first witness for the prosecution was Dr. Quint Quincy of the State of Alabama Crime Lab. After being sworn in, Mr. Chris Clock open the direct.

"Dr. Quincy, what is your education and title?"

"My title is Doctor. My degree is in criminology. I graduated from the University of Alabama. I then took two years of medical technology, and another two years to get my master's degree in criminology from the University of Alabama Medical Center."

" Dr. Quincy, did you examine the gloves found at the Mansion on the Hill?"

Yes Sir, I did. The glove found at the Mansion on the Hill was a left hand rubber glove."

"Describe for the jurors the left hand glove found at the crime scene," said Mr. Clock.

"The left glove had a four inch cuff, and was of heavy rubber. The glove is popular with farmers who butcher their own livestock, packing houses and meat markets who do butchering. The glove had a hole cut in the middle at the tip. Around the outside of the hole, we found type A negative blood, and after turning it inside out we also found type A negative blood. On the outside of the glove we found three types of blood, type O positive, type O negative and type A negative.

"Dr. Quincy, did you have the sample of Mr. Samson's blood?"

"Yes Sir."

"What type of blood does Mr. Samson have?"

"Mr. Samson has type A negative blood."

"Dr. Quincy, tell the jurors if the blood on the glove found at the crime scene and Mr. Samson's blood matched."

"Yes Sir, the blood from the glove found at the crime scene and Mr. Samson's blood are a perfect match."

"What about the glove found at the Sad and Happy Drive-In?" asked Mr. Clock.

"The glove at the Sad and Happy Drive-In is the mate to the one at the crime scene. It had some O positive and negative type blood on it and also some type A negative blood."

"Did you also examine the plaster of Paris cast of the tire treads found at the crime scene and compare them to cast of the tires of Mr. Samson's car?"

"Yes I did, I found that the cast of the tire from the crime scene matched the cast taken from the right front tire of Mr. Samson's car."

"What brand was the tire, Mr. Quincy?"

"It was a Kelly-Springfield, and the serial number was 37-2-18769-13."

"Did you attempt to identify the store that sold the tire?"

"Yes Sir, the tires were purchased from Moates Garage. The serial number was listed as being sold to Mr. OJ. Samson and mounted on a 1937 Hudson Terriplane in April 1937. The first two serial numbers refer to the year they were manufactured which is 37 or 1937, the second number refers to the month, which is two or February, and the last two numbers refer to the day of manufacture which is the thirteenth, so the tire was manufactured on February 13, 1937. The records show that this and other tires were shipped to the Alabama Tire Wholesale, Inc., Montgomery,

Alabama, on March 2, 1937. Alabama Wholesale, Inc., records show that Moates Garage purchased 16 tires from them on March 20, 1937. On April 15, 1937, Mr. Oscar James Samson purchased four Kelly-Springfield tires with one tire having the serial 37-2-18769-13 on invoice 003412 and signed by Mr. Samson."

"Your Honor," Mr. Clock said, "I would like to submit for evidence the records of Kelly-Springfield, the Alabama Wholesale, Inc. and the Moates Garage, showing the serial number of this tire."

"Mrs. Nation, number the documents and enter them into evidence."

"Your Honor, I have no further questions of this witness."

Mr. Barry Kall cross examined Dr. Quincy, but could not shake his testimony.

It was now time to recess for the day.

The State had only two more witnesses, and both would only be on the stand a short time.

Chapter Twenty-Nine

Mr. Flip Moore called Mr. Kaylow Kala to the witness stand.

"Mr. Kala, on the night of June 12 were you employed by the Sad and Happy Drive-In?"

"Yes Sir, I was hired by Mr. OJ Samson to manage the Sad and Happy Drive-In and was working there."

"What time did Mr. Samson leave Three Notch on his tour bus for Shreveport?"

"He left at five minutes after nine that night."

"How can you be sure it was five minutes after nine?"

"I was cleaning up when the bus pulled off, I looked up at the Jax Beer clock and it read 9:05.

"Are you sure the Jax Beer clock had the correct time?"

"Yes sir, Mr. Samson set the clock at six o'clock that evening."

"Now, Mr. Kala, I want you to think, what time was it, by the Jax Beer clock, before Mr. Samson set the time to six o'clock?"

"I didn't notice."

"Do you have a watch Mr. Kala?"

"Yes Sir."

"Did you reset your watch on the twelfth?"

"Yes Sir."

"What time was it by your watch when you set the time?"

"It was 7:20 by my watch when I looked at the Jax Beer clock, and it read 7:30 thirty, and I changed it to 7:30."

"Has your watch ever run slow before?"

"No Sir, I checked it every day with the Jax Beer clock and it was always on time. This is the first time it was not the same."

"Do you have any reason to believe Mr. Samson set the Jax Beer clock a head by 10 minutes?"

"No Sir, unless he made a mistake."

"Mr. Kala, what do you mean unless he made a mistake?"

"Well, I closed the Sad and Happy Drive-In and stopped serving drinks at 8:30. When I called time each of the three people in the bar said it was only 8:20. I didn't believe them. A lot of times customers will tell me the clock is wrong, so they can get another drink."

"When did you find out your watch and the Jax Beer clock were 10 minutes fast?" asked Mr. Moore.

"The first time was when the detective, who came out looking for Mr. Samson the next morning, asked me what time Mr. Samson left on the tour bus. I said five after nine. Then he asked how I knew the time, and I said by the Jax Beer clock. He asked me if I knew the clock was 10 minutes fast. I said no, Mr. Samson set it at six o'clock the night before. Both detectives watches were 10 minutes slower. The Nehi delivery man came to deliver the soda and they asked him the time. His watch was 10 minutes slower than the Jax Beer clock."

The defense's cross-examination was very short and Mr. Kala was dismissed.

Miss Kluck called the Nehi delivery man to confirm the time. She also called the customers in the bar that night to confirm the time.

There was very little cross, and recess was called for lunch.

The jurors again made the familiar walk to Rooster's Cafe. Today it looked as if the trial was taking its toll on the jurors. They were quiet and had very little conversation.

"Court was called to order at 1:15 PM and the prosecution called four witnesses testify to the beatings and abuse of Nike Samson."

The defense cross-examined the witnesses, but could not get them to alter their testimony.

The prosecution called their last witness, Mr. Evans Lee, the gentlemen who castrated Mr. Samson's bull.

Mr. Lee stated he castrated the bull and asked Mr. Samson if he could borrow the gloves for a few days.

"Mr. Lee, for what purpose did you borrow the gloves?" asked Mr. Moore.

"I was going to buy a cow and butcher it and take it out to the packing house to freeze some of the meat. As it turned out, I couldn't get the cow I wanted, so I didn't use the gloves and gave them back to Mr. Samson two days later."

"Was there any blood on the gloves when you carried them home with you, Mr. Lee?"

"No Sir. Before I asked to borrow them, I cleaned them real good with lye soap inside and out."

"Did anyone else have access to the gloves while they were in your possession?"

"No."

The defense asked a few questions and dismissed Mr. Lee.

"Your Honor the prosecution rests."

It was getting late in the afternoon, and Judge Ego adjourned the court until 10 AM, the next day.

That night Donny visited OJ at the jail.

"OJ, at this point things are not going as well as planned. Tomorrow I will try to get the blood expert to put a hole in the blood theory, and see if we can't tear down the sheriff's office, especially Deputy Burman. We will introduce reasonable doubts by the watch fob that was found, since they cannot find the owner. Do you know anyone who has a watch fob similar to the one that was found?"

"No, Donny, I don't. I tell you I am plenty worried abut the way the case is going. I did not kill Nike and that fellow. The Lord is my witness."

"I know OJ. Sometimes the clouds look darker than they are. We are not finished yet. Take care and I'll see you tomorrow."

Chapter Thirty

Miss Kluck hurried to her office, asked her secretary, Sarah Perapay, to call the State's Attorney in Chicago and get Mr. Don Yaley on the phone.

When Mr. Yaley was on the phone, Martha explained the situation she was in. She asked if he would be kind enough to make a background check on Dr. Nickolas Bloodgood, giving all the information she had, full name, company's name and address and the reason she needed this information by seven AM. Also she asked if he could subpoena the records of the Bloodgood Analysis Laboratories. She needed the records of Oscar James Samson, and anyone else who had been tested for Sickle-Cell Disease since the lab had been in business, which was about three years.

"I surely hope you can help me and get me the information by seven AM. I will be most grateful, I owe you one."

"When the annual convention of the N.A.P.A. (National Association of Prosecuting Attorneys) is held here in Chicago you can buy me a drink."

"I'll do more, I'll buy you dinner and drinks at your favorite restaurant."

"It's a deal Martha, at the Stock Yard Inn. Talk to you later."

Martha worked through the night until four AM, but did not get a sound sleep. When Big Ben jarred her awake with the loud ringing at six, she dragged her still sleepy and energyless body into the bathtub. A lot of work had to be done by 9:30. Why in the hell did Judge Ego have to start that early.

To save time Martha thought she would go by Rooster's Cafe and get breakfast. As she entered the cafe, the usual crowd of early morning merchants, clerks, and farmers in town for business, were having their coffee and some were eating.

She took a table in the back of the cafe, near the long table that seated about eight to 10 people. The regulars gathered there for their morning coffee, rolls or breakfast, and gossip. This morning, she ordered two over easy eggs, grits, country link sausage and biscuits, more than she usually ate. "Gad," she thought, "I ordered enough for an army." Then she realized she had not had dinner the night before. As she looked over some notes, she heard the words "nigger lover" float over from the long table. She looked at the notes but didn't read them as she eavesdropped on the gossip table. At the table was, Len Thigpen, owner of Thigpen Horse and Mule Stable, Charlie Hawkins, owner of Hawkins Jewelry, Seth Bradley, owner of a large farm, Shorty Dunn, a hardware store manager, Slim Duncan, manager of the Western Union, Kirk Newberry, owner of Newberry's Women Clothes, and Dago Russo, who owned the Standard Oil Station.

Kirk Newberry said, "That Nike Samson sure was a knockout. I can't see her slipping around and seeing a nigger. Doesn't that knock your ego down below your belly button."

"Maybe the nigger was a farm hand who was doing some work there and tried to get smart," said Shorty Dunn.

"I don't know, but this will set old OJ free. I have missed him coming in for gas," said Dago.

Martha thought, "Damn, my case is going to hell in a hand basket. I have got to get to the office and stop the bleeding."

She finished her breakfast and was at the counter paying her check when Dorothy Sue Pyle asked, "Miss Kluck, how long will OJ be in jail, now that they found out a nigger killed Nike?"

"Dorothy Sue, they have not proven anyone other than OJ Samson killed Nike."

"What about that watch fob that was found? Mr. Hawkins said it looked like the one he sold to that nigger Fred Floyd, who works out at the Three Notch Country Club?"

"Just rumors, Dorothy Sue," she said as she left the cafe and hurried over to her office.

When she arrived at the office, Mattie, who was asked to come early to take any messages, had some messages from Don Yaley in Chicago. As Martha looked over Yaley's messages and the others that she had gotten through the night, things began to look up. The gods were smiling on her again. She went into her office after leaving a message that she was not to be disturbed for any reason until 9:15, and to notify her that she had to be in court.

It only seemed like 10 minutes when she was notified that it was time for court. She gathered up her papers, stuffed them into her brief case and took off to court with a spring in her step.

On the way Detective Otter came up along side of her and matched her stride. "Miss Kluck, we have a lead on the watch fob," said Detective Otter.

"I know, but Fred Floyd has not been charged."

"How did you know that, Miss Kluck?"

"Hell, everyone in Three Notch County knows every fart that has been let and by whom. Get with it, Van, we are not stopping the trial to let a guilty man go."

Chapter Thirty-One

When court convened at 10 AM Judge Ego asked Mr. Kockran to call the first witness for the defense.

Mr. Kockran called four of OJ's and Nike's friends to verify that they had never seen any violence, between the couple. They all testified that OJ and Nike were a loving couple. Two said they thought the breakup of their marriage was due to the concerts and traveling.

The prosecution asked a few questions, getting one of the friends to admit that they did argue once in a while, but he had never seen any physical violence between them.

Mr. Kockran called a Lt. Lon Beesley of the Sheriffs's Department, who was Deputy Burman's supervisor, and had subpoenaed his work record and history.

"Judge Ego, I would like to enter into the record Deputy Burman's work history as evidence."

The record was entered as evidence in the court.

"Lt. Beesley, looking at Mr. Burman's records, have there been any reprimands?"

Yes, Sir, there have been three."

"Were the reprimands before or after Deputy Burman was made acting detective?"

"Before he was acting detective."

"What were the three reprimands for, Lieutenant?"

"One was in April of last year, when he was assisting in an investigation of a house burglary. He entered into evidence material he took from another suspect, a radio, that was not connected to the case he was investigating."

"In plain English, Lieutenant Mr. Burman was careless, wasn't he?"

"Yes Sir."

"Lt. Beesley, I am looking at the record, page two, second paragraph, the State vs Oscar Myers. It reads, 'Deputy Burman arrested Mr. Oscar Myers for rustling hogs from Frank Farmer'. Now Lieutenant, read to the jurors the rest of the story."

"Deputy Burman is hereby reprimanded for falsely entering into the record the following entry. Deputy Burman arrested Mr. Oscar Myers for rustling hogs from Mr. Frank Farmer. The entry should have read, Deputy Burman arrested Frank Farmer for rustling cows from Mr. Oscar Myers."

"You are telling this jury that Deputy Burman arrested a man for stealing his own hogs, and that Mr. Burman did not know a hog from a cow."

"He made a mistake Mr. Kockran."

"Lt. Beesley, if the deputy made a mistake such as entering into the record and arresting the man who owned the cow, not the hog, couldn't it also be a mistake if the same deputy found a boot and entered it as a glove? Can the jury believe this man? Lt. Beesley, what is the other reprimand on Deputy Burman's record? Please read from the record book."

"It reads as follows, 'Leon Crook was arrested for moonshining at the still. Leon said he didn't give a Tinkers Dam. Deputy Burman was given a reprimand for incorrectly entering into the record book an arrest. It should have read, Leon Crook was arrested at his still in the Tinker Dam area for moonshining."

"Lt. Beesley, again you are asking the jurors to believe that Deputy Burman found a glove and not some other object like a boot or shoe. Did he make a cast of a tire or was it a wagon rim?"

"I object," shouted Miss Kluck."

"I am finished with this witness, Your Honor," said Donny Kockran.

Judge Ego called a lunch recess until 1:30.

The jurors took their usual route to Rooster's Cafe and went into the meeting room for lunch.

This day the blessing was said by Miss Shirley Pimple who said" I pray you take some meat; for this is for your health- Acts 27:34."

Today's menu was Catfish a la Rooster, with hush puppies, and french fries. The catfish was caught above Tinkers Dam where the mash from the moonshine stills run into the Tinker River. They were big and plump, rolled in corn meal and deep fried. This was topped off with banana pudding.

The jurors walked back to the courtroom for the afternoon session.

Judge Ego called the court to order after the jurors were seated, and asked for the next witness.

"Mr. Israel Zolowit, the attorney, whose specialty was fingerprinting and blood analysis called Dr. Nickolas Bloodgood to the stand.

"Dr. Bloodgood, tell the jurors your educational background."

"I attended college at The University of Illinois, majoring in medical sciences. Afterwards I attended the School of Medicine at Harvest. Upon completion I was appointed Assistant Coroner at the Illinois Coroner's Office. I studied nights at the School of Medicine at Harvest, the subject bloodology."

"Dr. Bloodgood would you explain, bloodology, and what you can tell by using it, and how you can be certain of a match?"

"Mr. Zolowit, the blood carries red cells and white cells. Under a high powered microscope, you can separate the cells. This is a new scientific work on the human blood embracing all parts of the blood and its cells. Poor erythrocyte or red blood cells will show jaundice, torpid liver and sallow complexion.

"Dr. Bloodgood, did you get the sample of blood from Mr. OJ Samson, analyze, and compare it to the type A negative blood that was found at the crime scene?"

"Yes Sir."

Dr. Bloodgood, in your professional opinion, did the type A negative blood at the crime scene match Mr. OJ Samson?"

"Sir, the erythrocyte count in the type A blood at the crime scene was somewhat lower than Mr. Samson's, showing the type A blood at the crime scene was not Mr. OJ Samson's."

"Were there any other tests that you performed that proved the type A blood at the crime scene was not Mr. Samson's?"

"Yes, Sir, I performed an Enegay test and the results were the erythrocyte showed distortion and fragility, the cells are lost rapidly from circulation. Mr. Samson's blood did not show this."

"Dr. Bloodgood, will you tell the jurors and the court in layman's language the significance of erythrocyte in the blood distortion and fragility?"

"Yes Sir. It is a hereditary chronic blood disorder, common among the Negro population, known as Sickle-Cell disease."

The courtroom got noisy, with people talking. Judge Ego banged his gavel on the desk to restore order. After the noise quieted down Judge Ego announced, "Ladies and Gentlemen, I want absolute silence in the courtroom. If there are any more outbursts, I will clear the room. Is that clearly understood? Continue Mr. Zolowit."

"Dr. Bloodgood, did Mr. Samson's blood sample show any erythrocyte distortion and fragility?"

"It did not".

"Then, Dr. Bloodgood, you are saying that the killer was a Negro?"

"I am saying, Mr. Zolowit, that the blood at the crime scene and on the glove was from a person with, a slight evidence, of Sickle-Cell disease."

"Thank you," said Mr. Zolowit. "That is all."

"Any cross from the prosecution?" asked Judge Ego.

Miss Kluck rose and said, "Your Honor, it is now three 3:45, by the time we take a break and return, it will be almost time to adjourn. If the court pleases, I would like to adjourn until tomorrow morning."

Judge Ego looked at the defense and received no answer, so he said, "We will adjourn for the day. Court is dismissed until 9:30 tomorrow morning. Good day, Ladies and Gentlemen."

Chapter Thirty-Two

Judge Ego called the court to order at exactly 9:30.

"Call the witness, Dr. Nickolas Bloodgood, to the stand. You are still under oath Dr. Bloodgood., You may start your cross, Miss Kluck."

"Good morning, Dr. Bloodgood," Miss Kluck said in her sweetest voice and gave the doctor a large pleasant smile.

"Good morning, Miss Kluck," the doctor answered, thinking,"What a pussy cat she is, and I do mean pussy."

"Dr. Bloodgood, what name did you use when you attended the University of Illinois?"

"Nate Anthony Conway."

"Dr. Bloodgood, or Mr. Conway, which name shall we use today, or what about Anthony Conrad, may we use that name?"

"There is an explanation for these names, Miss Kluck," he replied, as he put on his most charming smile.

"Pray tell the jurors and the court, why almost everyone in our great county has one name but the great Dr. Bloodgood has three. Are you that important?"

"My name was changed from Anthony Conrad to Anthony Conway when I was adopted. Before I entered the University of Illinois, I legally changed my name to Dr. Nickolas Bloodgood for professional reasons."

"I am holding in my hand a message from the State's Attorney Office in Chicago, that you legally changed your name to, David

Robert Nickolas Bloodgood. Do you use the initials of your first two names with your third and last names, making this Dr. Nickolas Bloodgood? I have the proof on the way. Now, David Robert Bloodgood," she raised her voice so that it could be heard on the street as the windows were open. A silent hush fell over the court room, "Answer YES or NO, D. R. N. Bloodgood?"

D.R.N. Bloodgood dropped his head and answered, "Yes."

"Mr. Bloodgood, what name did you use when you served time in the Illinois Penitentiary, and what was the crime you were convicted of?"

"I object," shouted Mr. Zolowit, "The type of conviction is not relevant."

"I will show my connection in his truthful answer Your Honor."

"Objection overruled, answer the question, Mr. Bloodgood."

Anthony Conrad said, "I was convicted of falsifying a medical record while I worked in the lab at Mercyless Hospital in Chicago, and I was sentenced to three years and paroled in 18 months. I falsified the blood test of a man who was accused in a paternity suit."

"You only went to The University of Illinois one year, is that correct Mr. Bloodgood? An answer of YES or NO is sufficient."

"Yes."

"Mr. Bloodgood, we have talked to the Attorney General in Illinois and he gave us the full report on your business, the Bloodgood Analysis Laboratories. He put those papers in the mail this morning. We called the State's Attorney last night and got a subpoena of your records. We asked the Illinois authorities to look them over and check to see if anyone else had a record where you analyzed for Sickel-Cell disease, or would you rather tell the jurors and this court the truth about finding Sickel-Cell disease at the crime scene and on Mr. Samson's glove. Which will it be Mr. Bloodgood?"

"I manufactured false reports, charts and analyses of the blood samples submitted to me."

"What was the reason for falsifying the blood samples and reports?"

"Money."

"Mr. Bloodworth, you are in serious trouble, do you understand this?"

"Yes Mam."

"Without getting in deeper and more serious trouble, tell this court who paid you the money for this job and how much?"

"I object," said Mr. Zolowit.

"On what grounds Mr. Zolowit," asked Judge Ego.

"There is no foundation that the money or the amount is connected to this case."

"The money was to falsify the evidence of this trial, and the person paying this money is equally guilty of this conspiracy. It has a connection. Objection overruled. Answer the question Mr. Bloodgood."

"I had a long distance telephone call from a person who said he was a close friend of Mr. Oscar James Samson, and he would like to meet with me. We made arrangements for him to come my office on the night of his arrival in Chicago. He arrived at LaSalle station from Three Notch, Alabama about four PM. We met at seven and he gave me an envelope with $2,000, more that my net profit for a month. We discussed the details of what to do. The Sickle-Cell disease was my idea. He had the blood samples, and background information. His name was Ferlin Williams."

Pandemonium went through the court room. Ferlin Williams was the drummer in OJ's band.

"Order! Order! We must have order in this courtroom or it will be cleared. One more outburst like this one and everyone will be removed," said Judge Ego.

"May we have a side bar, Your Honor?" asked Mr. Zolowit.

At the side bar Mr. Zolowit, Mr. Kockran, Mr. Kall, and Mr. Dash told Judge Ego that the revelations that Mr. Bloodgood revealed were a surprise to them, and that they would like a recess until Monday morning. It was now 11:10 AM on Friday, and Judge Ego adjourned the court until 10 AM on Monday.

OJ was escorted back to his cell, but before he left the courtroom, Donny said he would see him at one o'clock.

During lunch Donny thought about the development that occurred that morning. Why in the hell would anyone try to pull a trick like this. It couldn't be Williams, for he was not that smart and did not have that type of money. Only OJ was smart enough or dumb enough and he had the money for a stunt like this. The case had really gone to hell. He would have to talk to OJ and regroup.

Donny arrived at the jail at one o'clock and requested an interview room to meet with OJ.

When OJ walked in the room he started apologizing for what he had done.

"I thought you were smarter than to pull this kind of trick. What in the hell did you think you were doing? I should walk away right this minute, and I will if you lie to me and don't have a hell of good reason."

With a trembling voice, and tears in his eyes, OJ said, "Donny, forgive me and don't walk out. I know now I did wrong, but the way the evidence was going, it looked like I was a dead man. I am innocent, yet the evidence is all against me. Everyone, but Ma and Pa think I did it. I had to do something. What can we do now?"

"Be honest, tell me everything. Who all is involved in this?"

"I talked Ferlin into doing this for me. He followed my instructions. He is the only one, I am to blame for that. See if you can keep him out of this. I'll pay for that."

"I don't know if I can get him off scot-free. I can try for maybe just a light fine or sentence. The big problem is you. I am going to the office and see how to approach this problem. I want you to keep your mouth shut and don't talk to anyone about any part of the case. I have until Monday to try and come up with something.

As Donny left the jail, he stopped by the office and asked that no visitors, except his mother and father be allowed to see OJ over the weekend. Maybe he could keep him out of trouble that way, however, they were in so deep, that it wouldn't matter much.

During the weekend Donny went over all the records, and made his plans. He notified Lt. Lon Beesley, that he would be recalled on Monday at 10 am. and to bring the records of Deputy Mack Burman.

Donny learned Ferlin Williams would be playing drums in a band at the Cholly Hoss Honky Tonk and Country Club on Saturday night. Being unable to find him all day Saturday, Donny went to the Cholly Hoss about eight o'clock. The band was playing, but would take a break at 8:15.

Donny sat through the loud band music, watching the customers who were on their way to being high. Several people recognized him and offered to buy him drinks. Most any other time they would have been welcome, but not tonight, not even for Lucy Locket Walker who was dressed in a red tight fitting skirt and white short sleeved blouse trimmed in red that was cut low in front, showing cleavage and the nipples of her breasts. She wore a little too much make up, but it showed off her delicate facial features, large brown twinkle eyes, and ruby red lips that looked as if they were always ready to give a sexy kiss. He remembered that pleasing smile that seemed to be for him.

She came over to ask about OJ, but kept getting closer to him. The perfume she had on was light and sweet, with an exotic fragrance. She wore just the right amount to arouse but not overpower him. When she sat down, she was a small person, and as he looked down he saw the cleavage, the round firm breasts, and the nipples showing through the thin blouse and wondered how the fragrance would smell when you were nuzzled in there.

When the band took their break, and he excused himself and went to find Ferlin Williams. Ferlin was a tall lanky fellow about 25 years old, with dirty blond hair, shifty blue eyes, wrinkled and soiled clothes. He was uneducated and his grammar was poor.

"Ferlin, I understand you did a job for OJ and had a trip to Chicago on the train. How did you enjoy the trip to the big city?"

"I shore liked it real good, but I ain't goin' to live no place like that."

"Tell me about it, Ferlin, and I want the truth. OJ told me some, and I promised him I'd help you out of this mess. The more truthful you are, the better it will be, because I am going to have a tough time keeping you out of jail."

"Mr. Kockran, I shore don't wanna go to jail. I only done what OJ told me to do. I toted the money and a letter to that doctor in Chicago and brought the papers back. OJ told me to give the papers to that deputy feller, Mr. Burman, with some money in a envelope."

"Where was Deputy Burman when you gave him the material and the envelope you brought back from Chicago?"

"He was over thar in that booth in tha corner."

"Now be honest with me Ferlin, was anyone with Deputy Burman when you gave him the material and money from OJ?"

"Yea, Barbé Paulieri, the girl sanger that sang here once in a while."

"Was Barbé Paulieri and Deputy Burman together a lot?"

"Yea. Mack and her were sort of a item. When he weren't workin' he would go on gigs with her, and some times sang."

"Thank you Ferlin, I'll do my best to keep you out of trouble. Watch yourself and stay clean."

As he was leaving, Lucy Walker came over and said, "Sugar, you aren't leaving are you? We can have some fun."

The perfume drifted up his nostrils, the fragrance and closeness of her body stirred his emotions. He wanted to stay, but the case was in too much trouble."

"Lucy, I have to go now, however, I would love a rain check. I think you and I could do some lovely things together. But I have to finish the Samson case first."

"How long will that be, Sugar?"

"Not too much longer. How can I get in touch with you?"

"Depending on where you want to touch me. Just joking, give me a pencil and paper and I'll write the address of my home and work."

Donny eased out of the Cholly Hoss Honky Tonk and was walking over to his shiny new 1937 Buick when he saw a figure in the shadow of the building. A person in dark clothes with a bandana over the lower part of his face called to Donny to come over or risk being shot. Donny slowly walked over to the side of the building. The man said, in a low disguised voice, "Donny, don't go any further with that Chicago business. If you do, this is just a sample of what you will get."

Just as Donny looked down his head exploded like a large firecracker had been stuck in both ears and he went down.

He became conscious of someone mopping his face with a sour smelling towel. He recognized the odor as whiskey and beer. "My God, they are washing my face with the bar towel," he thought. He slowly got up, and saw it was Lucy Walker who had the towel.

"How are you feeling, Sugar?"

"I feel like some damn mule kicked me up side of the head. Did you see who did this?"

"No, Sugar. Ginger, my girl friend, and I was headed for home. When we came out we saw somebody hitting someone, which turned out to be you. He had something over his face, and he ran and got into a car."

A crowd was standing around, and one or two said they saw the figure but failed to recognize him. One person said the car looked like a Ford coupe, a 1934 or 1935 model.

"Sugar, are you married?"

"No, divorced."

"Good, Ginger can take my car home and I'll drive you home. You will need your head taken care of, and I can do that Sugar."

As Lucy was driving, Donny laid his aching head on the back rest, closed his eyes, and tried to remember what had happened. As he was going down he saw the shoes of the man who was assaulting him. They seemed familiar, but he couldn't place where he had seen them before. He drifted in and out of sleep until he felt soft hands rubbing his face and head. He was home.

Lucy took off his coat and helped him to the bed. She got a pan of warm water, a wash cloth, iodine, gauze, adhesive tape and petroleum jelly and gently washed the side of his head where there was an ugly, deep gash about two inches long. She cleaned this well, and told Donny that she was going to put some iodine on it.

"Before you do Lil Thang, look in the kitchen and get the bottle of White Ribbon Vitae, and look in the ice box and get that bottle of water, marked spring water and two glasses, that is if you will have a drink with me?"

"Sure, Sugar, but I'll take soda pop with mine."

"There's some Nehi Cola in the cabinet."

Lucy assembled the items, and fixed Donny a stiff drink of White Ribbon Vitae. She handed it to Donny, who put about two tablespoons of spring water in the drink, explaining, "I don't want to ruin a good drink with too much water."

While Donny had his second real stiff drink of White Ribbon Vitae, Lucy sipped hers and began to work. She mopped out the wound again and put some iodine on it. Donny let out a big whistle, as Lucy handed him another big drink. She put more iodine on the gash, then petroleum jelly. She put some gauze over the wound and taped it firmly in place. She added a damp cloth on his head, and being finished had another White Ribbon Vitae.

She took the rest of his clothes and his shoes off, and as he lay naked, she started removing her clothes. First she unhooked her stockings from her garter belt, sliding them down over her perfectly shaped legs. Then she unbuttoned her skirt, let it fall to the floor and stepped over it. She undid the buttons on her blouse and pulled it over her head.

Donny was transformed into a zombie. He was so taken back at the beauty of this girl. Lucy winked at Donny and pulled her white satin slip over her head. As she did, Donny saw the beautifully shaped, creamy skinned body, clad only in red panties and bra. When she reached behind her back to unfasten her bra and remove it, Donny's head was throbbing rapid fire, but not from the hit on the head. The Lil Thang slid her thumbs on top of each side of her panties, slowly lowering them to her feet and stepped out of them. There she stood in all of her glory. My God, Donny thought, I have died and gone to heaven. Then he saw her pubic hairs. The hairs were light brown, the color of her head, but trimmed in the shape of a heart. Now he knew the blow had killed him, for this was too good to be happening on earth.

When Donny awoke the next morning, it had not been a dream, for the Lil Thang was laying there beside him, looking just as beautiful as she had the night before. He tried to recall all the details of the past night but because of the blow to his head and the White Ribbon Vitae, things were not too clear. Well, he was well enough now. Besides he was more horny in the morning than at any other time.

He slid his hand gently over those pointed breasts, down her smooth stomach, toward the heart shaped hairs. Lil Thang slid her hand down along his leg as she turned over on her side. He was in lala land with the smell of the exotic fragrance still lingering from the night before.

About noon Donny and Lil Thang got out of bed and took a bath together. It was a little tight in the tub, but a real pleasure. While eating the meal Lil Thang had prepared, eggs, sausage, and coffee, they discussed the night before.

Donny couldn't get the shoes out of his mind, and Lucy kept trying to place the car. While this discussion was taking place, a knock came at the door. Donny answered and there stood Billy Kidd, a guard from the jail. He had a note from OJ that Billy had agreed to drop off on his way home from work. He handed the note to Donny, but it missed his hand and fell on the floor. As Donny bent over to retrieve the note, he noticed the shoes that Billy was wearing. Donny slipped Billy a dollar, then sat down on the sofa to read the note.

The note from OJ said he wanted to see him before court tomorrow. When Donny finished reading, he laid his head back, closed his eyes and thought about the image of the shoes. He sat upright with a start, he now knew what kind of shoes the guy had on last night. They were shoes worn by the personnel of the sheriff's department, local police and jail guards. He could only think of one person who would want to do him harm, Deputy Burman.

"Lil Thang, have you ever seen the private automobile of Deputy Mack Burman?"

"Sure have, Sugar. One afternoon I was coming home from work and ran out gas. This car stopped and it was Mack. He took me up to Dago Russo's gas station to get some gas."

"Think now, little one, the car you saw last night, could that have been Mack Burman's car?"

Lucy tilted her back, closed her eyes, wrinkled her brow and started thinking.

While she was doing this Donny observed her. Gosh, how cute she was.

After she lifted her head, she answered, "Yes, Donny, I am sure it was his car, because when I went for gas I noticed that his rear bumper was hanging lower on the left side. The bumper on the car I saw last night was also hanging lower on that side."

"Lil Thang, I have to go see OJ, and run a few other errands. Can we have dinner to night?"

"Tell you what, Sugar, I'll get Mr. Sasser to go to his store and get me a couple of steaks, and potatoes, and I'll cook dinner. What time will you be by?"

"That's great. I'll be over about six and I'll bring the White Ribbon Vitae. Get dressed and I'll drop you at Ginger's on the way over to see OJ."

OJ told Donny that he had asked Wyatt Herp, the same guard who delivered his notes to Barbé for credit at the Sad and Happy Drive-In, to help him. Wyatt put me in touch with Mack Burman, who said he could get someone to alter the blood samples for me.

I gave him $5,000, $2,000 for D.R. Bloodgood, $500, plus expenses, for Ferlin Williams, and the balance was for him and any other costs. I wasn't thinking clearly, Donny."

"Is this all that you have done in the way of tampering with the evidence in this case?"

"Honest to God, Donny, it is."

"OK, I have some errands to do. I'll see you in the morning."

Donny left the jail walked and over to the sheriff's office in the courthouse. He asked the duty officer if Deputy Burman was on duty and was told no. He asked for Burman's home address and it was given to him. The address was about a mile outside of Three Notch.

As he drove the Buick down Route 21, he mapped a plan in his head. Then his thoughts turned to the Lil Thang and to earlier this morning. All at once he was at the address of Burman. He saw a 1935 Ford sitting in the yard with the left side of the bumper hanging lower than the rest of the car.

Donny walked up to the house from the side where there were few windows to see from. He climbed over the porch bannister, and crawled under the porch window to the door. Standing to one side, he knocked and disguised his voice saying, "Mack, hey, it's me, Ferlin."

Donny could hear the foot steps coming and he leaned against the wall. The door was opened by Mack and just as he pushed the screen door outward, Donny jumped and caught Mack by surprise. He kneed Mack in the gut, and as he bent forward in agony, Donny caught his chin with his right fist. Mack went out like blowing out a kerosene lamp, flickering on the way down. He heard a noise inside and ran in catching Barbé by surprise. He grabbed her by her pretty neck with both hands and slammed her against the wall. Barbé cried out in pain, gasping for breath. He turned her loose and with his left hand he backhanded her so hard she fell to the floor. He turned as Mack was groaning and trying to get up. Donny grabbed a handful of Mack's hair and pulled him up, slamming him against the wall holding him there. "You low life son of a bitch, I should beat your ass until it's up around your mouth." He gave him one swift blow to the belly, so there would be no marks on his face. The breath went out of him like a big fart.

"Get over there and sit down beside Barbé," he shouted. She was now sitting on a couch whimpering. Now, Mack, tell me the truth, and if I think you are lying, I'll bust your mouth so hard you will feel your teeth biting your ass. NOW TALK."

"Don't hit me again, I'll tell you the truth. As a deputy, I have access to the jail. One day OJ saw me and wanted to talk. He told me the evidence was too strong against him and he needed to do something to even up the sides. He told me of the doctor in Chicago that some inmate told him about. He gave me the address. He offered me $5,000 and I figured when I payed out the money to the doctor and Ferlin, I could make more than I make in about a year and a half working for the county. I talked to Barbé and she said 'Take the bastard's money.'"

"OK Mack, let me lay this out for you. I have identified you to several people. I want the two of you to keep your mouths shut. You may be arrested, but I will never forget this gash on my head. And as for you, Barbé, you have gone too far, so you two, chill it."

Donny got up and walked over in front of Mack and asked him to stand. Mack stood up and just as he got in an upright position, Donny put another right in his gut.

As Mack doubled over in pain, Donny went out and got into his Buick. As he drove down the country road, with the dust flying up behind the car, his thoughts went to the Lil Thang, who was waiting for him with White Ribbon Vitae, steaks, and her heart shaped sex machine.

Chapter Thirty-Three

Donny awoke early and alone, took a bath, shaved and dressed, and was at Rooster's at 6:30 AM. After breakfast, he took a cup of coffee with him in a borrowed cup from Rooster's. He had asked his secretary, Nell, to be in as early as she could on this Monday.

Nell arrived at 7:20 and began getting things in order. Donny asked her to prepare the papers to get subpoenas for Deputies Wyatt Herp, Matt Millon, Billy Kidd and Mack Burman. "I don't know if I will call them, but I want them to be ready and sweat", he told her. "As soon as the papers are ready, I'll take them to the court and file them the minute the courthouse opens. I want the deputies to be there by the time court reconvenes after lunch."

At 8:30 AM Donny went over to the courthouse, and filed the subpoenas, then headed for Sheriff Jenkin's office. As a courtesy, he told Sheriff Jenkins about the subpoenas he had just filed. He told the Sheriff that he wanted the deputies to be in the courtroom by one o'clock.

"By the way, Sheriff Jenkins, have you investigated the watch fob that Mr. Hawkins said he sold to Fred Floyd?"

"Yes I did. Mr. Hawkins gave me the serial number of the watch, and Fred Floyd still has the watch with that serial number and the fob. We still don't know who this fob belongs to."

Sheriff Jenkins said, "Deputies Herp and Millon are scheduled to be on duty as escorts for OJ at the courthouse. I will send two other deputies over to relieve them."

Billy Kidd was in the office and the Sheriff told him to stick around that a subpoena would be issued shortly.

At 9:30 everyone was ready when the judge called the court to order.

Donny stood up and said, "Your Honor, the defense recalls Lt. Beesly to the witness stand."

"Lieutenant, my question to you about Deputy Burman is not in the record book, but rumors are floating around, and I am sure you have heard them. For instance, Deputy Burman is dating a fairly well known singer. They take trips to Pensacola and the beach, eat at fine restaurants, and stay at the finest hotels."

"I have heard this, but I haven't actually seen them."

"Lieutenant, you have heard about this, yet you have not tried to verify any of these rumors, why not?"

"Well, I just didn't believe it, because that is more money than a deputy makes."

"Lieutenant, have you heard of any other deputies spending more money than they make or living beyond their means?"

"No Sir."

"Lieutenant, there are at least three deputies hanging out at the Sad and Happy Drive-In, and they put their drinks on a tab and never pay the tab. Do you know of this?"

"No Sir."

"Lieutenant these are the deputies that have taken an oath that they found certain items pertaining to this murder investigation. Let me ask you Lieutenant, when we prove the deputies have done this, and we have evidence, would you want them to investigate your case if you were charged with murder?"

"I object Your Honor, Mr. Kockran is making a statement, irrelevant to this case and asking for an opinion."

"Mr. Kockran, you know you cannot ask for an opinion. The objection is sustained. Ladies and Gentlemen of the jury, disregard the question and statement by Mr. Kockran."

"That is all of this witness, Your Honor," said Donny.

Miss Kluck had no recross.

A 10 minute recess was called, and Donny went out to check on the witnesses. He spotted Mack Burman and told him that he was the next witness.

When court convened, Mr. Kockran asked the court to recall Deputy Mack Burman. Because Burman was the witness for the prosecution, Donny asked if he could treat him as a hostile witness for the defense.

At the side bar, when both sides heard the law as read, the witness was called as a hostile witness.

Mack Burman took the stand. Judge Ego told Deputy Burman that he was still under oath, but had been declared a hostile witness.

"Deputy Burman, I want you to answer yes or no to this question. Have you ever taken a bribe in connection with this case?"

"Yes."

"Deputy Burman, did you accept the bribe for getting a witness in this case to submit false evidence, lie, or both? Answer yes or no."

"Yes."

"Deputy Burman, did this witness submit blood evidence in this court?"

"Yes."

"Deputy Burman, you know that your record was read in court on the three reprimands you have received?"

"Yes."

"Deputy, with three reprimands, accepting a bribe to get a person to alter crucial evidence and lying on the witness stand, do you expect the jury to believe you found a bloody glove?"

"I object," shouted Miss Kluck.

"Sustained," answered Judge Ego.

"I have no further questions for this witness, Your Honor," stated Mr. Kockran.

"Bailiff," said Judge Ego, "You will hold the witness in contempt or court, for lying on the witness stand, taking a bribe to have a witness lie, and for bribing a witness to submit a false document. It is now 11:30, we will recess for lunch until one o'clock. Court adjourned."

The jurors were led over to Rooster's Cafe to their usual room. The group was a little upbeat, because they could see the end was near.

Spencer Macy asked the blessing, and they began their meal of meat loaf, boiled new potatoes, string beans, fried okra and corn bread. While eating they began talking about the weekend.

Reverend John Paul Pope, said that he held revival meetings in the community of Sasser. They were on Arron Sasser's farm. While he was on jury duty the fine people of that community put an arbor down near Yallar Creek." Lord, did we ever have grand time," he said. "About six people came to the Lord and were saved."

Leroy Rodgers said he went down on Saturday night. "Boy I do love to hear the Holiness preach their hell and brimstone sermons, and the real good singing. I sure thought Daisy Tilley was having a fit when they started singing, 'The Rock of Ages'. She held her hands over her head, started shouting and trembling and jumping up and down, and murmured things I didn't understand. She gave a big shout and sank down grabbing at me as she fell. There she lay on the ground trembling and kicking. The Reverend Pope here, was preaching for the sinners to repent. Everybody was a jumping, shouting and having a good time."

"Yes," said Reverend Pope, "We saved six people, but Sunday afternoon was even better. We had a baptizing down at the beach on Yallar Creek. All of the six was there, and four others found the Lord and were baptized. What a glorious day it was."

Iola Bridges said she had always enjoyed going to church. She said she was a Baptist, and Baptists always had a good time at church, singing the old gospel songs and listening to the hardshell preaching. She went to a Holiness arbor meeting once, and they really put on a good meeting. She was thinking about joining, but she didn't go back.

Reverend Pope said, "Iola, we will be holding an arbor meeting Saturday night, and baptizing on Sunday afternoon at Oliver Patterson's place. He will put us up an arbor at the creek that runs across his front 40. Be my guest Saturday night. If you find the Lord, I will be happy to baptize you on Sunday."

Iola said she just might do that.

The jury was back in the jury box and the court was called to order at one PM.

Mr. Kockran called Wyatt Herp to the stand, and after taking the oath, Mr. Kockran addressed the witness.

"Mr. Herp, you are under oath. I am going to ask you some questions, and I want you to answer, yes or no, unless I ask for an explanation, do you understand?"

"Yes, Sir."

"Mr. Herp, have you taken any money for doing favors for any person connected to this case?"

"Yes Sir."

"Have you taken money for this act more than one time?"

"Yes, Sir."

"For more than six times?"

"Yes, Sir?.

"What were the favors Mr. Herp?"

"For carrying notes to Barbé and bringing in White Ribbon Vitae to the jail."

"I have no further questions your Honor."

"Any cross, Miss Kluck?" asked Judge Ego.

Donny was nervous inside as he waited for Martha to confer with her team.

"Yes, Your Honor," answered Miss Kluck.

Donny thought, "I rolled the dice hoping she would not cross. I won't put Millon and Kidd on."

"Mr. Herp, I'll asked you some questions. Please answer yes or no. The person you took the money from, is that person in this courtroom now?"

"Yes Mam."

"Mr. Herp," she said as she raised her voice and walked over close to and pointed at OJ, "Is that the person?"

"Yes Mam."

"No further questions, your Honor."

The court recessed for 10 minutes.

Donny and his defense team had a discussion and decided it was best not to call any more witnesses and rely on closing argument to sway the jurors. They knew they could not win, maybe the closing would help.

When court reconvened after recess, the judge asked Donny to call his next witness.

"Your Honor, the defense rests."

This took everyone by surprise.

Judge Ego said, "We will adjourn until 10 am tomorrow, when we will start the closing arguments."

Chapter Thirty-Four

Donny arrived at the jail a few minutes after OJ was locked in his cell, and they began to talk about the trial.

"OJ, we are in a bad spot. Things aren't going as I planned."

"I know, and I am afraid. I am innocent of these crimes and someone is trying to convict me. Is there anyway we can stop this insanity and get me out of this?"

"Let's be honest, OJ, first you interfered in this case. Remember, I told you to trust your attorney, no matter who that attorney was. Also, you said you would not do or say anything unless you had your attorney's permission. From the beginning you were bribing the guards to sneak notes to Barbé, and God only knows who else. Then you got that dumb Ferlin Williams and Mark Burman in this thing. Not only that, your involvement with Burman almost cost me my life. I haven't told you, but I found out about the deal when Burman beat the side of my head. That is what this bandage is about, except now it is much smaller. I do not have the slightest idea why a seemingly intelligent person like yourself would pull such a dumb stunt. You put your neck in the noose. By doing this, you suggested to the jurors that you did it and now are trying to bribe your way out."

"But Donny, I was being railroaded."

"No, you were not, the evidence fell that way. Sometimes, it seems impossible to get people off whether they are guilty or innocent, that was my job, not yours. We are going through some rough times. Because of your interference we went backward. But we can't quit. Before I tell you what I think is the best plan, I am going to give you the opportunity to find yourself another attorney. It is up to you."

"No Donny, I don't want another attorney. I promise I will not do anything without your permission if you will stay on the case. Honestly, is there any hope?"

"The hope is slim, and the time frame is long. Here is what we can do. I will give my closing argument to the jury, trying to show police corruption, to show they were trying to frame you. I may work Burman in by trying to set you up on the D.R. Bloodgood caper. I will try by throwing suspicion on someone else through the watch fob that has not been identified. If this does not work after the sentencing, we can go for a retrial."

"But Donny, I am innocent. Why should I go to prison for any amount of time."

"The evidence is strong and with the screw up you did, this is the best we can hope for. I see a number of things we can appeal on. Trust me, this is the best way. I know you will be in prison for awhile, but we will have you out in a few months."

"OK Donny. Will you explain this to Ma and Pa. It is going to nearly kill them."

"Yes, OJ, I'll talk to them tonight. See you in the morning. I have to prepare my closing argument."

After Donny left the jail, he thought he should go out to Mr. Samson's farm and tell OJ's parents the bad news, so he could get to work and not be interrupted. God, it is going to be difficult to tell Lil Thang that for the next few days he would be busier than a one armed cotton chopper in a cotton chopping contest, and wouldn't have time to see her.

Mr. and Mrs. Samson took the news very hard. Mrs. Samson almost had a heart attack. Donny told them they had to be strong, as OJ needed them more now than at any time since he was in school.

Donny arrived back at his office, made a quick call to Lil Thang and went to work. He got home at three o'clock, walked into the kitchen to make a cup of coffee, but found the pot on the stove and the coffee ready to drink. He walked into the bedroom, and there on the bed lay the Lil Thang, stretched out on her back, without a stitch of clothing on her beautiful body. Even laying on her back her breasts stood up to a point, and, of course, the heart shaped sex machine was gorgeous. Oh well, who wanted coffee.

Chapter Thirty-Five

The alarm sounded like a freight train whistle at six o'clock. Donny got up, took a bath and shaved. As he was dressing, Lil Thang got up and went to the bathroom wearing just a smile. Man did she look good, but he had to get moving. Lil Thang made some coffee and they had two cups, then Donny headed for the office arriving at 7:15.

Donny worked on his closing argument, refining it and adding some to it. After having some coffee that his secretary, Nell, had gotten from Rooster's Cafe, he carefully put his papers in order, put them into his brief bag, walked into the bathroom, washed his face, combed his hair, put his coat on and went to the courthouse to roll some dice. He thought," I sure hope to hell they don't come up snake eyes."

Donny arrived in the courtroom at 9:45, spoke to everyone, sat down at his table, and looked around at the other attorneys, wondering if they, too had butterflies in their stomachs. The prosecution team was smiling and chatting with everyone. Martha Kluck looked cool and calm. Donny walked over to Kall and Cobb, the only defense attorneys he had asked to be present. The others were not needed. He asked Kall and Cobb that they display a cool and confident attitude, smile and make conversation among the other attorneys in the court room, and by all means, remain calm all throughout the closing arguments of both sides, and at all times when the jurors were in the courtroom.

After a few minutes, the bailiff came in and called the court to order. Judge Ego entered, and then the jury. The jurors were looking very serious and solemn.

"You may start your closing now, Miss Kluck," said Judge Ego.

"Thank you, Your Honor. Good morning Ladies and Gentlemen of the jury. We have come to the phase of the case where we look at the evidence, and summarize the proceedings of this trial. Then you the jury will decide the fate of Mr. Oscar James Samson."

"Here in this courtroom before you is a double murderer, Mr. Oscar James Samson. He did murder two innocent people in a horrible, brutal and frenzied killing. We have proven far beyond a reasonable doubt that the person sitting at that table," pointing to OJ, "did this. You have seen the evidence and heard testimony of the beatings that Mr. Samson gave to Mrs. Samson. You remember the testimony of Charlie Spinks of the Cholly Hoss Honky Tonk and Country Club, that he knocked her to the floor, and was quoted as saying, 'Hell I wouldn't pee on Nike's leg if she was on far.'

"Before that he threw her in Snit Creek and drove off leaving her to drown. Luckily she came to and walked home."

"You looked upon the photographs of the brutal slashing and stabbing of the victims. Would a stranger kill someone in this fashion to rob them? No, this was an act of revenge and hatred."

"Ladies and Gentlemen, think of the photographs of the once lovely Mrs. Samson laying in a muddy hog pen, throat cut, from ear to ear, cut under her breast almost severing the breast off, her bowels ripped open and some of her intestines laying in that muddy hog pen. Mr. Hooper, a poor innocent person, doing a good deed, who tried to protect Mrs. Samson. A big price to pay for doing a good deed. You saw the scene, the photographs of Clem Hooper's body, his stomach where this," again pointing to OJ, "murderer took a castrating knife used on animals, stuck it in his stomach so hard the butt of the knife imbedded in his flesh. Remember the glove which had the two victims blood and the blood of the defendant. You heard the evidence from Dr. Mack Davis, of the coroner's office, who has years of experience as a respected physician, who testified that blood from the victims was also on the inside of the glove. Would you under any circumstances, consider anyone else putting Mr. Samson's blood in the gloves? What about the knife? Even though it has not been found, the letter from Sears, Roebuck, confirms the purchase of the castrating knife by Mr. Samson. Mr. Evans Lee, who castrated the bulls for Mr. Samson, confirmed Mr. Samson owned the knife. What about the tire tracks at the murder scene, of which a plaster of Paris cast was made, matching the right front tire of a 1937 Hudson Terriplane, owned by Mr. Samson which was parked at the Sad and Happy Drive-In? The gloves contained the blood of both victims and of Mr. Samson who owned the gloves, one of which was found at the crime scene, the other at The Sad and Happy Drive-In where Mr. Samson has an apartment. Ladies and Gentlemen, how do we know Mr. Samson owned these gloves? You heard the testimony of Mr. Evans Lee who borrowed the gloves and returned them to Mr. Samson a few days later."

Martha walked up and down in front of the jurors, over in front of OJ and stopped, and as her voice rose she said, "Ladies and Gentlemen of the jury, Mr. Samson asks that you believe that he did not have time to go out to the Mansion on the Hill, murder these two innocent victims and return to the Sad and Happy Drive-In in time to leave on his tour bus at 9:05. Remember Mr. Kaylow Kala, who on the witness stand, under oath, stated that Mr. Samson set the clock to six o'clock on the night of June 12. At 7:20 Mr. Kala looked at his watch and the Jax Beer clock that Mr. Samson reset. The clock read 7:30 and Mr. Kala reset his watch from 7:20 to 7:30. How do we know that the clock was 10 minutes fast? Remember the next morning Mr. Otter, Mr. Burman and the Nehi Soda Pop driver all had watches that were ten minutes slower. Now, Ladies and Gentlemen can we believe that Mr. Samson's, Jax beer clock was correct and the detectives, the Nehi Soda Pop driver and Mr. Kala had watches that were all exactly 10 minutes slower? No, we can not believe this murderer on the time. He deliberately reset the Jax beer clock 10 minutes fast. The testimony of Detective Otter, gave the time line as 30 minutes to go out to the Mansion on the Hill, kill two people, change clothes and wash up. What is the time that Mr. Samson had when you add 10 minutes to the clock?" Mrs. Kluck walked over in front of OJ and again pointed her finger at him and said, "This man had 40 minutes to do the deed. If anyone else had been there, he would have had the time to kill a couple more people."

"What about the shoe prints of which Dr. Davis had plaster of Paris casts made? The shoes were never found, but the casts matched a set of foot prints near the left front running board of the Hudson Terriplane owned by Mr. Samson. There were three prints that matched, that formed a path from the door of Mr. Samson's apartment to the Hudson Terriplane's left front running board."

"Ladies and Gentlemen of the jury, do you think an innocent man would pay a large amount of money to a laboratory and bribe the director to lie on the witness stand and change someone else's blood on the gloves and alter evidence? Only a murderer would do this."

"Ladies and Gentlemen, the law is that we must prove beyond a reasonable doubt that Oscar James Samson is guilty. I have proved beyond a reasonable doubt his guilt. You have heard the testimony, seen the evidence, seen the photographs of Mrs. Samson and Mr. Hooper in a muddy hog pen, their throats cut from ear to ear. You have seen innocent people's blood all over the hog pen. A bloody glove contained both the victim's and Mr. Samson's blood on the outside and inside. You can be assured that the prosecution has proved it's case beyond reasonable doubt. I ask that you find Oscar James Samson guilty of murder in the first degree of Nike Brown Samson, and I ask that you find Oscar James Samson guilty of murder in the first degree of Mr. Clem Hooper.

"Your Honor, that concludes my closing argument to the jury," Miss Kluck addressed Judge Ego.

The judge announced that the court would recess until 1:30 for lunch.

The jurors took the familiar walk to Rooster's Cafe. As they walked in the door all eyes were upon them trying to read their eyes, expressions or body language. Everyone wondered what they were thinking, how they would vote and what the verdict would be. The jurors did not look at anyone and went straight to their table.

All of them were under great tension. Al K. Haul asked Mr. Kit Carson to say the blessing.

"Oh Lord, as we gather for our daily bread, guide us in our quest for the right decision in our deliberations on the case before us as we serve the Lord our God and he shall bless this bread. Amen."

They had chicken, baked in dressing, corn fritters, baked sweet potatoes, lady peas and okra. It was a solemn lunch, with talk about their families, and what they would do the first week after the trial was over. Most said they would visit with their family and friends, rest and go shopping and, back to work.

After lunch they made their trip back to the courthouse and in front of the jail. Thelma Jitter looked up to the top floor and wondered what OJ was thinking at this moment. It sure didn't seem as if the man sitting in the courtroom could do what they showed. Maybe the defense will show that he didn't do any of those terrible things.

Thelma had never heard OJ sing. On a recent shopping trip to Montgomery, she was in the S.S. Kresge 5 & 10¢ store and saw some of his records. She purchased two of them and after she got home, she closed the door to her room put a record on her Victrola, lay down on the bed and closed her eyes as she listened. Gosh, he had a beautiful baritone voice. She would play his records for hours on the weekends, but now she must decide OJ's fate.

Chapter Thirty-Six

After everyone was in place, court was called to order and Judge Ego asked Mr. Kockran if he was ready for his closing argument. Mr. Kockran answered in the affirmative, slowly walking over in front of the jury.

"Ladies and Gentlemen of the jury, the prosecution wants you to believe that this case is cut and hung out to dry. First, let me remind you, as will Judge Ego when he charges the jury, that as you see Mr. Samson sitting over there, you are looking at an innocent man. For the law states, and I quote, 'The status of innocence is presumed until guilt is proven beyond a reasonable doubt in a court of law.' This procedure requires the government to bear the burden of proof. Mr. Samson sits in this courtroom innocent until the state proves all reasonable doubts regarding the defendant's guilt. Ladies and Gentlemen, let me read you the instruction the judge will give you in this matter. And I quote, 'Reasonable doubt, the term referring to the amount of certainty that a juror must have before deciding on the guilt of a criminal defendant. The defendant is presumed innocent until doubt regarding the defendant's guilt has been removed.' Remember the words, all doubt of the defendant's guilt has been removed, not some doubt, not 75 percent doubt removed, but ALL, Ladies and Gentlemen. ALL, means 100 percent.

"Let us look at some of the allegations made by the prosecution. An allegation is an assertion that is made by a party, in this case the prosecution. It is their statement of what they intend to prove. It is circumstantial evidence or indirect evidence, presented from which other facts or evidence are to be inferred. If you look in the Webster's Dictionary, you will see that the word infer means, (1) to derive as a conclusion, (2) guess, (3) surmise, (4) hint, (5) suggest.

Let us look at some of the things, the prosecution inferred to as facts. No.1, the castrating knife. Yes, Mr. Samson purchased this knife. But the knife was in an unlocked barn for weeks or months before this tragedy happened. Any number of people knew it was in the barn and could have taken it.

Inference No. 2. The persecution guesses it was Mr. Samson who used it. Not dozens of other people who knew it was there or literally hundreds of strangers who could have found the knife in an unlocked barn when they attempted to rob or rape Mrs. Samson.

"Inference No. 3, surmise. The prosecution could have surmised Mr. Samson used the knife because he purchased it. Why not surmise the person who owned the watch fob, the owner of which has never been found, committed the murders?

"Ladies and Gentlemen, it could have been inference No. 4, hint. Mr. Samson committed the deed, because he purchased the knife, but no hint that the owner of the watch fob did it.

Inference No. 5. Let's suggest that Mr. Samson did it, and not suggest that the owner of the watch fob did the murders, not suggest a rapist did it.

"We can do the same with inferred excuses on the gloves. But, you, may think, Mr. Samson's blood was on the glove? Yes, how and when did that blood get on the gloves? Inference No. 2. We guess because the lab said it was type A negative blood and Mr. Samson has type A negative blood. But don't guess it was my blood. I, Donny Kockran, also have type A blood. Don't guess it was the owner of the watch fob, he may also have had type A negative blood. They don't know who the owner is. Have they tried to find him? Don't guess it was the thousands of other people with type A negative blood. Only guess Mr. Samson, as he was the only one tested.

"Inference No. 3. Let us surmise it was Mr. Samson who wore the gloves, because he is close, and we don't have the owner of the watch fob.

Inference No. 4. Let us hint that it is Mr. Samson's blood in the glove, because our detectives or deputies would not plant evidence of blood. However, they will bribe a lab to falsify a blood report and they will testify on the witness stand to the effect that the blood of a Negro, long ago dead, was on the glove.

"Inference No. 5. Suggest that the tire tracks that the cast was made from, were left at the scene the night of the murder. The prosecution did not consider the possibility the tracks were left there the week before when Mr. Samson visited his children. And remember the weather report, it had not rained in twelve days, therefore the tracks could have been left at that time.

Inference No 3. Again, surmise. Let us surmise Mr. Samson did not get any blood on himself or his clothes. If we surmise this we won't need to explain, why no blood was found on Mr. Samson or on his clothes.

"Well, Ladies and Gentlemen of the jury, we want the answer to, where the bloody clothes are. The clothes had to be bloody, you saw the photographs. A man or woman could not have done those killings without getting blood on themselves. If they don't have Mr. Samson's clothes, then lets surmise Mr. Samson is innocent as the law states he is, until all doubts have been removed.

"Inference No 4 again, hint. Let us hint that Mr. Samson is an expert driver, and made the trip to the Mansion on the Hill, killed two people, returned, washed up, and buried the bloody clothes. Sorry we can't say anything about the bloody clothes, because of No. 3, surmise. The prosecution has not found any bloody clothing, only surmised there are some.

"The prosecution had Detective Van Otter, who as a law enforcement officer has been trained to drive at high speeds, testify that he made the trip from the Sad and Happy Drive-In to the Mansion on the Hill in eight minutes. Do you remember the description Detective Otter gave of Route 3 going out to the Mansion on the Hill? He stated the roads on Route 3, after you leave the city limits, are sandy ruts, except for a small area with clay hills leading to the bridge at Snit Creek. Now Ladies and Gentlemen, I dare anyone in this courtroom, except law enforcement officers to drive it in the stated time. I believe most of you have been out Route 3, on the way to Slap Out, Burntout, and Rose Hill. In those communities a good many of you have been to the all day singing and revivals at the various churches. Could any of you drive to the Mansion on the Hill and back in 16 minutes? Also, remember you have to brutally murder two people who are putting up a struggle for their very lives. Could you murder two people in the fashion you saw in the photographs in 15 minutes? I say you could not. Why? Inferrence No. 2, guess. I guess you are not professional drivers, nor professional killers, and neither is Mr. Samson. Let's go back to surmise, as the prosecution has done a lot of this. They surmised that the blood found on the glove at the crime scene was Mr. Samson's. Who bribed the lab in Chicago? A police officer. Who took bribe money to contact the crooked lab? Another police officer. In all, four police officers have been arrested for misconduct in this case. All of the inferrences added up to No.1, 'to derive at a conclusion with only circumstantial evidence.'

"The prosecution has presented only circumstantial evidence, as I have outlined to you. Not one bit of evidence has been presented to show that Mr. Samson had any reason to commit the murders. The prosecution has not entered anything into evidence showing premeditation, or a distinct intention of conscious purpose to kill these two people. Mr. Hooper was unknown to Mr. Samson, and Mrs. Samson, while no longer his wife, was still the mother of his children. Why would he murder the mother of his children?

"When you go into the jury room to deliberate the case of the State of Alabama vs OscarJames Samson, you must keep in mind reasonable doubt, and you have more than enough to render a verdict of not guilty."

"Your Honor, the defense rests," stated Mr. Kockran.

"Ladies and Gentlemen of the jury, as it is now four o'clock, the court will adjourn until 9 a.m. tomorrow, at which time I will charge you with this case and give you your final instructions," said Judge Ego. "I caution you not to talk about this case to anyone. Court adjourned."

Chapter Thirty-Seven

After court was adjourned, Donny went over to the jail to see OJ. As he entered Mr. and Mrs. Samson were in the visiting room also waiting for OJ. Donny walked into the room, shook hands with them and sat down to wait. Mr. Samson said, "Mr. Kockran, I want you to tell us the truth about OJ's case, no matter what you wish the outcome to be."

"Yes, Mr. Samson, I will tell you the truth as I see it, but let's wait for OJ."

After some small talk, OJ entered the room and hugged his Ma and Pa. "Donny, you gave a great closing argument. Do you think it swayed any of the jurors?"

"I think it helped us a great deal. I noticed the jurors were very attentive to the points I wanted to make regarding reasonable doubt, although, some of them had a look of puzzlement on their faces. But, yes, I think we made some headway."

"Donny," OJ asked, "What will the verdict be, as you honestly see it?"

"I have a lot of optimism, but I want you to be prepared for any verdict. On anything except not guilty, we have several options. A mistrial, and if that, by any stretch of the imagination is denied, we have openings for appeals on several accounts. However, let's be very optimistic about the verdict the jury will render. You folks have a nice visit, I have to run along and prepare some work for tomorrow. All of you rest easy tonight and I'll see you in the morning."

Donny was going home, but he did not want to be alone. He needed someone to talk to. After he got home he planned to call Lil Thang, but as he entered his home, his telephone rang and Lil Thang was on the line.

"Hi, Sugar," she said, "How did it go in court today?"

"The closing argument went very well, but I am afraid that when OJ butted in, it threw a lot of suspicion on him and his credibility went way down. I don't know how my closing went over with the jurors, but it was good, if I do say so. I will be biting my finger nails tonight."

"Look, Sugar, do you want some company?"

"Yes, that sounds great, I'll run out and get a couple of steaks and be back by the time you get here. A couple bourbon Kool-aides, steak and a roll in the sack should do wonders. By the way, have you had your trim today?"

Martha had gotten home, kicked off her shoes, and was trying to wind down. She felt that her team had put on a good case. In fact, it was damn good. She believed that the jury would bring in two counts of first degree murder. While her thoughts were on the jury, the telephone rang. She started not to answer it, but grabbed the phone and a sexy voice, said "Hello." It was Brad Larson, her old boyfriend.

"Hello, Brad, how are things going?" This was a hell of a way to start a conversation, but she didn't want to sound eager. She hoped to hell he would give some hint about getting together.

"Fine, Babe, just wondering how you felt after the big day?"

"Well, I should feel better, but something seems to be missing. I don't know, except I have felt like I unloaded a big burden and I am exhausted."

"Look, how would you like for me to go by Shorty's Barbecue, pick up some ribs and bring a bottle? You need to relax. How does that sound?"

"Brad, love, I need you tonight. It sounds perfect."

Barry Kall and Rufus Cobb dropped by Skeeter's Sport Bar, just outside the Three Notch City limits. Being out of the city limits they could only sell beer, but you could pay a $2 cover charge and bring your own bottle. Skeeter's was a popular meeting place for fishermen, golfers, Auburn and Alabama football fans and baseball fans who came to relax and trade whopping lies. Skeeter would even lie to your wife or girlfriend if you asked him to.

Barry and Rufus sat in a back booth sucking on Regal beer, going over the trial.

"Rufus," said Barry, "I think Donny has lost the case. I say Donny, because he did almost everything. We were talking one night and I wanted to dig into the background of Mack Burman. I told him I had heard rumors of Burman's sloppy and careless work. Also, I told him that I learned Burman took kickbacks. But Donny said it wasn't necessary to investigate, that the deposition he gave did not indicate there was anything else. I also asked Donny to hire a private detective to investigate the watch fob."

"You are right, Barry, I also asked Donny to get someone to investigate the watch fob. I think Donny was afraid that the fob might be connected to OJ."

"Well, I think it's too late now. Let's have another Regal. I just hope we get all of our fees from Donny. When this is over, let's get together in Montgomery and knock around some ideas on setting up a law partnership up there."

Chapter Thirty-Eight

Judge Ego had not yet made his appearance in the courtroom. The attorneys for both sides were a little upbeat and confident. They mingled with each other making small talk.

"All rise," announced the bailiff, as Judge Ego came in and took his seat.

At nine o'clock court was called to order.

OJ entered the court room. He was well dressed with a light gray suit, white shirt, red tie and gray shoes. He looked out over the courtroom and saw his Ma and Pa. He gave a thumbs up sign to them.

"Good morning Ladies and Gentlemen and members of the court."

Judge Ego looked at the jury, and said, "Ladies and Gentlemen, today I am charging you the jurors, with the case of the State of Alabama vs Oscar James Samson.

"Charging the jury means instruction or command as to the law. Mr. Samson was indicted for murder one for Mrs. Nike Brown Samson, and murder one for Mr. Clem Hooper. The burden of proof is on the State of Alabama since the defendant is presumed innocent.

"Murder is the unlawful killing of one person by another. You must find the defendant guilty in the first-degree, if all reasonable doubts are removed. First-degree murder requires proof of premeditation. You may find the defendant guilty of second-degree murder, if the defendant can show provocation by the victim's actions or words that would make a reasonable person lose self control. As you look at the evidence you must determine, if the defendant so murdered these two people without provocation, and if the State has the evidence to show proof of premeditation. Manslaughter is the unlawful killing of a human being in circumstances less culpable than murder. For example, when the killer suffers extreme provocation, is in some way mentally ill, which is diminished responsibility, did not intend to kill but did so accidentally in the course of another crime or by behaving with criminal recklessness.

"The other verdict would be not guilty. If the State has not proved by a preponderance of the evidence, and all reasonable doubts are not removed, then you must bring in a verdict of not guilty.

"If you need to have a copy of a statement by a witness, ask the bailiff to secure this from the court. If you need to see any exhibit that was entered into evidence to the court, ask the bailiff. If there are any legal questions you need to ask, write them on a piece of paper and give it to the bailiff.

"Only the evidence that was entered in court is to be considered. Only the testimony you heard from the witness stand is to be considered. You are not to take as the truth the remarks made by the attorneys of the prosecution or defense in the opening or closing statements of this case.

"The jury may retire to jury room number one. The alternates will retire to jury room number two and will remain in that room for the term of deliberation, unless you are called upon to replace one of the jurors. The jury will select a foreman for your deliberation.

"When you have reached a verdict fill out the form. The foreman will sign it and give it to the bailiff. Knock on the door once to give the bailiff a note or a request. Knock twice when you have reached a decision, and completed the form. Hold your verdict form until you are in court, at which time you will give the verdict form to the clerk, who will bring it to me and I read the verdict and hand it back to the clerk to read in open court."

The jury was escorted to jury room number one, the alternates to jury room number two, and all of the attorneys went across the square to the Robert E. Lee Hotel to wait for the verdict.

The Robert E. Lee Hotel was built in 1901, and last refurbished in 1921, some 16 years before. It wasn't run down, just old. Some of the furnishings had been replaced as they became frayed. It was well maintained, and the atmosphere was friendly. The restaurant was clean and served good food. The defense team rented a room, for Mr. and Mrs. Samson, OJ was escorted back to his cell to wait alone.

Everyone had to be in the courtroom before the verdict would be read.

Chapter Thirty-Nine

When the jurors entered the jury room and were seated, Iola Bridges passed around a slip of paper to each juror and asked them to vote for a foreman to head the deliberation of the case.

After the slips were returned, Kit Carson counted them and passed them on to Tom Mix. The count was 10 for Al K. Haul, one for Kit Carson and one for Spencer Macy. Al K. Haul was named the jury foreman.

After this business was completed, Al K. Haul asked if anyone wanted to start the discussion.

"I would like the court to give us the meaning of preponderance of the evidence," said Rhett Cutler.

Al K. Haul said, "They will, but they would like us to work it out. It would take too long to ask the meaning of every word, unless one of us can't explain it. To me preponderance of the evidence means, the evidence for guilt must outweigh the evidence of innocence by a huge amount. It means there is no reasonable doubt. Does anyone have a different opinion?"

After some discussion they agreed with Al K. Haul's explanation of the meaning of preponderance of the evidence.

Al K. Haul addressed the jury by asking if there was any one type of testimony or evidence they would like to discuss.

Several were brought up and the jury spent time going over those that were mentioned. After a recess and more discussion, it was time for lunch. They knocked on the door and advised the bailiff, they would break for lunch for one hour.

Rooster's Cafe was packed as the jurors filed into their room in the rear.

Al K. Haul asked that they talk as little as possible and speak in low tones, so no one could hear them, and eat quickly so they could go back to the jury room, out of the public's eyes.

Back in the jury room they began their afternoon discussions. They spoke of the witnesses and the physical evidence. They agreed on some things and disagreed on others. They worked all afternoon except for a short break. By 4:30 they were completely exhausted and knocked on the door to tell the bailiff they were through for the day. The court adjourned for the first day of deliberations.

The attorneys for the prosecution, thought that this was a good sign. The jurors were deliberating, meaning they were looking at the strong evidence.

The defense thought that this was a good sign, because the jurors were looking at the weak evidence.

Day two started out the same as the day before, with a discussion on the testimony of Detective Van Otter and the drive to the Mansion on the Hill. The discussion got quite heated as Miss Iola Bridges said that no one could drive that fast on Route 3, because the ruts are deep. Mrs. Mae East said she lived a mile past the Mansion on the Hill and she rode in a car pool with four other people, and they made the trip from her house to the shirt factory five days a week. She said it took her 15 minutes to pick up the four people and it was fives miles to the shirt factory. She timed the trip one Saturday when she had to work, and did not pick up any passengers. She was a little late and she drove 30 to 35 miles an hour, and after she got to city limits, she drove 45 miles an hour. She got to work on time and it had taken her 10 minutes. Therefore, anyone who drove that road regularly, such as the detectives and OJ, could easily make the trip from the Sad & Happy Drive-In to the Mansion on the Hill in seven or eight minutes. "We don't know where OJ started from. I've heard that he went to Skeeter's Sport Bar a good bit. He could have gone from there and it's closer to the Mansion on the Hill than the Sad and Happy Drive-In," said Mae East.

This type of discussion went on until it was time for the lunch break.

After lunch the jurors asked to see some of the photographs of the crime scene, to see if the scene was consistent with the testimony the detectives. After viewing the graphic pictures some of the jurors had to go to the bathroom.

They asked the judge to excuse them at four o'clock as one or two of the jurors were still a bit woozy from viewing the photographs.

Day three started at nine o'clock. Al K. Haul asked that a vote of guilty or not guilty be taken in the Nike Samson murder.

Ballot slips were passed out and each juror marked their verdict. Al K. Haul counted and called out the ballots, while Iola Bridges wrote the tally down. Of the twelve votes, there were nine to convict and three acquit.

"Has anyone a question, so we can come to some conclusion?" asked Mr. Haul.

Thelma Jitter was the first. "I don't think OJ had a motive to kill them. He didn't even know Mr. Hooper."

"You have a point, Thelma, let's have one of the others give their viewpoint," answered Al K. Haul.

Iola Bridges said, "I also have doubts of motive, plus I still have doubts about the time frame."

"What about the other juror, what determined your vote?"

Spencer Macy said, "It seems to me that someone else could have done it. The watch fob has not been tied to OJ. Besides Detective Burman and two or three others were taking bribes."

"All of you have very good points. Let's look at each one," said Mr. Haul.

They discussed the points in question until the noon hour, had an uneventful lunch, returned and discussed the three juror's concerns until 4:30 PM when they adjourned.

On day four the jurors were asked to vote again on the guilt or innocence in the murder of Nike Samson.

After the votes were counted, Al K. Haul called out the vote and Iola Bridges tallied the votes. Haul read the tally. We still do not have all twelve votes alike. Again Haul asked if anyone had a viewpoint they wanted to discuss.

Thelma Jitter said she still had doubts as to OJ's motive. Mr. Spencer Macy stated he conceded to the detective taking bribes, but the matter of the watch fob still bothered him.

"OK," said Al K. Haul, "Let us take each point one by one for a discussion. First, Miss Jitter's concern is about motive. Would someone like to start the discussion on this?"

Kit Carson said, "I have known people who became stars and became so possessive of their wives or girl friends, that no one could talk to the wife or girl friend without the star's permission. They became abusive. We had witnesses tell us of OJ's abuse of Nike. Remember, at Cholly Honky Tonk and Country Club, when Charlie said OJ came in and found Nike and some fellow named Potter in a booth. OJ went over and grabbed her, pulled her out of the booth and hit her so hard he knocked her to the floor. He was going to kick her, but Charlie Spinks stopped him. He was mad and as he stood there with Charlie Spinks holding him, he said to Charlie, 'Hell, I wouldn't pee on Nike if she was on far.' Then there was the time he threw her in Snit Creek. It was 12 o'clock at night, and he hit her and knocked her cold and then threw her in the creek. If she had not come to, she would have drowned. To me these two incidents and a few other spats tell me he was insanely jealous."

"Yes," said Minnie Curl, "There was the witness that stated, he had asked Nike to remarry him and she refused the day before the murder."

"Yes," said Thelma, "I see that now, that is the point I didn't understand. I have never seen any abuse like this, and it is horrible."

"Let's go to lunch and when we return we'll see if we can clear up Mr. Macy's concerns.

After lunch the jury took up the concerns of Mr. Macy.

Mr. U.R. Short, who had been quiet up to this point, said, "As no one has identified the watch fob, I don't see how this can come into play. It could have been OJ's, one he had purchased on one of his tours. But, as I see it, it does not tie him to the crime, nor does it eliminate him. There are many more items of evidence to incriminate him, even without the watch fob. The blood at the crime scene, that matched OJ's blood, and the victim's blood on the gloves, the ground and fence rails. The tire tracks that matched his car. Witnesses who said he never parked at the barn or near the hog pen on his visits to see his children."

Al K. Haul asked if there were any more questions before calling for another vote.

Since there were none, they took another vote, and as before Miss Bridges tallied the votes as Al K. Haul called them out. At the completion of the count Mr. Haul called out, "The twelve votes are all the same, guilty."

"Now Ladies and Gentlemen, let us vote on the degree of guilt, first degree murder, second degree murder or manslaughter. Remember the judge's instruction that, second degree murder was when the defendant can show provocation by the victim, in action or words that would make a reasonable person lose self control. He was indicted on first degree murder. Have we found a cause for second degree murder, or have we found him guilty? Please vote for guilty or not guilty of first degree murder. A vote of not guilty of first degree murder would mean that Mr. Samson is guilty of second degree murder or manslaughter. If the vote is guilty of second degree murder, then Mr. Samson is found guilty of second degree murder. If found not guilty of second degree murder we will vote on manslaughter."

After the votes were tallied Miss Bridges called out the result.

"We still do not have twelves jurors that agree."

"May we have more discussion. Who would like to start?"

"I would," said Thelma Jitter. "I don't think it was proven that he wasn't provoked and he lost control."

"Miss Jitter, you are young and I admire you for accepting jury duty at your age, however, not only is the testimony and evidence very important, a juror must use common sense to weigh the results. Now let's take OJ as he drove up to the hog pen. Did he jump out and start slashing and cutting the victims, or did he wait for the victim to say something like, OJ you are a good for nothing bum, or curse him? What could they have done to provoke him to murder both of them the way he did? Would you murder your boy friend and another girl on something bad they said? How bad would it have to be?"

"You are right, Mrs. Curl, I am glad you explained it to me the way you did. I couldn't murder anyone by being provoked."

The vote was again taken and this time all 12 votes were alike.

"It is now five-thirty," said Mr. Haul. "We have to vote on guilty or not guilty for the defendant in the murder of Mr. Hooper. The question is, do we want to stay and try to finish this tonight or wait until tomorrow?"

"I suggest," said Kit Carson, "We take one vote tonight, and if that is agreed upon by all of us we will give out the verdict. After one vote if we are not in agreement, we will finish the voting tomorrow."

Everyone agreed and the voting slips were passed out.

The tally showed not all were in agreement as to the verdict.

Mr. Haul knocked on the door at six PM and told the bailiff they would like to adjourn for the night.

When the prosecuting team saw the jurors working late, they thought a verdict might be near, so they sent down for coffee to ride the time out. Before the coffee arrived, they saw the lights go out and rushed to the courtroom to hear that the jury had retired for the night.

Donny went over to the jail with Mr. and Mrs. Samson. After they were seated in the visitors room, OJ broke the silence with, "Well, Donny, what do you think is happening?"

"The longer the jury stays out the more favorable it is to the defendant. If they deliberate tomorrow, and maybe the next day we are home free. Get some rest tonight, see you tomorrow."

Donny had placed a call to the Lil Thang. He needed to be with someone tonight, for he had a gut feeling things were not going well for OJ.

The court was buzzing the next morning, the fifth day of the deliberations.

The jurors were led into the jury room.

"After a night of rest, let's start over by taking a vote to see where we stand," said Haul.

The votes were counted and the outcome was in agreement of a guilty verdict.

Mr. Haul asked, "We took the final vote, is everyone in agreement on this ballot?"

Everyone answered in the affirmative.

Mr. Haul filled out the verdict form and went to the door and gave two loud knocks. Everyone jumped, for it had only been about 10 minutes since the jurors went into the jury room. Judge Ego told the bailiff to assemble the interested parties.

After everyone was assembled, Judge Ego called the court to order. The jury was seated. The judge asked, "Ladies and Gentlemen, have you reached a verdict?"

"Yes we have, Your Honor," answered Mr. Haul.

Judge Ego told the bailiff to accept the sealed verdict and bring it to him. He read the verdict, resealed it and called a recess for ten minutes.

Donny thought, "God, what a fingernail biting time this will be for the next ten minutes."

Chapter Forty

Martha Kluck was as nervous as a hen at Easter time. She and the other prosecuting attorneys talked it over and decided that the jurors had come to the verdict the day before and slept on it. From the short time they were in the jury room this morning, they had not changed their verdict. This looked as if they had won.

At 9:40 AM the court reconvened, and the players were in their places. It was like they were sitting in an outhouse on a cold December morning.

Judge Ego entered and asked the bailiff to bring in the jury. After being seated the judge asked the jurors if the verdict that was handed to him earlier was agreed to by each and every juror. All nodded their heads in agreement.

The judge opened the verdict and read it again, while the audience looked as nervous as Auburn footballs fans when the Alabama cheerleader took over for their quarterback. God, why won't he hurry it up thought OJ.

Judge Ego handed the verdict slip to the clerk, Mrs. Shirley Nation, to read.

Mrs. Nation read the slip to herself and then out loud.

"On the first count, the jury finds the defendant, Oscar James Samson, guilty of first degree murder in the death of Mrs. Nike Samson. On the second count, the jury finds the defendant, Oscar James Samson, guilty of first degree murder in the death of Mr. Clem Hooper."

The judge looked at the jury and asked again if everyone was in agreement. Every head nodded yes.

Mrs. Jim Paul Samson fainted, OJ went limp and almost fell.

Chapter Forty-One

The noise level in the court room was very high. Judge Ego banged his gavel and shouted, "QUIET! QUIET! QUIET!" Then a hush fell over the courtroom as the reality of the verdict slowly sunk in.

OJ was being helped up, where he almost fell to the floor. As he straightened up he began waving his arms and hollering "I'm innocent. I'm innocent."

"Bailiff, will you have the guards calm the defendant or return him to the jail."

After OJ had settled down and the courtroom was quiet, Judge Ego addressed the jurors, "Ladies and Gentlemen, the court thanks you for the job you have done. However, there is more to do. That is, the sentencing phase of this trial. You have found the defendant guilty on two counts of first degree murder. One count for the murder of Nike Samson and the second for the murder of Clem Hooper. The sentencing options for first degree murder are, one, life in prison for each count or two, death in the electric chair for each count. You will retire to the jury room to deliberate the sentencing of the defendant Oscar James Samson."

After the jury had retired to the jury room, Judge Ego told the prosecuting attorneys and the defense attorneys, that he would have the final ruling on the sentence, but would give the jurors recommendations a great deal of weight. After the jury had sent notice of their decision on the sentencing, he would notify all parties, giving them three hours notice to return to court. Judge Ego then adjourned the court.

Donny went to the jail to see OJ. He had been moved from his original cell to a maximum security cell, with visitors by special permission only. His attorney was the only one without special permission that could get in to see him and that visit could be in his cell.

When Donny was let into his cell, he saw a broken man. He babbled in place of talking. Donny said very sternly, "OJ, snap out it, all is not lost. Look at me and sit up straight. You have to be strong for your Ma and Pa. I will try to get them special permission to see you before you are sent to Kilby Prison in Montgomery."

"I don't want Ma and Pa to see me now. I am too upset and can't get myself under control. Wait a day or two."

"That will not help. The jury is out considering a recommendation on a sentence, and they won't be out long. We have three hours after they reach a decision to be in court for the formal sentencing."

"But, Donny, the sentence is automatic life isn't it?"

"It will be that, I expect, but there are two sentences for first degree murder. The other is the death sentence. The prosecutor has asked for the death penalty, however, I don't think they will give you that type of sentence.

"In any event we have a very good cause for an appeal, maybe even a mistrial. I want you to settle down so you can help me with the appeal. Get some rest, I am going to the office to do some paperwork."

As Donny was walking to his automobile, he thought, "I sure hated not to be completely honest with him, but I need to get him out of the mood he is in."

When he arrived at the office a message was waiting for him, to call Judge Ego's clerk, Mrs. Shirley Nation.

Donny called Mrs. Nation and was informed that court would convene at nine the next morning. He called the jailer and told him when OJ was to be in court. The jailer had already received the message from Mrs. Nation, and just relayed it to OJ.

At nine the court was called to order. Everyone was present, and the jurors seated. Judge Ego asked the defendant to stand. OJ and all of the attorneys stood, as the judge opened a folder and spoke, "Ladies and Gentlemen, the court has received the decision of the jury for the sentence of Mr. Oscar James Samson. I have looked over the decision and agree. Therefore, I sentence Mr. Oscar James Samson to death, by electrocution, for the first degree murder of Mrs. Nike Samson. Furthermore, I hereby sentence Mr. Oscar James Samson to death, by electrocution, for the first degree murder of Mr. Clem Hooper. MAY GOD HAVE MERCY ON YOUR SOUL. The defendant will be transported to Kilby Prison in Montgomery, Alabama, where the death sentence will be carried out in six months on June 12, 1938 at 8:30 PM."

OJ had slumped to the floor, crying out, "I am innocent. I am innocent. Won't someone listen to me, I am innocent, I tell you." He was a pitiful sight from the once carefree, handsome singer. Mrs. Samson had fainted again and had to be carried out.

Donny went over to the sheriff's office and talked with Sheriff Jenkins. He asked the jailer to put a guard on watch to prevent OJ from committing suicide.

Chapter Forty-Two

Two months passed since OJ received his sentence. His prison cell, on death row, was eight feet by eight feet, with three solid walls and an open front with steel bars. A prison guard sat at one end of the prison block of six death row cells. Every five minutes a guard would pass the cell. In the cell was a bunk made of wood. Springs were not allowed, as they could be used as a weapon or suicide tool. A wash basin stood in one corner, and open toilet in the other. A chair and table, used as a writing desk, with a small radio completed the furnishings. The cell on the right was empty. He could talk to the man in the cell on the left, but could not see him. The man next to him was convicted of murdering his wife and her lover. His name was Comer "Bear" Braswell. The nickname came from his size, six feet five inches tall and weighing 275 pounds. He was also innocent, according to him. His wife and her lover were beaten to death by another of his wife's, lovers a midget, and if they catch him they'll hang him not so high. So here sat two men on death row who were innocent. Bear fell out of a stupid tree, and hit every branch on the way down. OJ would hear Bear talking. He asked Bear one day who was he talking to.

"Well," Bear answered, "I'm talking to my pet. It's jest lak de one I had when I wuz a lil youngon, tis a cockaroach. Somebody done told me it wuz a Cuban cockaroach called cucaracha or something. I call dis one Cuca. I got him trained lak my dog, Meathead. I got him on a string, and when old frog face, de guard, pass, I reach out and I gonna give you de string. De cockaroach is trained and will follow de string. Jest talk to him, and he'll talk back."

Well, thought OJ, what the hell, old Bear is happy, I will go along. It wasn't too long before he liked Cuca, so Bear and OJ would send Cuca back and forth.

Donny visited OJ in the second month and told him that the State Supreme Court was going to hear his appeal in March. "It looks good from here," said Donny. After Donny left, he told Bear what Donny said.

"Well, buddy, if dey don't give you a appeal, let's ask fer twin electric chairs. Thada blow the lights out of Mongomery."

Chapter Forty-Three

After four months of tracking the watch fob, Detective Van Otter got an ever so slight lead that he almost passed it up.

One Saturday night, a big fight broke out at the Cholly Hoss Honky Tonk and Country Club. Four deputies went out and arrested four of the people in the fight. As they were booked and turned in their possessions, a watch with about three links of a chain was put in the envelope of Jeff Cook. The next morning the deputy who booked Jeff Cook told Van Otter that the chain looked familiar, he had seen it or a picture of it somewhere. Van Otter pulled the envelope of Jeff Cook, and pulled out the watch. Sure enough there were three links of chain on the watch. Van pulled the case file on Oscar James Samson and pulled the photograph of the watch fob found at the crime scene. It was Sunday, but he called the coroner Mack Davis and asked him if he could take a look at it.

"Hell, Van, this is Sunday. Can't it wait until tomorrow?"

"I would like for you to look at it today. The person it belongs to, could be bailed out and leave today. I really would appreciate it if you would look at it."

"OK, meet me at the office in 30 minutes."

Van carried the photographs and the watch with the short chain over to Mack Davis' office.

When Mack came in, they went to the lab table where he got out a microscope and put the watch with the chain part under the scope. On the side of the lab table he laid the photograph of the watch fob with the short chain. After looking at them for a few minutes he said, "Van, I think we have a match. The fob came off of this watch and chain. Let's set up the camera and take some close-ups of the two. You can take this back and I will come by after I develop the film and make some prints. It will take about an hour."

Van went back to the jail and asked that Jeff Cook be brought to the interrogation room. While they went to get Jeff Cook, Van called over to see who was on duty. Deputy Don Mack Browne was on duty.

"Send him over on the double to the interrogation room."

Deputy Browne arrived just as Van, the jail guard and Jeff entered the interrogation room.

Van spread the contents of Cook's envelopes on the table, and asked about the various items and where he got them. When they got to the next to the last item Van picked up the watch, looked at it, laid it down and picked it up again and slowly slid it across the table in front of Jeff Cook.

"Jeff, what were you doing at the Cholly Hoss Honky Tonk last night?"

"Well, you see Sir, I am a drummer and I was playing my drums, when some jerk came up and hit our lead singer. I jumped up to help and all hell broke loose."

"You took this watch off of one of the guys you hit, why?"

"Hell, Detective, Ott.

"Otter, Van Otter."

"Well, Detective, I didn't take that watch from anyone. That is my watch."

"Can you prove it Mr. Cook?"

"Yes Sir, all the members of the band can tell you it is my watch."

"Where did you buy the watch, Mr. Cook?"

"About six months ago a Pentecostal preacher I met, needed some extra money. He said his collections wasn't coming in too good. He just took over a new church in Fairfield, California. I gave him $5 for it."

"What did you do with the fob?"

"It didn't have one. I asked him about the fob and he said he lost it. He didn't know where."

"How did he happen to ask you to buy the watch?"

"I dated a girl that was going to his church and she introduced us. When he found out I was from Flomotan, Alabama, he said he had lived in Three Notch, Alabama for a while.

Van's heart began to beat faster and about this time Mack Davis came in the room with the photographs.

Van covered the fob up and left the chain showing in the first photograph, and in the other photograph covered up the watch and left the chain showing.

"Mr. Cook look at these two photos and tell me if the two chains look the same to you?"

Jeff looked at the chains and began to get that queasy feeling in his stomach. He thought, "What the hell is going on. It was only a honky tonk fight."

"Yes, Sir, they look alike to me."

Van Otter uncovered the watch fob, then the watch.

"The fob was on this watch before it was lost, Mr. Cook. "You do know where we found it don't you?"

"No, sir, I never seen that fob before, honest."

The detective slid a photo of the crime scene showing both bodies and all the gory details.

"Mr. Cook you lost this fob at this site last June."

Jeff Cook almost fainted. He turned pale and was about to get sick.

"No, sir, I was in Fairfield in June and July. I ain't been back to Alabama since Christmas a year ago."

"Mr. Cook you could be in lots of trouble, so I want the truth. First, what is the name of the person you purchased the watch from?"

"It was a Preacher Ludlow Potter, and he said he was from around here."

"Did the preacher tell you about anyone in this area?"

"No, sir, he was quiet about where he came from."

"Was there anything said, no matter how insignificant it may sound, a word may help, about anything in this area?"

"Well, there may be something. He said he liked to stay at some fish camp on a river. But I can't think of the name of the river. Maybe if I heard it or read it, it might come to mind."

"Well, let's see," said Van, "There is Gant River, Snit Creek, a small river, Black Water River and Yallar River."

"That's it, Yallar River, a fish camp," Jeff, said.

"Thank you, Mr. Cook, when you are released, do not leave town, until you clear it with me, OK?"

On Monday, Van took Deputy Don Mack Browne and they drove out to a fish camp by the name of Tatum Fish Camp and Cabins. They found Joe Tatum down near the river fixing some fishing skiffs.

"Hi, Joe, how is the fishing business these days?"

"Not too good. The fish is biting good, but nobody wants to spend nights much, so most of our trade is daytime, renting boats and selling bait. Not much money in that."

"Well, Joe, spring is around the corner and your business should pick up then. By the way, last summer in June you had a Preacher Potter stay here, remember him?"

"A preacher stayed here one night, but I don't think that was his name. He didn't do any fishing or eat anything. He paid only fer the cabin fer one night and left early in the morning."

"You remember the date?"

"Not off hand, but I may recollect if I look at my ledger, cauz he gave me $3 and I owed him $.75, and I only had a quarter. I told him I would give him the half dollar change the next morning, but when I went over to his cabin he was gone."

"What time was that?"

"Oh, I think about seven o'clock."

When they got to the cabin Joe looked at his ledger and found that on June 12, a Preacher Ludlow stayed in cabin four and was due a half dollar refund.

"Can you recall if the preacher left the camp that night?"

"Yes, Sir, he did, said he was holding a revival, some place over near Slap Out, and would be back late, but he got back about 9:30 or 9:45."

"How did you know about the time?"

"Jack Sprat and two friends were going cat fishing that night and was supposed to be here at eight, but didn't come til 9:15. I was down at the river helping them get the boat in the water. He went into the cabin and came down to the beach over there and took a bath. I thought it was strange, cauz most folks take a bath before they go off."

Did you find any clothes or anything bloody around the cabin or outside after he left?"

"No Sir."

"Have you ever found any bloody clothes or knife anytime after the preacher stayed?"

"Yes, but it wuz over yonder behind the outhouse. Ole Jake, that's my dog, wuz a scratching out there and brung in some clothes, that was bloody. A pair of blue serge pants, and a white shirt all tore up."

"Do you remember what date?"

"No, sir, it was sometime in August."

"What did you do with them?'

"I buried them behind the outhouse and put some rocks on top so Ole Jake wouldn't dig them up again."

"Show me the spot where you buried them and the spot where Ole Jake first dug them up, and I'll need a shovel."

Van and Don dug up the old bloody clothes. They were almost rotted away. Some blood stains could be seen on the foul smelling rags that were left.

They then went over the spot where Ole Jake dug up the clothes the first time. Joe wasn't exactly sure, so they dug a circle of about 10 feet. On the outer edge of the circle, they found a castrating knife, a pair of socks and a handkerchief. They were rotten and moldy, but maybe the lab could pick up something. They put everything in a bag, not touching the knife and left, telling Joe that if he thought of anything else, to call them and he gave Joe a card.

Upon returning to town, Van went over to the jail and had Jeff Cook brought down to the visiting room. He asked Jeff if he knew where the Reverend Ludlow Potter was living.

He did not, but knew his church was the Fairfield Pentecostal Church on the outskirts of Fairfield.

Van thanked him and went back to his office and called the Fairfield, California. Sheriff's Office. He spoke to the sheriff, a George Haban. He told Sheriff Haban his problem, and said he felt sure he could get an indictment, but would need time. Van asked the sheriff if he could check on the Reverend Ludlow Potter. He asked for all the information he could get and some type of surveillance until the paper work was done in Three Notch. Sheriff Haban was very cooperative and said he would keep him posted.

Van Otter carried the bloody clothes, the knife, socks and the handkerchief to the Coroner's Office to have Mack Davis check out the blood type and see if any fingerprints could be picked up from the knife. He said he needed a rush on the analysis as he didn't want Ludlow Potter to get wind of anything before the reports were in. He would write to Sears, Roebuck and Co., sending the serial number to verify that this was the knife OJ purchased.

It took two weeks for all the tests and paperwork to be done. They had the letter of verification that this was the knife OJ Samson purchased. The blood on all the clothing and the knife was type A negative, type O negative and type O positive. Van had asked Mack Davis to check the blood, type O negative and positive and compare it with the blood of Nike Samson and Clem Hooper found at the crime scene, and to check the type A negative blood found at Tatum's Fish Camp and that of the type A negative blood found at the crime scene.

Mack Davis reported the type O blood, negative and positive were the same as Nike Samson and Clem Hooper, but the type A negative blood was the same type A negative blood found at the crime scene, but not the same type A negative blood as Oscar James Samson. Mack Davis' reports read that he concluded that Oscar James Samson's blood was not at the crime scene.

Van called Donny Kockran and asked that he drop by his office immediately. Donny's office was across the square from the detective's office and he was there in 10 minutes.

After Donny was seated, Van said, "Donny I have some news that could make you happy, if it comes off as I think it should. However, you must promise you will not tell anyone, at this time, as there are some loose ends to tie up. Do I have your word?"

"Yes, I give my word that I will not tell anyone, unless, of course, it would jeopardize my client."

"OK, here is what I have. We have found out who the person is who owned the watch fob. We have traced his movements to Three Notch and we found his bloody clothes covered with Nike's and Clem's blood. We found the castrating knife with both victim's blood type O negative and positive, and type A negative blood that does not match OJ's. Also there are fingerprints that were partially lifted. I think enough to make a match. We know who that person is and have contacted the authorities in California to keep him under surveillance until we can tie up the loose ends. If everything falls into place as I visualize, the outcome of the case will make OJ a free man. If it does not check out, then he is no worse off."

"Can you give me the name of the person and more of the details?" Donny asked.

"No, I can't. The fact is, I shouldn't have given you any of the details, because if this does not work out, and if knew the full details, it would be devastating to you both. But I'll keep you posted as the case progresses.

Two weeks later, Van called Sheriff Haban in Fairfield, California to tell him he had a warrant for the arrest of Preacher Ludlow Potter on two charges of first degree murder.

"Sheriff, I will send by Western Union Telegraph, a warrant, the number and charges. This should be enough for you to hold him until Deputy Don Browne and I arrive there. We will be leaving Three Notch as soon as we hear that the Preacher has been arrested, and we should arrive there in four days. I will have extradition papers to bring him back with us. Let me know when you pick him up. Thanks."

The next day Sheriff Haban called to let Van know he had the preacher in jail.

"He hasn't said anything. He's keeping a tight lip, but we can hold him for one week. If you are not here with the warrant and extradition papers, we will have to release him."

Four tough days later, driving though the southwestern states, into northern California, Van and Don checked into a motel in Fairfied at four o'clock in the afternoon. They were so tired they went to bed without eating and slept until five the next morning.

Up, feeling rested and optimistic about the preacher, they ate a large breakfast and arrived at Sheriff Haban's office at eight AM.

They went into the interrogation room. Waiting for them was the preacher. He was not a big man, 5'11" and about 175 pounds. He needed a hair cut as his blond hair came into a duck tail in the back. He had blue eyes, high cheek bones and a ruddy complexion. He was well built, a nice looking clean-cut man. He seemed nervous and avoided looking into the men's eyes.

Van quickly sized up the preacher, decided to go easy and put the pressure on gradually.

"Good morning, Reverend Potter, you are a minister aren't you?"

"Yes, I was ordained a minister and I am a pastor of a church here in Fairfield."

"You were the pastor of a church in Three Notch County, Alabama, in the community of Turnip Hill, were you not?"

"Yes, I was," answered the preacher, "But I fell into sinful ways, backslid and my whole life changed."

"Yes, I know life can easily change. When I was in my last year of high school I fell in love with the most beautiful girl in the school. Everybody wanted her for their girl. Anyway, Dolly Mae paid, I thought, more attention to me. Man was I in love. Dolly Mae got me to do more things than my Mama and Daddy taught me. I stopped going to church, lost the Lord, started drinking, going to honky tonks, and even stole to get money to impress Dolly Mae.

"One night I stole my Daddy's car and went over to pick up Dolly Mae, but she had gone to a girl friend's house. I decided to go to the Riverside Inn for a drink or two and come back and pick her up later. When I went in the Riverside Inn, I saw Dolly Mae and Bosefus Grimes dancing, and they were real close. My heart almost stopped, because I thought I was the only one. I went down to the end of the bar and had two big drinks of Jessie's special moonshine. It hit me like a bale of cotton fell on my head.

"I walked over to the booth and told Dolly Mae to come with me now. She said no, and as Bosefus jumped up, I put an upper cut in his gut and a left in his eye as he was falling. Dolly Mae came over and slapped me so hard I saw stars. She told me to get lost, as she bent over Bosefus. I can never forget how mad and hurt I was. I even thought about killing Bosefus, but, hell, he was doing the same as me, loving Dolly Mae. I felt so bad and hurt I moped around for weeks thinking of all kinds of ways to get Dolly Mae back and to run Bosefus off.

"My dear old Mama knew something was wrong with me, but she never asked. One Sunday as they were getting ready for church she said, 'Van why don't you go to church with us today. You can sit in the back.' Well, I went to church and found the Lord and my heart was free of Dolly Mae."

Van looked at Ludlow and saw the pained expression on his face.

"Ludlow, may I call you Ludow?"

"Yes, I don't need to be called Reverend any more. I have been through what you just told me. I met a beautiful girl when I was preaching at the Turnip Hill Pentecostal Church. She was beautiful, about 5'2", a little over a 100 pounds, long blonde hair, blue eyes. Did I ever fall for those blue eyes.

"But she fell for someone else and I lost her. It was so bad I took up drinking, secretly, and it got worse until I back slid. I left Alabama and came to California, but I could not forget her. I wrote her letters. She wrote back after she got a divorce, and I thought I had a chance. One of the letters said she would like to see me and talk over old times.

"I drove to Alabama to see her. I went by her house and she told me to come later after it got dark, because she didn't want anyone to see us together just now. Just like you, when I went back that night I saw her coming out of the barn with another man. I visualized what took place in the barn and I lost it. Detective, I went further."

"Ludlow, we know what happened next. We have the knife, your old bloody clothes, fingerprints, and blood samples. We, of course, know where you stayed. You know, Ludlow, I believe you have found the Lord again and he would not want an innocent man to die for the sins you have committed. Let me show you some photographs of the scene you left," said Van, as he slipped the murder scene prints across the table in front of Ludow.

Ludlow took a quick look at them and turned his head and said, "Let me have a few minutes with my Lord, is all I ask?"

Ludlow went over to the corner of the room, kneeled down and the officers could hear him speaking in a low voice, not loud enough for them to understand.

After a few minutes he came back to the table and said he had made peace with his Lord and was ready to tell everything.

It was even harder going back to Alabama, with Ludlow under the watch of one of them at all times. Ludlow prayed for 2,732 miles.

Chapter Forty-Four

Donny had kept OJ informed of the events, after the return of Ludlow Potter, and on this day he and Mr. and Mrs. Samson were on the way to Kilby Prison in Montgomery to pick him up.

OJ was in the visiting room waiting for them. After hugs and kisses from his Ma and Pa, they headed to Three Notch, where, for the first time in almost a year, he was traveling without handcuffs and leg irons.

Donny dropped the Samson's off at their home and left to go by and see the Lil Thang. He felt real good about himself.

After a great meal that night with only his Ma, Pa and his two children, Oren and Nita, OJ was beginning to feel free. After everyone was asleep, he lay in bed looking out of the window at the full moon. He got up, and in his underwear walked out on the front porch, looking at the full moon and remembering back to when he was a little boy. When he had to go to the outhouse at night, he would stop on the porch. He stood there a moment then pulled out his penis and peed off of the front porch, just like he did when he was a boy. He looked up at the moon and shouted to the world, "FREE AT LAST!"

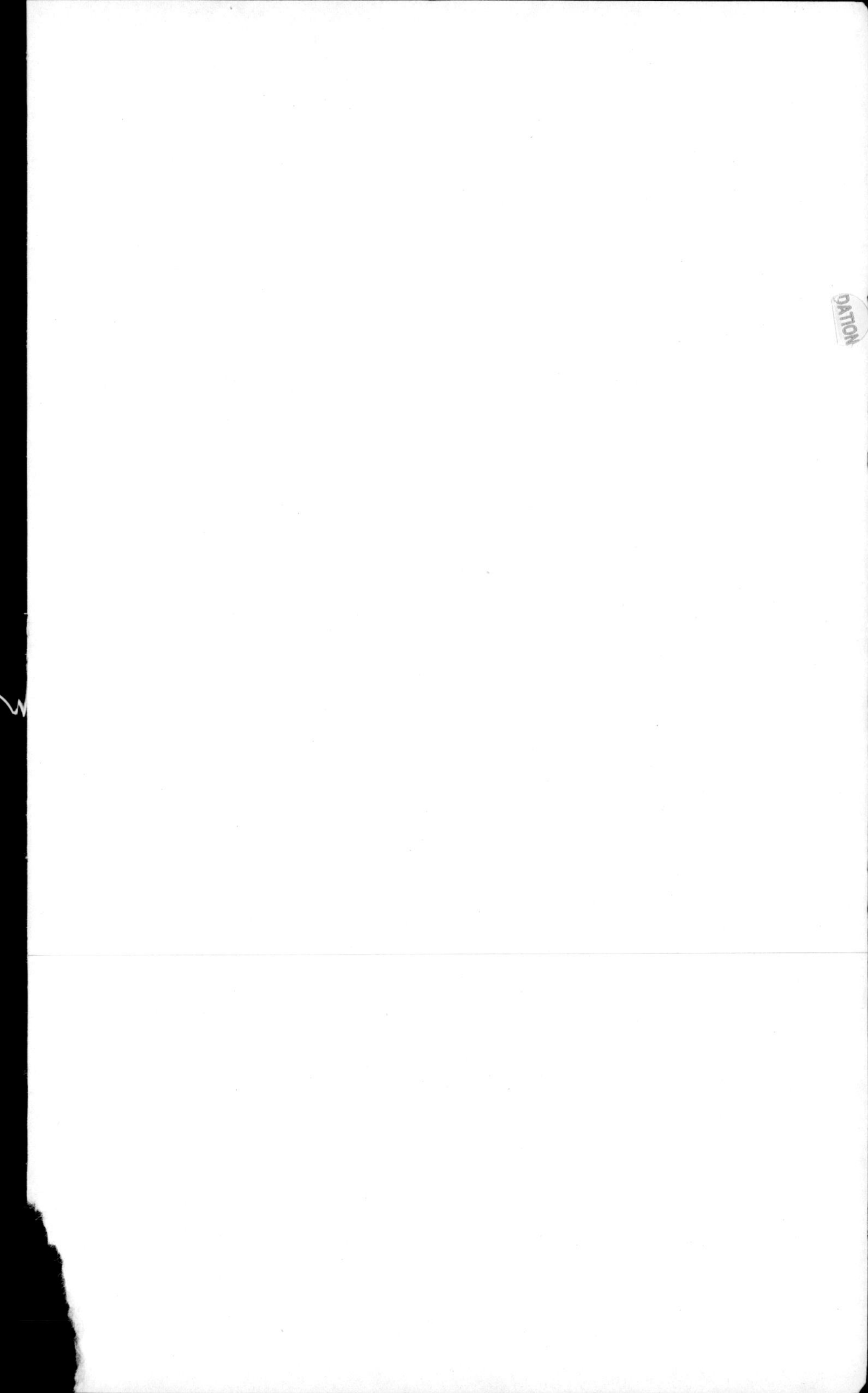

9 781893 652767